TREASURE & TROUBLE

Troubles of the Heart - Book One

BETTY WOODS

Scrivenings
PRESS
Quench your thirst for story.
www.ScriveningsPress.com

Published by Scrivenings Press LLC
15 Lucky Lane
Morrilton, Arkansas 72110
https://ScriveningsPress.com

Printed in the United States of America

Paperback ISBN 978-1-64917-389-8

eBook ISBN 978-1-64917-390-4

Editors: Ann Harrison and Linda Fulkerson

Cover by Linda Fulkerson www.bookmarketinggraphics.com
Back cover photo by Bob Swafford

All scriptures are taken from the KING JAMES VERSION (KJV): KING JAMES VERSION, public domain.

All characters are fictional, and any resemblance to real people, either factual or historical, is purely coincidental.

My late mother-in-law, Mavis, who gave me the idea of Eugenia hiding her notes behind a loose stone in the column at her gate. She was absolutely sure I'd be a published writer.
My first agent, the late Mary Sue Seymour, and my mentor, Lena Nelson Dooley, who told me not to give up on this story and that it would find a publishing home one day.

Chapter One

1832

Outside Murfreesboro, Tennessee

Eugenia Hampton urged her mare Belle into a gallop as her favorite trail through the woods widened. She lifted her face to the warm spring sun as the honeysuckle-scented breeze caressed her face. Better to enjoy the beautiful May day than worry about her troubles. Her top hat slipped over one ear, but the chattering squirrels wouldn't scold her the way her mother would.

A startled crow flew within inches of Belle's head. The horse spooked and reared. Eugenia fought to stay in the saddle. She screamed just before slamming into the ground. While she struggled to quit shaking long enough to sit up, horse's hooves pounded toward her.

"Whoa!" a masculine voice commanded. A man quickly dismounted and knelt beside her. "Are you all right?" He tilted his hat back as he studied her.

She sucked in several shaky breaths. "I-I think so. A crow— at least it looked like a crow—spooked my horse."

"So I saw. If you're sure you ain't hurt, I'll go catch your horse. Don't move before I get back."

"I'll be still." Her trembling legs wouldn't support her anyway.

Swinging up into his saddle, he galloped off to retrieve the mare.

The few minutes the man was gone gave her a little time to gather her wits and assess her situation. She raked a gloved hand across the moss she'd landed on, shuddering at the sight of a fallen log lying only a foot or so away. How fortunate she'd been dumped in a soft place.

After the big man returned with her horse, he slid from his saddle and crouched in front of her. "Does it bother you to move, Miss Hampton?" He cocked his head as he scanned her face.

She shook her head. No pain for now. That had to be a good sign. Tomorrow might be another story. "I should be fine once I calm down."

Resting his arm on his knee, he continued to watch her.

She smiled, hoping to reassure her anxious-looking rescuer. "How do you know my name when I don't know yours?"

"Sorry. My name's Paul Stuart."

"Are you related to the Stuarts in this area, particularly John Stuart, my papa's overseer?"

He nodded. "He's my pa. I was at church this morning with my folks and saw you with your ma. That's how I figured out who you are."

"Oh."

The more she gazed into his fascinating sky blue eyes, the more she wished she'd paid closer attention to the Stuart family's pew near the back of the church. Wavy carrot-red hair falling almost to his collar drew her attention to his broad muscular shoulders. She would have to be more observant the next time she went to services.

"You sure you're all right, miss? You're awful quiet."

Nothing pained her as she took another deep breath. "I'm all right. I lapse into my own thoughts at times. I do appreciate your help."

"A lady riding sidesaddle shouldn't be galloping through the woods as if she's trying to outrun a fire. You weren't much more than a blur when I saw you, and this trial narrows down not too far from here."

She stiffened. This stranger had no right to rebuke her like a child no matter how gentle his tone. "I'm an excellent rider. Papa bought my first pony for me when I was six, and I've been riding in these woods ever since."

"Excellent riders still need to be careful. Look where you are now." His lips almost formed a smile, accenting a very interesting cleft in his chin

The man sounded too much like her overly watchful mother.

"Always being careful is quite boring. Are you cautious every moment of your life?"

He chuckled as he looked into her eyes. "No, so I guess it wouldn't be fair for me to be too hard on you."

"No, it wouldn't." Her mother did enough of that sort of thing. One person who didn't understand about the thrill of unexpected adventures was enough. She didn't need or want anyone else taking Mama's place.

When she glanced down at the dirt and debris on her riding habit, she gasped. Mama must never see all this. She whisked away a few leaves. "I must be a frightful mess after taking such a tumble."

"You don't look too bad."

Did not looking too bad mean not too disheveled or was he

admiring her as he studied her? After all, he'd noticed her in church and remembered her. She'd have to worry about his intentions later. For now, she needed to be sure Mama would never be able to tell Belle had thrown her. She patted her hair, trying to feel how many hairpins remained. "I'm certain my hair is a terrible mess, but does my appearance tell anyone my horse threw me?"

His eyes narrowed. "Only the good Lord knows why you didn't break something or worse, and all you're worried about is how you look?"

The good Lord? Mama was the only one in her family on speaking terms with God, but that was none of this man's concern. How dare he be so blunt with someone he didn't know? She'd dismiss him this instant except that might prove his assumptions about her misplaced pride.

"I'm not as vainglorious as you think. Mama would never allow me to ride alone again if she knew Belle threw me. I couldn't bear losing this little bit of freedom." She gently removed a twig snagged in the lace trim on the collar draped over her shoulders. The current fashion of such large collars was a definite inconvenience today. "You have no idea how cumbersome it is to be a proper lady all the time."

"I don't guess I do."

Judging by the sarcastic tone of his voice, his patronizing thin smile perhaps bordered on disgust or mockery.

"Being a lady isn't as much fun as most people think. Sometimes I feel as if I'm smothering."

His eyes widened as he shook his head.

How useless trying to explain her situation to a man dressed in homespun who had no idea what her life was like. "I suppose I've bored you long enough. You must have more pressing things to do than listen to me ramble on."

"You're too hard to figure out to be boring."

Oh, and why is that? Regardless of what he thought of her, she was quite intrigued with her plainspoken rescuer. Not one of her suitors had ever dared speak his mind to a woman with a dowry as generous as hers. She couldn't help but admire this man's forthright behavior, especially the way he seemed so unimpressed by her status. How refreshing.

"You've helped me more than you'll ever know. Thank you." She shifted her position. "I should go home now."

"I want to be sure you can stand as good as you think you can before I leave." He rose and then offered his hand to assist her.

His large strong hand swallowed hers. Thoughts of dismissing him flew away more quickly than the crow she'd startled. His earthy scent and butternut-colored homespun shirt bespoke a common laborer, yet his confident stance signaled he'd hold his own with General Andrew Jackson if necessary.

"It ain't every day I get stared at the way you're doing." His eyes twinkled.

"Pardon me. You must be almost six feet tall. My papa and my brothers aren't tall, and I'm not accustomed to it."

That was. the best explanation she could manage. She dared not tell this stranger how much she liked his uncommon self-assurance and commanding appearance in spite of his gentle rebukes.

He grinned. "To someone as small as you, I must look pretty big."

If he was so unimpressed with her, why did he continue smiling? Was he friendly by nature or did his intriguing, sparkling eyes indicate a deeper interest? Under different conditions, she'd enjoy discovering the answers to the questions tumbling through her mind. But her focus for now must remain on being sure her parents never discovered Belle had thrown her.

She stooped to retrieve her top hat. Considering the circumstances, it appeared to be in surprisingly good shape "If I get the rest of the leaves and grass off my clothes, will I truly look all right?"

"Dirt don't show too bad on your dark green dress. You should put your hair up a little better and get the leaves out before you put that sil—that hat back on."

Had he started to call her top hat silly? His flushing cheeks suggested he had. She couldn't blame him for thinking such a thing, but Mama wouldn't allow her to ride without the proper attire. She wished for a mirror while she tucked her hair behind her ears and partially pinned the other strands. At least she didn't have to see what she was doing to put her hat on.

"I'll have my maid repair the damage to my hair when I get home. You may help me up on my horse now."

His eyes narrowed to slits as he clamped his open jaw shut. He hesitated another moment or two then cupped his hands together to make a step for her and boosted her up onto her horse.

"Thank you, sir."

"You're welcome." He swung up in his saddle, looking much too serious.

Not a single hint of his former teasing in his now terse voice. His warm blue eyes had turned frosty cold. She'd puzzle over such a sudden change later. "Mr. Stuart, would you do one more thing for me?"

"If I can."

"If you see either of my parents, please don't tell them what happened this afternoon. I'm not exaggerating when I say they'd both be terrified for me. Mama might never allow me the freedom to ride alone again."

He shrugged. "I won't say anything, not even to my pa in case he might say something to your pa."

"I'd appreciate that. I hope we can visit again sometime. Good day." She smiled.

"Good day to you." He tipped his brown hat.

With a gentle pull on the reins, she urged her horse forward. He didn't return her wave. She hoped her rescuer was a man of his word and wouldn't tell a soul about this afternoon. Even her indulgent father might forbid her to ride alone if he'd seen her crashing to the ground.

* * *

PAUL KEPT an eye on the woman until she rounded the next bend in the trail. She rode away quickly enough. Maybe she was telling the truth about not being hurt. She must not be as fragile as she appeared. Her light blonde hair falling around her narrow shoulders made her look as delicate as the lace decorating her clothes. He'd really enjoyed watching those lively green eyes of hers that talked as much as she did.

Plumb crazy thoughts. He shook his head to clear his mind. She'd ordered him to help her up on her horse as if he were one of her father's slaves but called him sir when she thanked him. What a strange woman. Promising not to tell anybody about her reckless behavior probably wasn't right, but going back on his word wasn't either. Except such a reckless woman would put herself in danger.

Instead of heading toward Murfreesboro and home, he turned his horse down the narrow trail leading to Hopeton, Titus Matthews's plantation. His best friend could probably help him decide about keeping his word to the lady. Maybe, for her own safety, he should tell someone how she'd been galloping through the woods. She could have been hurt—even killed—if that crow had been a low branch hanging in her way.

A few minutes later, Titus grinned at him as they seated themselves in the wooden chairs on the front porch of Titus's columned mansion. "I didn't expect to see you here this time of day. You usually don't like to be this late going back to Murfreesboro."

"I didn't expect me here either." Paul stretched out his legs and propped his elbows on the wooden chair arms. "I figure you know Eugenia Hampton."

"Our families have been friends since I was a boy. How do you know her?"

"I don't." He gave the one person he trusted to keep a secret a quick version of how he'd helped the lady. "Should I keep quiet about her?"

Titus nodded. "Her parents are every bit as overprotective as she said."

From what Paul had seen, they should be, but he had better manners than to say something so impolite about a friend of Titus. "Then I'll keep her secret."

"She'll be sure to thank you if she gets the opportunity. From what my sister says, Eugenia often rides on Sundays."

Paul shook his head. "I don't always take that trail on my way home."

"In case you do, Eugenia could use more friends. She's lonelier than you'd guess."

As spoiled as she was, Paul could understand why she needed friends. "I can't see a lady like her ever wanting to be friends with a man like me."

"Then I promise, she'll surprise you." Titus's eyes twinkled as if he'd said something hilarious.

Just what, Paul couldn't figure out. Miss Eugenia Hampton had acted like any other highfalutin lady he'd ever met. He couldn't say that to Titus, so he'd better think of something nice. Staring toward the well-tended lawn gave him a moment to think.

"She was calmer than I thought she'd be after taking such a spill."

Titus chuckled as he shifted in his chair. "That can't be the first time she's fallen off a horse."

"Probably not, if she rides like I saw today."

Paul swatted at a fly while trying to figure out why a lady so unlike him would bother saying one word to him if she didn't want or need something. "She'd gallop that horse the other direction from me if she knew I won't own slaves. You're the only person around here I can be honest with about that."

And he couldn't be completely truthful with a slave owner like Titus. He dared not tell anyone the real reason he'd left Nashville in such a hurry. Since he wanted to get to Murfreesboro before dark, he talked with his friend only a little bit longer.

During his ride home, he couldn't shake thoughts of Eugenia Hampton. He liked her spirit, even if she had challenged him when he told her it wasn't safe for her to gallop her horse through the woods. Without whining once about her fall, she'd gotten to her feet. A woman with that kind of gumption would fit right in on the frontier farm he hoped to own someday.

Such ridiculous thoughts made him laugh out loud. She's too spoiled to even think about. Her riding clothes were fancier than his mother's best Sunday dress. A woman with everything money could buy should count her blessings, not complain about being smothered by her wealth. God could smother him like that any day, and he'd never fuss about it.

Still, it had been a long time since he'd come across a woman with such a perky spirit and so much nerve. But she'd talked an awful lot without saying one thing important, no matter how much he'd enjoyed watching her expressive green eyes. He liked and didn't like the woman, all at the same time. If such an aggravating lady needed friends, someone else would have to help with that.

Except God called Paul a friend, no matter that he could never deserve such a precious friendship.

His thoughts jolted him in his saddle. "All right, Lord. I'll think about being her friend if I ever see her again. I hope You understand, I ain't in a hurry for that to happen."

He'd run from enough problems in Nashville. He didn't need woman trouble added into the mix.

Chapter Two

While Eugenia and her mother sat in the ornate parlor of Mama's dear friend, Mrs. Martha Browning, Eugenia swallowed a sigh along with her tea. She would rather fall into an icy pond on the frostiest day in January than be here gazing down at the rose-patterned carpet while Mama and Mrs. Browning visited with each other.

But she must appease Mama. Her mother had been so aghast at Eugenia's unkempt appearance when she'd returned from her ride yesterday that she hadn't noticed the scratches on her daughter's cheek. Eugenia had conveniently lost her balance walking in the rose garden soon thereafter and now had a perfect excuse for the scratches and some stiffness.

If only she'd been too sore to come calling. She hid her frown by looking down to stir her tea while Mama and Mrs. Browning exchanged pleasantries. With any luck, the two older women would soon be chatting away as if she weren't in the room.

A welcome breeze scented the parlor with the tangy-sweet smell of magnolia blooms. The Browning's tree-shaded front yard beckoned to her as she gazed through the window edged by blue velvet drapes. Mid May in Tennessee should be enjoyed out of doors.

"I'm delighted you've come calling with your mother, Eugenia."

Mrs. Browning's words yanked Eugenia's attention from the gorgeous view outside. "As Mama said, we had to see how you're faring."

"I'm doing quite well now."

Eugenia almost choked on her tea. These couldn't be the words of the lady who feared contracting every latest illness. "I'm glad you're feeling so sound."

"I've felt wonderful since Jonah came back from college saying he plans to stay close by."

The cup in Eugenia's hand halted in midair. *Jonah? Oh, no.* She wanted to see Jonah Browning as much as she wished to run into a porcupine with extended quills. If given the choice, she'd face the porcupine. Unlike Jonah, the porcupine would offer her some sort of adventure and excitement. She offered a fake smile before sipping her now tasteless beverage.

"I thought I recognized your voice, Eugenia." Jonah stepped into the parlor as if he'd been summoned.

A black cloud of doom descended on her. She loosened her grip on the handle of her cup, lest she damage the delicate china. As often as Mama visited with her friend, she probably knew when Jonah was coming home. No wonder her mother had been so thrilled when Eugenia offered to come calling with her.

"Could I interest you in a walk outside on such a nice day? That is if you don't mind, Mrs. Hampton."

Jonah's smug smile made her feel as if she were a mouse cornered by a cat.

"Of course not." Mama's round face glowed.

Eugenia rose and walked out of the room with him. Before allowing Jonah to escort her outside, she took her time tying on her bonnet, then fluffed the lavender bow just right. What a dreadful way to waste such a beautiful afternoon.

"The weather has been delightful the last few days." How she wished she could ignore the man assisting her down the front porch steps. "Yesterday was perfect for a vigorous ride."

His brow furrowed. "I suppose it was."

Peering into his much-too-serious face, she stifled a laugh. Jonah hadn't approved of her galloping Belle through the woods when she'd told him about it the last time he was home.

Perhaps she could irritate him enough to make this a shorter walk than he intended. She suspected her dowry was what really attracted such a business-oriented man to her, especially since his older brother appeared to be the preferred son to someday take over their family plantation.

"Has Mother told you of my plans to move to Nashville, now that I've finished my studies?"

"No." She watched a squirrel scamper up a nearby oak tree and wished she could join the creature. How easy to picture herself perched on a branch pelting Jonah with acorns until he ran away.

He spent the next few minutes talking of his plans, not appearing to notice she did nothing but nod or smile as they walked among the shade trees. How boring to be so predictable. Like a horse with blinders unable to see anything else around him, he'd mapped out his entire life and intended to follow that path only. Not one syllable uttered about the warm sunshine or the heavenly perfume of roses blooming nearby.

"Once I have a secure position, I'll build my own home and

settle down with the right lady." His thin lips almost turned up into a smile as he glanced at her.

I'll not be that right lady. Not if she could manage it. And manage she would. She couldn't imagine enduring a lifetime with a man who didn't understand or accept her any better than Mama did. Living with her mother was hard enough.

"Oh! Ouch!" Grimacing, she halted and stared down at her foot. "I think I have a pebble in my slipper."

"May I be of assistance?" He reached over as if he'd take her arm.

"If you'd be so kind as to turn around, I'll remove my slipper and shake out the rock."

He did as she asked. Eugenia leaned against an oak tree and removed her right slipper. Just in case he tried to steal a glance her direction, she shook out the pretend stone before putting her shoe back on. "You may turn around now."

When he looked into her eyes, she placed her weight on her foot and winced. "For such a tiny rock, my foot feels quite bruised. I'm afraid I need to return to the house."

"I'm sorry you're in distress." He offered her his arm.

She pretended to be in too much pain to notice his gentlemanly gesture and limped toward the house.

Not long after Eugenia hobbled into the parlor and sank into the nearest chair, Mama ended her visit. If only they'd managed to leave before the Brownings issued a personal invitation to the ball they planned for Saturday next. What a terrible way to start the month of June.

"Of course, we'll come." Mama's brown eyes shone like a child receiving a new toy.

"May I be so bold as to ask if you'd promise the first dance to me?" Jonah smiled at Eugenia from the gold upholstered chair next to hers.

She struggled to swallow the lump in her dry throat. "I'd be delighted."

After a few more remarks about the ball, Jonah and his mother walked with Eugenia and Mama to the door.

"I do hope that bruise doesn't pain you too much." Mrs. Browning fanned herself as vigorously as if she were the one in agony. "I know how dreadful something like that can be."

Leaning against the wall, Eugenia managed to maintain a serious expression. "I'll be fine. Thank you for your concern."

* * *

THE BRUISED FOOT healed well enough for her to call on Clarisse Matthews, her best friend, by the next afternoon. "You mustn't mention to my mother about our walk today." Eugenia soaked in the sunshine as they stepped off the front porch of the spacious Matthews home.

"Oh?" Clarisse's eyes widened as she glanced over at her.

She told her friend everything that happened at the Browning's house yesterday, including the invitation to their upcoming ball. "I had to remember which foot to limp on the rest of the day."

Shading her eyes from the early afternoon sun, Clarisse grinned. "Shall we walk toward the back yard where we'll be out of the heat some?"

Eugenia nodded. Her friend's smile and sparkling blue eyes looked wonderful. Poor Clare had endured so much heartache since the death of her fiancé. Eugenia wasn't ready to risk such pain for herself. Another reason not to rush into any marriage, even if she had a likeable suitor.

"I wish I could have declined Jonah's request for the first dance, but you know how Mama and Papa adore the entire Browning family."

Clarisse nodded. "Especially Jonah since he's such a fine prospect for a husband."

"As long as someone doesn't mind living with a walking business journal." Eugenia groaned.

"But that business journal is in line for a good inheritance." Clarisse playfully pointed her finger at her friend.

Eugenia rolled her eyes. If or when she was ready to think about marriage, she'd like someone to offer her his heart rather than his money or status. She saw nothing wrong with wanting someone to accept her for who she was not what she had.

"I'd much rather discuss the interesting man I met Sunday afternoon."

"Oh?" Clarisse's dark eyebrows arched up.

She gave Clare a brief description of the mishap on her Sunday afternoon ride plus a glowing report of her intriguing rescuer. "I don't know what I would have done if Mr. Stuart hadn't come along. He's quite nice and helpful."

"My brother would agree with you." Clarisse grinned as she fanned herself.

"He would?" Waiting for more information, Eugenia paused next to a magnolia tree.

"Titus had problems with a carriage wheel while he was in Murfreesboro a while back. Paul is a wheelwright, so he repaired it for him. Titus was impressed with the man's workmanship and the man himself. They've become good friends since then."

If Titus thought so highly of the man then Eugenia's impressions of him had to be right. How nice. "Then I can be certain Mr. Stuart will keep my secret."

As they neared Mrs. Matthews' fragrant flower garden, filled with a rainbow of colorful blossoms, Eugenia took a deep breath. She'd rather concentrate on the beautiful verbenas and roses than think about her troubles.

Clarisse slowed her pace. "Do be careful with Jonah."

"Oh, I am." Eugenia stooped to smell a beautiful pink rose in full bloom. If only she could enjoy this wonderful spring day and not be concerned about Jonah.

"Good. Jonah and my brother crossed paths a few days ago. Titus was appalled by the man's statements."

Eugenia jerked up so quickly, she almost pricked her finger on a thorn. Judging from Clare's serious expression, she'd better pay more attention to her friend's words. "What did Jonah say?"

"Since everyone thinks a married man is more stable and reliable, he's decided marriage is a good way to further his business plans. He never mentioned affection, much less love."

"Oh, dear. I do have a dilemma, don't I?" Eugenia slumped onto the black wrought iron bench next to the rose bush.

"I fear so. He wants a refined yet spirited lady." Clarisse sat next to her. "He might as well have called you by name."

"If I can manage to stay on good terms with Mama for the next week or so, then I could have a horrific headache the night of the Browning's ball."

"I won't be surprised if I don't see you there." Clarisse's eyes twinkled.

"If that doesn't work, I'll think of something that will." Eugenia laughed in spite of the problem hovering over her. "I've become quite adept at dodging unwanted suitors. And Jonah is definitely of the unwanted variety."

Eugenia enjoyed her best friend's company as long as she dared stay. Such a friendship comforted and cheered her. Only Clare would warn her about Jonah instead of considering him a wonderful beau.

Chapter Three

The Saturday of the Browning's ball arrived much too soon, but feigning a headache was not an option. After much pleading, Papa had agreed—even insisted—she should have a new gown. Even Mama, who usually objected to unnecessary clothes, had agreed with Papa. Which meant she was stuck sitting in front of her mirror, fighting not to fidget while Lily finished doing her hair for the ball.

If they couldn't see how mismatched she would be with a man like Jonah, her parents' eagerness couldn't bode well for her. The placid life he planned was the opposite of what she wanted. The man had no idea what she thought or felt and didn't care. Visions of dancing with Jonah sent prickly shivers through her body despite the warm early June evening. She couldn't imagine a marriage with someone like him.

"Miss Eugenia, you has to sit still." Lily, her maid, admonished her while trying to finish putting Eugenia's hair up.

She forced herself not to squirm. If only she *did* have a headache. The pale orange silk gown reflected in her mahogany-framed dresser mirror gave her no joy. Their seamstress had fitted the dress flawlessly. The bright orange sash accented her narrow waist to perfection. Her pearls were just the right highlight for the scooped neckline. How awful to waste such a lovely ensemble on such a horrid occasion.

Lily fluffed the last curl. Eugenia stood and twisted to survey the back of her head in the mirror. "Oh, I want my good beige fan."

As her maid rushed to retrieve the fan, a soft knock on the door prevented Eugenia from thinking of another method of delay.

"The carriage is waiting, dear girl." Her father's voice drifted from the other side of the door.

"I'm coming." She took the fan from Lily and then trudged into the hall.

By the time the Hampton carriage rolled up the drive to the Browning home, the entire lane was lined with parked, empty vehicles. With any luck, some other lady had already captured Jonah's attention. Every mother in the county considered such an ambitious man a fine catch for their daughters.

Jonah stood in the entrance hall with his mother and father when the butler ushered Eugenia and her parents inside. He looked so proper and stiff, she might have mistaken him for a statue if he hadn't moved.

She stifled a sigh when the image of Mr. Stuart popped into her head. What a contrast between her unassuming rescuer, so at ease in his homespun clothes, and the rigid formal Jonah, clothed in a fashionable black coat and trousers. The simple Mr. Stuart intrigued her enough to hope for another chance meeting with him, while Jonah made her wish she could run from the room and never return.

"Good evening, Gerald, Anna, we're pleased you've come."

Mrs. Browning flashed a glowing smile at all three Hamptons despite leaving out Eugenia's name.

"We wouldn't think of missing your ball," Papa replied.

"Good evening, Mr. and Mrs. Hampton." Jonah made a slight bow to them. "May I steal your lovely daughter away? She has already promised the first dance to me."

"Yes, indeed." Papa's beaming smile turned up the ends of his white mustache. "You young people enjoy yourselves."

Feeling like a bird trapped in a gilded cage, Eugenia walked with Jonah down the brightly lit hall and into the large parlor serving as the ballroom. The furniture had been removed, leaving the sparkling crystal and gold chandelier as the main feature in the room. The festively dressed people against the background of the polished mahogany-paneled walls would have been a breathtaking sight if she had been with different company.

"You are a vision of loveliness in that dress." Jonah's grating nasal voice interrupted her thoughts.

She hid her frown behind her fan. "Thank you."

"I've missed our lovely Southern ladies while at college. Northern women cannot compare to our local jewels."

"Then you must reacquaint yourself with everyone you've so direly missed." Eugenia hoped to divert his attention from her while they walked across the room.

"I prefer your company." He smiled into her eyes.

Before she could think of a suitable reply, the instruments sounded the notes of the first dance. Jonah took her hand. Discordant prickles radiated up and down her spine.

Dodging her unwanted suitor consumed too much of her evening. She and Clare stepped outside for some fresh air as often as they could manage. When inside, Eugenia accepted dances with any man who asked. Otherwise, Jonah would have cornered her for every dance.

Luke Williams walked up to her after she'd finished a waltz with a man who could double for milk toast. "I've had a difficult time telling you so much as a quick hello tonight."

"I've never lacked for friends." How nice this friend rescued her at just the right moment.

"May I have this dance?"

"I wouldn't think of telling you no." She gave Luke what she hoped was a dazzling smile when Jonah glanced her way.

Luke led her onto the floor as the first chords of another waltz began. "You've danced with Jonah more than anyone else tonight. Have I missed something between the two of you?"

"Oh, no!" Her reply was much too quick to sound polite, but she didn't care. No one would pair her off with Jonah.

"Since you're so popular, I'll ask in advance for the last dance. Would you give me the honor?"

"Of course." She hoped her fake smile appeared more convincing than she felt. The sooner this night ended, the better.

"Thank you. I missed you while I was away at school."

"Oh, really?" She gazed up into his earnest blue eyes. His rapt attention and remarks too closely echoed Jonah's actions.

"Yes, really." As they moved to the music, his beaming smile lit up his entire countenance.

The moment Mr. Browning announced the last dance, Eugenia spied Jonah striding toward her. She delighted at his frown when Luke claimed her before Jonah could finish making his way across the parlor.

"I have relished what little time I've managed with you." Luke glanced toward the advancing Jonah as he led her in the other direction.

"We've enjoyed each other's company since childhood." She managed not to wince as she gave him another well-rehearsed smile. Her head hurt from feigning happiness for so long. This long night of charades couldn't end soon enough.

"Yes, but I enjoy the woman I'm dancing with now so much more than the little girl I teased when she came to play with my sister." He squeezed her hand.

Looking into his adoring eyes made her mouth go dry. She would drive such a mellow man to distraction. His unadventurous outlook would frustrate her. Luke needed to pursue someone more like himself. More important, such a fine man deserved someone who loved him—not liked him as she would another brother.

"I don't believe I've ever seen you so quiet." He gazed into her eyes as they glided past another couple.

"I'm tired from dancing most of the night."

He nodded. "I suppose you are."

She forced another smile, glad this man didn't need to talk every minute, which allowed her to keep her true thoughts to herself. Any serious relationship still frightened her after Clarisse's painful loss of her intended.

Add to that her frustrating situation with unwanted beaus, who cared more about her dowry than her, and she had a plethora of reasons for her exhaustion. She was so weary of dealing with men like Jonah, who wouldn't accept her for herself. Even a friend like Luke didn't truly understand her.

The last sincere conversation she'd had with a man had been the day Paul Stuart had assisted her. True, he'd dared to chide her about galloping Belle, but his bold honesty impressed her. Such a confident man would never want a wife as a mere bauble to show off his accomplishments. When she was ready for marriage, she'd thrill at being courted by a man with the qualities Mr. Stuart possessed.

If only he were the son of a prominent landowner instead of the son of her father's overseer.

Jonah stepped up behind Luke and tapped his shoulder, sending Eugenia's pleasant thoughts of Paul Stuart skittering across the room like shattered shards of glass. "May I intrude and finish the dance with this lovely lady?"

Gentle Luke released her hand to the boorish Jonah and walked away, leaving her to seethe in silence. After such a brazen move, the whole county would assume Jonah was courting her.

Chapter Four

Squinting at the bright sunlight streaming through the lace curtains of her bedroom window, Eugenia groaned. She vaguely remembered her maid trying to shake her awake earlier this morning. Mama had wanted her to go to church, but she'd resisted Lily's efforts and gone back to sleep. The Browning's ball had ended after midnight. Only Mama would go to services with so little rest.

An unwelcome image of Mama marching off alone flitted through her mind. Her mother's sweet smile and honey-coated comments to friends would show no hint of how perturbed she was with the daughter who had missed church two Sundays in a row.

After a late breakfast, Eugenia strolled through her mother's flower garden at the edge of the backyard. The early June sun warmed her tight shoulders. She stooped to check the rose bushes and filled her lungs with the sweet scents of the pink and white blossoms. Such a satisfying balm for her troubled spirit.

She'd lost count of how many times she'd danced with Jonah or Luke. She sighed. Why did everyone think she should have matrimony as her prime objective in life? Perhaps she was in danger of being a lonely spinster, but only a union with mutual respect and love would be worth risking her heart.

Someone tapped her shoulder. She jumped.

"Miss Eugenia, yo' mama is home and say for you to come in for lunch." Her maid interrupted her melancholy musings.

"Mama's home already?" Eugenia shot to her feet.

By the time she scurried up to her room to wash her hands in her basin and check her hair, Mama and Papa were seated in the dining room waiting for her.

"I'm sorry I'm late." Eugenia slid into the chair the butler held out for her.

Her mother's furrowed brow and slight frown sent unwelcome silent signals. Bowing her head, she waited for Mama to pray over the meal.

"Dear Father, thank You for the many unrecognized blessings You've given us. Help us to always be mindful of You and everything You do for us. Amen."

"Amen." Before settling her napkin in her lap, Eugenia smiled at her mother.

Papa's green eyes twinkled when he nodded at her, but he knew not to show too much cheerfulness when Mama was this unhappy.

"You missed a wonderful sermon on how God continues to love us regardless of what we've done, Eugenia."

Papa coughed. "Anyone who danced almost every dance last night needed extra rest."

Knowing Papa's views on God, Mama didn't continue on about the sermon. Instead, she attacked her chicken with a vicious stab of her fork. "Clarisse was disappointed not to see you this morning."

Her mother's unspoken words about her own disappointment hung in the warm room like a stifling wool blanket. Eugenia ducked her head, pretending a greater interest in her food than she felt. Her late breakfast had little to do with not being hungry. The almost constant warring with Mama curtailed her appetite much too often lately.

"I'll call on Clare tomorrow."

"You appeared to have a delightful time last night, especially with Jonah." Mama's observation finished ruining Eugenia's waning appetite.

Since her mouth was full, she used that as an excuse not to reply. Then grabbed her water goblet in hopes of ending Mama's comments. If such a disease as marriage fever existed, her mother suffered from it in the worst way. She'd be the intended victim of Mama's malady if she weren't careful.

As the meal progressed, Eugenia felt as if she were a rabbit trying to elude baying hounds. She lost track of how many times her parents mentioned Jonah or Luke. Both of them had spent too much time observing her dance partners last night.

"I thought Mrs. Browning's gown was exquisite in its simplicity. Didn't you, Mama?" Exquisitely dull to tell the truth, but she had to say something to change her mother's focus.

"I've always admired Martha's taste." Mama finally smiled.

After lunch, Eugenia made her best effort to remain in the parlor with her parents, but the sunshine and flowers all but called her name when she stared out the lace-curtained window. She'd have to practice being a demure lady another day.

"I must enjoy this beautiful weather. I promise to be back in plenty of time for supper."

"Before supper." Her father's no-nonsense tone didn't match the sparkle in his eyes. "Go on. You'll only be young once." His wide grin lifted both ends of his mustache. A welcome sign.

"Thank you, Papa." She smiled at her parents before making her escape from the room.

Her ride this afternoon would be much tamer than the one two weeks before.

"You can't gallop, Belle. I must come home in a much better state today." She sighed. "Mama loves me dearly, but we have such a difficult time getting along. I try so hard to be ladylike and mature, but I don't succeed at either most of the time."

Low masculine-sounding chuckles coming from somewhere close behind startled her. She slowed her horse and turned to see who the unexpected eavesdropper could be.

"Is someone there?"

* * *

PAUL GROANED TO HIMSELF. Too bad he hadn't kept quiet and ridden off. He'd heard Miss Hampton talking to someone. Shading his eyes, he squinted through the trees trying to see who was with her. If only he hadn't laughed, but he could have sworn she'd called her horse by name and then started talking to the animal like a real human being.

He'd told the Lord he'd be her friend if he saw her again, and he didn't take a promise to God lightly. But God could have picked a better day to put this woman smack dab in front of him. He'd almost had words with his pa over slavery again and didn't feel like talking to anyone right now.

Maybe he could just say hello and go on. Maybe he'd heard wrong, and she was chattering like a squirrel with a friend hidden by the trees and wouldn't be interested in talking to him. He blinked as he rode up close enough to see her. The lady was alone and talking to what—the air or her horse? He hoped her horse.

"Does your horse ever talk back?" He said the first thing that came to mind, wishing he'd come up with something more clever.

Her face turned red. "Uh, no."

"That's good. I didn't think your horse talked like that donkey did to Balaam in the Bible."

"I've never heard of such a story." She glanced over at him, wide-eyed.

"It's somewhere in the book of Numbers. You can look it up and read it."

"Perhaps I'll do that." She loosened her hold on the reins. "Judging by your solemn expression, you now think I'm daft as well as vain."

He shook his head. "If I knew what daft was, I could tell you better what I'm thinking."

"You must think me a little crazy. I'm afraid most normal people don't talk to an animal the way I do."

"Maybe not, but I don't think you're crazy." *Leastwise, not completely.*

"I'm glad to hear that. I get very lonely, and Belle doesn't mind listening."

He was happy he could talk to Titus instead of his horse. Before he managed to think what else to say, she started jabbering again.

"You see, my sister and brothers are so much older than I am that it's almost as if I'm an only child with no one to talk to. My eldest brother was the only one I really knew, but he died two years ago. The others all live in or close to Nashville with their families. I hardly know them."

He stared at her, amazed at the details she went on to give him about her sister and brothers, down to their ages and how many children each one had. If she talked like this all the time, no wonder she was lonely. This woman could make a man's ears sore, regardless of how pretty she was in her dark green riding habit.

Have I ever not listened to you?

The answer to that was as clear as the cloudless sky above his head. *No, Lord.* He hunted through his mind for something kind to say. "You don't ever meet a stranger, do you? I mean you're telling someone you don't know all kinds of things about yourself."

"You're a gentleman who came to my aid, not a stranger."

What crazy ideas she had. He laughed so hard he almost choked. No gentleman he knew lived in a one-room cabin with homemade furniture. "I'm the son of your pa's overseer. Remember?"

"You're polite and kind as a gentleman should be. You've also kept your word not to say anything to anyone about helping me."

He stared slack-jawed at her. Surely she didn't really think of him as a gentleman. Yeah, she did. Her serious expression signaled she must mean every word. "Why don't it bother a lady like you to talk to someone like me?"

"We don't have an aristocracy in this country, especially with Andrew Jackson as president."

Shading his eyes from the sun, he stared at her. This woman was harder to figure out than the weather.

She laughed. "I surprise you, don't I?"

"Yeah."

"Some people think I shouldn't converse with you like this, but I don't care. I enjoy making new friends, and their station in life doesn't bother me."

He guided his horse around a fallen log. "Just the same, if you see me at church, you don't have to act like you know me."

"I would have to do that if I were with my papa, but Mama probably wouldn't mind if you're my friend as long as you're a good Christian man. Since you go to church, I assume you're a Christian." She let her horse pick its way around the log and kept chattering until she was riding beside him again.

"I been raised in church, but that don't make me a Christian any more than walking into a barn makes me a horse."

"Whatever do you mean?" Eyes wide, she stared at him as if she couldn't wait to hear his answer.

"Believing in Jesus makes me a Christian, not going to church."

He couldn't believe he needed to explain such things to the daughter of a Christian woman. He didn't see her in church too much, but she had to have heard the preacher's sermons when she came.

"I'll think about what you've said."

This woman needed to think about a lot of things.

She tightened up the slack reins in her gloved hands. "For now, I must return home. If I see you at church, please don't be offended if I pretend not to know you. I dare not explain to my mother how we met. I hope you don't think me too forward for counting you as a friend so soon."

"Picking friends as fast as you gallop that horse can be dangerous. You don't know me."

"No, but Clare tells me you're a good friend of Titus. I trust her brother's judgment."

So did he. "Titus is a good man."

"Then you'll admit my opinion of you isn't faulty."

He couldn't help but grin at her. She'd bested him as soon as she'd mentioned Titus's good opinion of him. Pity any man who tried to win an argument with her. He didn't stand a chance, and she knew it judging by the mischievous smirk on her pretty face.

Those dancing eyes of hers would cause him all kinds of

trouble if he weren't careful. Better not spend any more time thinking about her looks, especially since she was spoiled beyond reason. "You don't like anybody to caution you about anything, do you?"

She stiffened. "My mother is cautious enough for me and at least ten other people." She glanced up through the trees toward the sun. "I can't return home late. I really must end our conversation. Good day, sir."

"Goodbye." He tipped his hat before she rode away. She'd called him sir. Again.

As he'd done the first time he'd met her, he watched her ride off until the trees hid her from view. He didn't understand why the Lord wanted him to be friends with someone who aggravated him so much.

Being a friend to someone he disliked and felt sorry for all at the same time wouldn't be easy, but he'd promised God he'd try. Since she was so lonely, he might be able to handle talking to her every couple of weeks or so until he left here for good next year. Rather, he'd listen while she yakked and yakked some more. She probably even talked in her sleep.

Yet, he liked how she spoke to him as if he was every bit as good as she was, even calling him a gentleman. Pa would get a good laugh out of that if he hadn't promised not to tell him he knew the woman.

Such a woman would probably never make sense to him. He'd best turn his thoughts and his horse toward Murfreesboro. Thinking too much about Eugenia Hampton would cause him more trouble than he left behind in Nashville.

* * *

As she rode toward home, Eugenia puzzled over the strange turn of their conversation. She had chosen the same trail she'd taken two weeks ago, hoping to see Mr. Stuart again, but she hadn't planned on a bewildering talk about God.

The direct, soft-spoken man and his ideas fascinated her. No man in her social circle dared to be so honest with her. He hadn't sounded eager to accept her offer of friendship. Why? Such a handsome, puzzling specimen of humanity deserved further study, even if it meant going to church.

When she walked into the house, her parents' discordant voices drifted from the parlor into the hall. She stopped just outside the room when she realized their strident discussion concerned her.

"You know Eugenia has no need for the other dresses she has begged you for. She needs to learn life consists of things so much more important than her wardrobe."

"I assure you she knows that, dear wife."

"How can she, as spoiled as she is? Perhaps we've even hurt her chances for finding a good husband by coddling her so."

To prevent her parents from hearing her moan, Eugenia covered her mouth with both hands. A new gown for the Browning's ball had been just fine.

Papa cleared his throat the way he usually did when he was upset. "Yes, we've pampered her, but as for marriage prospects, she looked to be the belle of the Browning's ball."

Thank you for defending me yet again, Papa. Eugenia closed her eyes and slumped against the wall.

Mama harrumphed in a most unladylike fashion. "I hope your assessment is correct. Please continue to remind me of that when she does such reckless things as she did Sunday before last."

Her mother's heavy sigh floated out of the parlor. "Grace rarely mussed her dresses or her hair, as a child, but Eugenia still does those things at eighteen. Perhaps it would have been better if she'd been our fourth son."

To keep from crying out in pain, Eugenia bit her lip. She'd realized years ago that her mother preferred her sister, Grace, over her, but had never thought Mama might regret her youngest daughter being born.

"God blessed us with each child for a reason. I believe I've quoted you correctly." Papa's gentle voice drifting into the hall did little to soothe her aching heart.

"You know you did."

The conversation ceased. The pages of Papa's newspaper rattled. Eugenia tip-toed back to the front door and then made sure her footsteps on the polished wood floor were loud enough to alert her parents to her return.

"I'm going to my room to change for supper. Would you send Lily up, please?" She rushed past the parlor toward the stairs.

While Lily helped her change clothes, Eugenia wished she could do more for herself. She craved time alone to think. To wonder how Mama could say such cruel things about a daughter she was supposed to love.

After everyone finished supper, Eugenia excused herself for a walk outside. She trudged around the entire flower garden and still couldn't bring herself to go in the house. Supper had been agonizing, pretending to be cheerful and acting as if she had not overheard her mother's remarks.

From the backyard garden, Eugenia walked to the front lawn and then down the tree-lined drive while watching dusky shadows chase away the daylight. Her heavy heart was as dark as the dimming yard. Even the fireflies couldn't fascinate her as they usually did. The crickets' chirping sounded harsh to her ears.

She turned toward the house and stared up at her parents' bedroom window. "Mama, don't you love me? I don't try to upset you on purpose, but sometimes I yearn for an adventure. Why do you think I'm so awful?"

Tears slid down her cheeks as she slumped against a sturdy oak tree and let the deepening shadows fall over her. Loneliness and emptiness engulfed her. She stayed outside until she saw candlelight flickering only from her parents' window.

After Lily helped Eugenia change into night clothes, her gaze fell on the Bible on her nightstand. Lily must have retrieved the book and dusted it off from where it fell under her bed. She kept it out only to appease Mama, but she'd welcome any kind of diversion for now. Dropping onto her bed, she grabbed the book.

Where was the story about the talking donkey Mr. Stuart had mentioned? Somewhere in the Book of Numbers. Curiosity compelled her to continue skimming, verse after verse. Finally, she located the story in chapter twenty-two.

The donkey *had* talked! She didn't understand much of the story. She'd ask Mama a few questions tomorrow. That should prove Eugenia cared for more than frivolities.

When she saw Mr. Stuart again, she'd thank him for telling her about this interesting story. Thinking of the quiet man with the gentle blue eyes made her smile. A man with his qualities would make such a wonderful and interesting beau. But even if the man liked her, she'd need one of Mama's miracles for either of her parents to accept someone of such humble means.

If miracles really happened.

Chapter Five

Eager to talk to her mother about the verses she'd read the night before, Eugenia made sure to be on time for breakfast. Joseph was just setting Papa's coffee in front of him when she entered.

"Mama, I was reading about Balaam last night and found things I don't understand. Could we talk about it?" Eugenia began her questions about the confusing Bible story as soon as Mama finished praying over breakfast.

Her mother's eyes widened. "Of course. Why were you reading about Balaam?"

"The talking donkey got my attention."

"I need to speak to Nancy about supplies in the pantry and see to a few other things. After that, we can chat as long as you'd like." Mama's face glowed as she took a bite of her eggs.

After breakfast, Eugenia went to her room to think and reread the verses she'd found the night before. She wanted everything fresh in her mind. Somehow, she'd prove to her mother she could be serious. Mama's remarks from yesterday still cut Eugenia's heart.

Worse was the realization the words held a small kernel of truth, but anyone growing up in such lavish surroundings couldn't help but be spoiled. Her parents also dressed in the latest fashions. Servants tended to their every whim as if the family were royalty.

She forced her attention back to Balaam's story. Reading for a while was much better than dwelling on disturbing thoughts she had no answers for. Life had become much too bewildering.

A short time later, a soft knock on her door interrupted her morose musings.

"May I come in?" Her mother's voice drifted into the room.

"Please do."

Mama's round face lit up when she noticed the Bible still in Eugenia's lap. "Do you want to talk up here, or go down to the parlor?"

"You would be more comfortable downstairs, wouldn't you?"

"Yes. When you reach my age, upholstered furniture is much better than the hard-side chair you have in here."

"Your age! You sound as if you're ancient."

Wishing Mama hadn't mentioned such a troubling topic, Eugenia followed her mother down the stairs. She didn't care to think about her beloved mother getting older or that Mama no longer went up or downstairs as quickly as she used to do.

"Fifty-five is not young. I can't deny my wrinkles, graying hair, or expanded waist." Mama kept a firm grip on the stair railing as she slowly set her foot on the next step.

Eugenia shoved her disconcerting thoughts aside and concentrated on the way Mama's eyes had shone when she saw Eugenia still reading the Bible. She'd have to ask other questions about the scriptures, if that would make her mother happy.

"Give me a little time to read the passage before I try to help you." A welcome morning breeze rustled the curtains as Mama settled herself on the beige tapestry couch beside Eugenia. "I don't often read in the Book of Numbers."

"God told Balaam not to go and curse the Israelites, then told him he could go. Yet God would have killed him if the talking donkey hadn't warned Balaam of the angel with the sword. That doesn't make sense to me." The instant her mother looked up from the pages, Eugenia began her questions. She'd be as thorough as possible to prove how deeply she'd been thinking.

Mama nodded. "I fear Balaam wanted the money he was offered more than he wanted to do God's will. Sometimes, God has to use drastic measures, such as a talking donkey, to get people's attention."

"I don't understand."

"God says His ways are not our ways. I'm not sure if I can completely explain, but I'll try." She patted Eugenia's arm.

"I'd like that."

By the time Mama finished her explanation, Eugenia cared more about understanding this strange story and why God would want so much to get someone's attention than she did about impressing her mother. Did God really care about anyone to such an extent? Papa didn't think so, but as usual, Mama spoke with unwavering certainty of God's love. Eugenia must find a way to learn which of her parents was right.

"I have much to think about. I never realized the Bible could be interesting."

Her mother's eyes sparkled as she pushed a strand of graying hair off her face. "Why did you start with Numbers?"

"I happened to open it to the part about the talking donkey and found the whole story intriguing." She dared not mention the intriguing man who had told her about the verses she'd searched for.

"You won't be disappointed if you take time to read your Bible. And if you have any other questions, I'd be thrilled to try to answer them." Mama's glowing smile wreathed her entire face. Closing her Bible, she leaned against the cushioned back of the couch. "I believe I'll lie down for a while before lunch. I've got an aggravating headache for some reason."

"Are you all right?" Eugenia focused her full attention on her mother. Mama never complained or gave in to pain.

"Except for the headache. I'm sure it will go away if I lie down for a bit." Mama rubbed her temples as she closed her eyes.

"Do you need anything?"

"No." Mama opened her eyes and smiled as if to reassure Eugenia.

Walking with her mother toward the stairs, Eugenia managed to grin back. If Papa wasn't out checking the fields today, she'd tell him at once about Mama. The instant her mother was out of sight, Eugenia returned to the parlor to watch for Papa. When he came home for lunch, she met him at the front door the way Mama often did.

"Is your mother still busy tending to servants?" Papa hung his hat on the hat rack.

"No, she went upstairs for a nap, complaining of a bad headache."

Papa's frown knitted his bushy white eyebrows together. "A headache?"

She nodded.

"I'll go see to her." He hurried toward the stairs, leaving Eugenia to wonder and wait until Papa escorted Mama into the dining room a few minutes later.

"I promise both of you, I'm fine now. I did too much this

morning. That can happen with any woman my age." Mama seemed determined to reassure her family.

In spite of her mother's bright smiles, Papa still looked as concerned as Eugenia felt. Mama never slowed down long enough for a nap, especially not in the morning. Eugenia reached for her water goblet to help her swallow a bite of tasteless cornbread.

A helpless dread crept into Eugenia's heart, alongside the restless feelings still residing there. If something happened to her parents, anything she could envision for her future would not be pleasant or peaceful.

Since her remaining brothers were so successful in Nashville, she assumed they'd sell the only home she'd known and insist she come to live with one of them or her sister until they could marry her off. All of them were more like casual acquaintances than family, and she didn't get along well with Grace, what little she saw her.

Where would she live if she couldn't stay with one of her siblings? Who would care about her—even a little?

* * *

TROUBLESOME THOUGHTS and doubts still plagued Eugenia the next afternoon. She welcomed the butler announcing Clare's call. Talking things over with her best friend would help her feel better.

"I had to get out of the house a while." Clarisse's voice sounded shrill as they strolled through the flower garden. "Mother is upset with Titus over the friend he asked to stand with him at his wedding next Friday. She even claimed Papa would disown him if he were still alive."

Eugenia gasped. "Why? Any of your brother's friends

should be acceptable to your mother." She couldn't imagine gentle Mrs. Matthews ever saying such harsh things.

Clarisse shook her head. "He asked Paul Stuart."

"Oh, I see." Eugenia watched a yellow butterfly land on a white rose. Such a beautiful sight amid such an ugly conversation. "It's a pity people won't accept Mr. Stuart."

"I know, but Mother thinks Titus should have chosen someone with a better social standing for such an honor. She's afraid people will talk." Clarisse wrung her hands.

A crow cawed from a nearby tree. Too many people could sound as unpleasant as the big bird. "If people can't gossip about your brother, they'll find someone else."

"Yes, but my mother acts as if everyone will remember my brother's wedding into the next century. I'm sure that's why Titus waited so close to the wedding to tell her he'd chosen Paul." Clarisse released a long sigh. "It isn't pleasant at my house right now."

"I'm glad you came here, then. I enjoy talking to you so much more than Belle." Eugenia fanned herself while wishing for any kind of breeze.

"I should think so." Clarisse laughed. "You'd better hope no one ever hears you talking to your horse as much as you do."

"So far, only Mr. Stuart has heard me, but he was kind, even as he teased me."

"He's always kind when he visits with Titus at Hopeton."

Eugenia balled her hands into fists and jammed them against her sides. "That's why it is so unfair for people to judge others by their vocation or parentage. Tell your brother I'll be glad to talk *to* Mr. Stuart and not about him at the wedding."

Clarisse's face brightened. "Thank you for cheering me up."

"You've come to my aid so many times. I'm happy to help you feel better."

Eugenia lifted her face to the sun, wishing its warmth

could somehow penetrate her troubled heart. She told Clare about her worries over her mother's health and the painful comments Mama had made about her.

"I don't want to be like Grace, even if I could. When she was here the last time, she made me want to scream. I'm not looking forward to her upcoming visit."

"Your sister could make anyone shriek." Clarisse swatted at a pesky gnat. "I wonder if she has her servants polish the *underside* of her table."

In spite of their serious conversation, such a silly idea made Eugenia laugh. "If only my sister worried about nothing more than dust. She delights in telling me everything I'm doing wrong."

Clarisse shook her head as they continued their walk. "Maybe this visit will be better. I'll pray about it if you'd like."

"That couldn't hurt. She won't hesitate to remind me I should have a serious suitor since she and David had wedding plans before she was my age." Eugenia wasn't sure if prayers would do any good, but they couldn't make things worse.

"But I'm eighteen and unmarried too."

"Yes, but you were engaged and all ..."

She left her sentence unfinished as she peered into Clare's sad eyes. Her dear friend still suffered from the death of her fiancé. While trying to think of a more pleasant topic, she reached over and patted Clare's arm. "Even though you came here to escape your problems today, I need a favor from you, please."

"It must be something good, judging from your sparkling eyes." Clarisse halted her fanning as if waiting to hear the request.

"Very good. Please ask your brother to properly introduce me to Mr. Stuart sometime on the day of the wedding. Then I won't have to pretend I don't know him if I see him at church."

"I'm sure Titus would do that."

Thinking about talking in public with Mr. Stuart gave her spirits a wonderful lift. If only she didn't perplex the man so. Perhaps she could change his opinion of her if she could speak more openly with him. Now she had a reason to look forward to Titus and Jenette's wedding.

Chapter Six

Paul followed Titus and Jenette outside, glad their ceremony and wedding supper were finally done. One Friday afternoon spent inside a fancy mansion where he didn't belong was one too many. He couldn't get out of Jenette's parents' house and away soon enough from so many uppity people, who thought they were better than him. He wouldn't put up with so many silent snubs or haughty looks for anyone but Titus. The evening breeze washed over him like a cleansing spring rain as they stepped onto the front lawn.

"There she is." Titus gestured toward Miss Hampton, who was standing beneath a tree, talking with Clarisse.

No need for Titus to point the lady out. He'd already noticed how nice she looked. Her yellow dress was perfect for her blonde hair and green eyes. The woman looked as tempting as his ma's sweetest cake. But she's so spoiled.

As they walked up to Eugenia and Clarisse, Titus interrupted Paul's thoughts. "My sister tells me you need a proper introduction to my friend." His brown eyes had a mischievous glint.

Eugenia laughed. "I assume you know why, judging from the sly smile on your face."

Titus nodded. "Miss Eugenia Hampton, may I introduce you to my best friend, Paul Stuart? Paul, Miss Eugenia Hampton, my sister's chief cohort and confidant."

"I'm pleased to meet you, Mr. Stuart. Now I won't have to lie to my parents and pretend I don't know you." She grinned as she fanned herself.

"Pleased to meet you, too, Miss Hampton." Gazing into her sparkling eyes, he wished for Eugenia's fan. Titus's borrowed suit wasn't the only thing making him hot.

She don't like lies. The woman has some good qualities. For what good that wouldn't do a poor wheelwright. He had to stop looking at the beautiful lady in front of him before he caused himself more trouble than he'd had in Nashville. Titus said something that caused all three ladies to laugh. Paul jerked his attention toward his friends.

The newlyweds stayed and talked for a few minutes before excusing themselves to get ready for their drive to Hopeton. Clarisse wandered off to speak with someone else, leaving Paul alone with Eugenia. Watching the light breeze tease the loose curls around her face was a pleasant sight he had no business enjoying. He stuffed his hands into his pockets and wished staring over her head wouldn't be rude.

"I hope everyone spoke kindly to you." Her solemn expression seemed to signal her words were sincere.

"Everyone was nice to my face, but that could change after they get in their fancy carriages to go home."

All those elegant folks could leave anytime for more than one reason. He couldn't wait to shed this borrowed suit. Titus's clothes fit a little too tightly, especially around his neck and shoulders. Sweat trickled down his back. Dressing like a gentleman was downright uncomfortable on such a warm late June day.

"I'm sorry. People shouldn't talk about you that way." Her kind words warmed him more than he wished.

"It don't bother me." Neither did this honest conversation. He'd never expected to hear such words from a lady like Eugenia Hampton.

"I admire your strength." She folded her fan and clasped her hands as she continued to stare up at him.

She had no idea how weak his knees had been while standing next to Titus with all those people staring at him. He was as out of place here as one of his sister's cornhusk dolls would be. No matter how friendly and accepting she was toward him, he'd better remember how out of place he was with this woman. "God's the one Who gives me strength. I prayed a lot." He'd best keep praying.

"You sound like my mother. I read the passage about Balaam and found it quite interesting." She fanned herself again.

You did? He clamped his mouth shut to keep from saying something so rude out loud. "That's good."

Some of the knots in his shoulders loosened at hearing her comments about the Bible. He leaned against the tree trunk to hear what else she might say. He could talk about God and maybe help her a little bit. Since she wanted to talk about something besides herself, this might be the first conversation with her he could enjoy.

When she glanced away from him, her glowing smile turned upside down. "I'd really like to speak with you more, but I think my father is ready to leave. I'm sorry to be so rude and walk away from you."

He looked toward Mr. Hampton. The older man's deep scowl couldn't be missed. "Go on with your pa. I understand."

"Perhaps I'll see you on one of my rides again." She whispered her words from behind her fan as her father approached.

He nodded. The closer Mr. Hampton got to Eugenia, the fiercer his glare got. The man looked at Paul like he was some kind of snake he'd like to shoot.

* * *

Eugenia flashed Paul a quick smile before walking away with Papa. "I hope I haven't kept you and Mama waiting. I failed to notice you sooner."

"So I saw." Papa said nothing more during their walk toward the carriage. He continued his silence, while the coach rolled toward home.

The slight remnants of a frown remained visible among the wrinkles on her father's face as Eugenia studied him from the seat across from him. "I'm sorry I didn't realize you were ready to leave."

"Keeping us longer is not the problem. I was shocked to see you conversing so freely with that man."

That man? Papa's condescending tones made her shudder. "Titus introduced Mr. Stuart to me. Since no one else was talking to him, I couldn't be rude and walk away."

Papa stiffened and looked straight into her eyes. "Every old woman in the county will be talking about this wedding. I don't want them gossiping about you as well."

"Titus says Mr. Stuart is an honest, hard-working man. Can't a common wheelwright be a gentleman too?"

"We don't socialize with the son of my overseer." His stern expression emphasized his terse words.

"Clare says he's a good Christian man and goes to church

regularly. Don't those things matter more than his vocation or parentage?"

She shifted on the cushioned seat that now felt more like a wooden bench with splinters, but she must defend the man she considered a new friend.

"The religious aspects have no bearing on this conversation. Young Stuart is not the same caliber of man as Titus."

"How many planters around here started out living in humble circumstances?" She returned her father's direct gaze. He sounded as if he'd forgotten his own modest beginning in Tennessee. Eugenia had been the only one of his five children born in the lavish house they now occupied.

Papa shook his head. "Talk to your daughter, Mrs. Hampton, and explain why a young lady has to guard her reputation and be careful about the people she is seen with."

Eugenia leaned forward. "But, Mama, isn't being a Christian man the most important thing? He wasn't asking to call on me."

"We'll talk later. I'm too tired to discuss it now." Mama closed her eyes as she leaned her head back against the black leather seat.

The tense silence hung like a heavy dark curtain dividing the carriage in two. Neither parent acknowledged her for the remainder of the drive home. Papa had never behaved like this with her, no matter how much she perturbed him. Since she was being a lady by not being rude to Titus's friend, Mama should have defended her.

For once, Eugenia was glad her parents were tired and went to bed not long after they returned home. She did the same. She needed time alone to think.

"I cain't remember you ever wanting to go to bed so soon." Lily shook her head as she helped Eugenia change into her nightclothes. "You sure you ain't coming down with something?"

"I'm fine. I've had a long day."

Lily didn't appear convinced as she smoothed the yellow silk dress before putting it in the wardrobe. "Dis dress be perfect on you. All the gentleman had to see that."

Her maid's remarks reminded her of the discreet but admiring glances Mr. Stuart had given her while they talked. But the other events of the day overshadowed such a pleasant time. She rarely had a difference of opinion with her father. "You may go now. I'm tired." Eugenia pretended to stifle a yawn.

After Lily left the room, Eugenia slumped onto the edge of her canopied bed. Papa had often told her being a female didn't mean she had to stop thinking for herself. Mama insisted it was her Christian duty to treat people kindly. Seeing her with Paul Stuart changed both parents' ideas, but she would continue to speak to her friend, no matter how her parents felt about him.

For reasons she couldn't explain, she wanted and needed Mr. Stuart's friendship. Something about the gentle, forthright man drew her to him. Since he hadn't looked so aggravated with her today, maybe he'd accept her as a friend in spite of their vast differences.

One day, she might even be able to talk with him in public. Surely her indulgent parents would change their opinions of a man with such a stellar reputation. And if they didn't, she'd—she'd do what?

She didn't know.

Chapter Seven

As soon as possible the next morning, Eugenia retreated to her mother's flower garden. She drank in the soothing colors and scents. Yesterday's disagreement with her parents still vexed her. If only her hopes for an open friendship with Mr. Stuart could be as bright as the flowers dancing in the summer breeze.

"I've been looking for you."

She jumped at the sound of her mother's voice coming from behind her. "Do you need me?"

"We have to talk about yesterday, dear. Let's sit in the gazebo where we'll have some shade."

Mama settled onto the wrought iron bench across from the one Eugenia chose. No matter how much Eugenia wished she was imagining it, Mama sounded out of breath. Normally, she enjoyed watching the sunbeams dance around the floor. Today, she clasped her hands in her lap and focused her attention on her mother's somber face. Whatever Mama intended to say must not be pleasant.

"Are you also upset with me for talking to Mr. Stuart?"

"The way you defended our overseer's son disturbs me." Mama fanned herself.

"But you've taught me since childhood that God loves everyone."

"The man *is* a common laborer. Your father is correct about guarding your reputation." Her mother's clipped tone left no doubt of her true opinion of Paul Stuart.

Eugenia gripped the arm of the hard bench. "I shouldn't have to guard my reputation when I did nothing more than be polite to a nice man with a good name."

"It isn't right, but people do talk. I don't want them gossiping about you any more than your father does." Mama slipped her handkerchief from her sleeve and dabbed at the beads of perspiration on her forehead.

"If they have nothing better to do, then let them talk. All our well-bred friends embarrassed me the way they shunned Mr. Stuart." Eugenia wanted to jump to her feet to emphasize her protest but forced herself to remain seated.

As if in need of support, Mama leaned against the back of the bench. "A lady's reputation is a precious commodity and easily besmirched."

"But it's all so unfair and wrong." Eugenia struggled to speak in a civil tone.

Her mother's hypocrisy galled her. God's love might extend to all mankind, but Mama had no love for a common man like Mr. Stuart. Both of her parents had forgotten her grandparents' once humble circumstances.

"I don't have the energy to continue this discussion. Please give serious thought to what your father and I have told you." Mama released a labored sigh.

"Yes, Mama."

Eugenia finally noticed the dark circles under her mother's eyes. She hoped something hadn't kept her mother from sleeping well last night. Every word she intended to say to prove her parents wrong stuck in her dry throat. "I'm sorry to tire you."

"It's not you. I've just had so much to do to get ready for Grace's arrival."

"We'll talk more when you feel better."

"Yes, we should. I believe I'll rest before lunch." Mama's voice faltered.

"Are you well?" Eugenia rushed over to her mother and laid a hand on her shoulder. "Could I do anything for you? Get you anything?"

"I'm fine, dear. I've just done too much after such a busy day yesterday." As she gripped the arm of the bench to stand, her smile looked more like a grimace.

Eugenia's heart raced as she watched her mother shuffle toward the house. Something was wrong with Mama, but she had no idea what. Lately, whenever she mentioned her fears to Papa, he assured her Mama never kept secrets from him and would tell him if she was ill. She hoped Papa spoke the truth and wasn't helping Mama hide something from her.

WHEN GRACE and her boys arrived for their visit on Wednesday, all of Eugenia's gloomy thoughts vanished. Such a wonderful way to begin July. Two chattering nephews jumped from their family carriage, instantly brightening Eugenia's mood. After a perfunctory greeting to her sister, she strolled into the house with a little blond boy holding each hand.

"Grandmother has fixed the same room you had last time for you both to stay in." She guided the boys into the room across the hall from her own. "Are you hungry? Our cook made a special cake for dessert."

Gerald clapped his hands. "What kind?"

"Applesauce, I think. You must eat your supper before you get any, though."

He wrinkled his nose. "Do we have to do that here like we do at home?"

"Yes, you do."

The boys' nurse walked into the room. "Yo mama says we got to get you bof cleaned up fo' supper."

"But I'm not dirty from riding in a carriage all day. See." Seven-year-old Gerald held out upturned hands.

"No dirt, Mammy." Four-year old Bradley held his hands out for inspection too.

The nurse shook her head. "I'm only doin' what the missus says."

Eugenia left the boys with their nurse and went to her own room to freshen up. The meal tonight would not be dull with her nephews at the table.

Whenever Eugenia glanced at her mother that night, Mama's round face glowed with happiness. She laughed often while enjoying her grandsons and eldest daughter. If only Eugenia could make her mother so happy. In spite of her difficulties, Eugenia slept better than she had the past two weeks. Mama looked well. That was what truly mattered.

* * *

THE NEXT TWO DAYS, her sister called on old friends in the afternoon, leaving Eugenia to play with Gerald and Bradley uninterrupted. What a pleasant way to avoid Grace and her lectures.

On Saturday afternoon, Eugenia sat upstairs on her bed with a small boy on each side. Lily knocked on the open door before she stepped in to interrupt the story Eugenia was reading.

"Excuse me, miss. You has a gentleman caller in the parlor waitin' for you."

"I'll be down soon. Send the boys' nurse up." She hadn't thought to ask who awaited her. Be it Luke or Jonah, she didn't care which one of her unwanted callers had come.

"Does this mean we don't get to hear the end of the story?" Gerald lifted his head from where he'd been snuggled next to her.

"Of course not." She smiled before resuming her reading.

Fifteen minutes later, Eugenia ambled downstairs. She could hear Grace prattling with Jonah in the parlor. He rose when she entered the room.

"Pardon me for taking so long. I had to finish reading a story to my nephews."

Jonah nodded. "I'm glad you enjoy children so much."

Like prickly thorns, shivers radiated through her body. She hoped his comment wasn't a veiled hint about the future he wished to have with her.

"You should have postponed the story." Grace frowned in her direction.

"We were so close to the last page."

"Next time the boys can wait." Her sister's scowl upended to a grin when she glanced back over at Jonah. "I'm sure you're much more interested in speaking with my sister than me."

"I enjoyed our conversation." Jonah's gaze remained locked onto Eugenia.

"Just the same, I'll investigate the books in Papa's office and let you visit with the lady you really came to see." Grace's sly smile made Eugenia wonder just what or whom her sister and Jonah had discussed.

Taking the maroon chair closest to the door, Eugenia cast

about in her mind for something else to say. She assumed Grace had ordered refreshments, so she should have a way to occupy her hands soon. "Again, I apologize for the delay."

"I don't mind waiting for you." Her unwanted caller's smile didn't reach his dark beady eyes.

"Oh, well, not everyone around here shares those sentiments. I'm not very punctual, I'm afraid."

Her comment sounded inane, but Jonah's remark flustered her. The way he watched her every move reminded her of someone assessing a fine horse for purchase. She wasn't for sale, and she'd find a way to show him that.

"I had a pleasant time waiting. Grace told me how your brothers are doing in Nashville."

"I'll thank her later for being so gracious."

While wondering just how close by Grace might be, she smoothed her skirt. Close enough to Papa's office door to eavesdrop on her conversation with Jonah, if she knew her sister. Still no signs of a servant bringing refreshments. She glanced out the window to avoid looking at Jonah.

"It's so nice outside. Would you like to go for a walk?"

"I'd welcome a stroll with you." His appraising gaze never left her face.

She forced a smile while they walked out of the parlor. How her parents could like this man so well was a mystery she had no intention of solving. "I'll get my bonnet, and we can enjoy the sunshine." Before allowing Jonah to open the front door, she took her time removing her bonnet from the hat tree and then fussed with the ribbon to be sure it was tied just right.

At the bottom of the porch steps, she stopped and took a deep breath, filling her lungs with the scents of honeysuckle and roses. What a shame to endure a walk with Jonah instead of soaking in the beauty all around her.

"I intended to call again before today, but I've been seeing to Mother." Jonah glanced over at her as they walked across the lush lawn.

"I heard she's been ill. How is she?"

"Much better. Have you been busy since your sister arrived?"

"Oh, not busy, just pleasantly occupied. My nephews are wonderful little boys."

"I'm sure they are. Any woman would be proud to have such fine sons."

Eugenia peered down at a beetle crossing her path. At this moment she wouldn't mind following the thing into the dankest recesses of its choosing—or anywhere else that would allow her to escape from Jonah and his hints about children.

"I intended to talk with you at Titus and Jenette's wedding, but I never got the opportunity." His piercing gaze reminded her of a hawk searching out its prey.

She focused on the tree behind him as she tried to think of something else to say. If only she dared tell him how hard she'd worked to avoid him the entire time. "There were so many people there I found it difficult to talk with everyone."

"I noticed you didn't linger long after the supper."

His words made her stomach burn as she returned her attention to him. She'd had no idea he'd watched her that closely. "Mama got tired. Papa was in such a rush to leave that I had to walk away from Mr. Stuart and leave him without a soul to talk to."

"I doubt a man like that was bothered by your leaving." He flicked a leaf from his sleeve.

She chafed in silence at Jonah's calloused attitude. "Almost everyone there snubbed the poor man."

"Don't you know who he is and why no one spoke to him?" A frown creased his forehead as he halted to look down at her.

"Yes to both of your inquiries and it still infuriates me every time I think about it." She swatted at a pesky fly, wishing she could shoo away her caller as easily as the offending insect.

"Infuriates you? Why should you be so concerned over someone like him?" The disdainful curl of his lip incensed her.

"He acted like a gentleman with me."

"That man is no gentleman. I was shocked to see you talking alone with him." His frown deepened, knitting his eyebrows together.

Lest she shout in anger at him, she balled her hands into tight fists. "It is not your place to voice such concerns."

"Oh, but it is." He brushed her arm with his fingers. "You shouldn't converse with people such as that. I care about you, which means I care what people think about you." His hand traveled down to grasp her fingers as he leaned his head toward her.

She gasped and stepped back so quickly, she almost stumbled over a tree root. She'd rather have a spider crawling on her than feel this man's touch, much less the kiss she'd just dodged. Behaving in such a forward manner must mean he had to be close to asking Papa's permission to court her.

"I'll speak with Mr. Stuart any time I please, and you will have nothing to say about any such conversations." Nor anything else in her life.

His jaw dropped. "I must be honest about my thoughts and feelings if we are to continue entertaining possibilities of more than friendship between us."

"I wouldn't think of such possibilities with any man who dares tell me whom I should or shouldn't talk with." She took another step back.

"Judging from the angry flashing in your eyes, we should discuss this later after you have time to think rationally about my concerns. I'll say goodbye for now." His tone of voice reminded her of someone trying to soothe an overwrought child.

Standing as straight and tall as possible, she looked him in the eyes. "You and I will have no further discussions about anything. No man will ever choose my friends for me. Goodbye, Jonah."

"I'm sorry you feel that way. I'll not trouble you further." Spinning on his heel, he headed toward the barn.

She stared at his retreating back. That solved the problem with one unwanted suitor who wouldn't accept her for herself. Mama would be dismayed, but she'd deal with her mother later. For now, she was free from the man who only wanted her as a trinket to show off to business associates.

After two or three deep breaths, she walked toward the house. Once inside, she tip-toed down the hall toward the stairs, hoping Grace wouldn't hear her footsteps. Her sister was the last person she wanted to speak with at the moment.

"Where is Jonah?" Book in hand, Grace stepped out of Papa's office before Eugenia reached the stairs.

"He left."

Eugenia forced a fake smile. Since the office windows afforded such a wonderful view of the lawn, she doubted Grace had read a single word the last few minutes. Her sister had to have seen Jonah's departure. Grace's wide eyes and thin smile didn't fool her.

"But I asked Jonah to stay for supper while you were still reading to the boys. Pansy has already set an extra plate."

"You should have consulted me before you extended the invitation." Eugenia gritted her teeth to keep her tone civil and prevent saying more than she should.

"It's the courteous thing to do for a gentleman caller." Grace's voice sounded too similar to the one she used when explaining something to her boys.

Summoning what little self-control she had left, Eugenia clenched and unclenched her fists instead of telling her sister what she thought.

"Perhaps you can invite him to stay another time." Her sister's tense smile didn't match her sweet-sounding words.

"He won't be back. I sent him away."

Grace's brown eyes widened while her nostrils flared in a most unladylike manner. "How could you do that to a man of his caliber?"

"It was quite easy, and I don't care to discuss the details." Eugenia fought to contain her rising anger.

Grace's grip tightened on the book. Her sister's good manners were probably the only thing preventing her from throwing the book at Eugenia no matter how much she looked like she wished she could do just that. "You'd best think before acting so rashly again. He's one of the most eligible men in the county."

"Not for me. I need to go to my room and assess any possible damage my bonnet has done to my hair." She left her slack-jawed sister standing in the hall and fled upstairs.

While Lily saw to her hair, Eugenia listened to family voices filling the other bedrooms as everyone prepared for the evening meal. She'd made a colossal mistake rushing to her room and leaving Grace alone downstairs to greet their parents when they returned home.

Mama had made calls. Papa had gone to look at a horse. They would hear Grace's account of what had happened before Eugenia could tell them some semblance of the truth. She dared not complain of Jonah's disdain for Mr. Stuart nor tell them she'd defended her forbidden friend again.

Eugenia didn't leave her room until she heard everyone else making their way downstairs. She paused just outside the dining room. No one was discussing her. But she doubted that mattered. Grace's earlier report to their parents had probably already done enough damage. As the butler seated her, she forced a smile.

"My, what a feast. Cook must have thought we were expecting company." Mama barely finished saying the amen to her blessing before commenting on the china platter heaped with chicken.

"No one extra tonight." Grace glanced across the table at Eugenia before taking a sip of water from her crystal goblet.

Papa coughed and frowned at first Grace, then Mama. "I'll always prefer the company of my family to entertaining a room full of guests."

Eugenia flashed him a grateful smile. Papa would listen to her later. And hopefully not too closely to Grace. She said little through the entire meal. Her favorite fried chicken tasted drier than stale bread.

"Aunt Eugenia, can we catch fireflies tonight?" Gerald asked as soon as Eugenia choked down her last bite of dessert.

Oh, yes, yes, yes. What an excellent way to avoid serious adult conversation in the parlor. She dabbed her mouth with her napkin to hide her delighted smile. "If your mother says yes, you may."

"Please, Mama." The boys begged in unison as they turned eager faces toward their mother.

"It isn't quite time for fireflies to be out yet."

"We can play outside until it's almost dark and then catch them, can't we? Please?" Gerald kept his innocent gaze fixed on his mother across the table from him.

"All right, but you may not stay out long past dark. Then you must go upstairs and get ready for bed."

In a few minutes, Eugenia trooped out the front door with Gerald walking on one side and Bradley on the other. She carried a cheesecloth-covered bottle for each boy to use to catch fireflies. Escaping the barely disguised frowns of her mother for a little while would be most welcome. No telling what Grace had told their parents about how Eugenia had dismissed Jonah.

She watched the boys play until dusk when the fireflies appeared.

"See if you catch them and put them in the bottle, they almost make a lantern." She laughed with the little boys in spite of her present troubles. The evening summer breeze, scented with honeysuckle and roses, helped ease the knots from her shoulders.

Once the darkness settled in, she watched her nephews play for a while longer. "Your mama said not to stay out here too long. Your nurse might already be waiting to get you both ready for bed."

"Just a little longer, please." Gerald clasped his hands together as he begged.

"No, you must obey your mama." She dared not aggravate Grace tonight by allowing the boys to stay outside too long.

She took them inside through the back door, hoping to avoid the rest of her family as long as possible. After the youngsters made their way upstairs, Eugenia had no choice but to walk toward the parlor, where she heard her parents and sister talking. No one sounded upset, and she didn't hear anyone mention her name as she approached.

"We caught quite a few fireflies." Eugenia seated herself in a maroon upholstered chair across from the sofa where her mother and sister sat. "Both boys should sleep well as much as they played today."

"I'm sure they will. You have entertained them royally." Grace's lips turned up slightly.

"I don't mind at all."

Eugenia hoped her forced smile didn't look too stiff. She

wondered why Grace wanted to keep the conversation civil now, but she was grateful for any small favor from her sister. "I love being an aunt."

"We can all see that, dear girl." Papa stifled a yawn.

Dear Papa. Still defending her. He was probably the reason why everyone was behaving so nicely toward her tonight.

Mama nodded. "You'll be an excellent mother someday."

The wistful tone of Mama's voice grated on Eugenia's ears. Hopefully, after Grace left, she could talk with her mother and get her to understand why Jonah was not the right man for her daughter's happy someday. She'd rather be a spinster than be miserable the rest of her life with someone else who didn't understand her.

"The boys should be ready for bed by now. I'll tell them goodnight and then retire myself." Grace kissed her mother's cheek before standing. "Rest well, everyone."

"I've had a busy day and could use some extra sleep." Mama covered her mouth as she yawned.

"I won't argue with you. My long ride made me tired." Papa helped Mama to her feet.

"Since I'm the only one who isn't sleepy, I'll go for a walk before retiring." Peering into her mother's tired, lined face, Eugenia tried to sound nonchalant.

"Then we'll bid you good night." Papa kissed her forehead. Mama kissed her cheek before they left the room.

Eugenia stayed outside until the candles no longer glimmered from any bedroom window. She wasn't sure why her sister had been so kind tonight. Perhaps Papa had kept her from bringing up Jonah again. Grace had never let Papa's cautions prevent her from speaking her mind before. Which made Eugenia wonder if Grace noticed how fatigued their mother seemed to be and decided not to trouble her.

Something was amiss, especially with Mama.

Chapter Eight

The next morning, Eugenia awoke in time to go to church with Mama. She cast covert glances at her mother during the entire service. Whenever their eyes met, Mama gave her a radiant smile. That part was normal. Mama was always thrilled any time Eugenia accompanied her to church.

Instead of visiting with some of the other ladies after the service, Mama hurried to the carriage to spend time with Grace, thwarting Eugenia's plans to talk with her friends. She'd seen Mr. Stuart in church with his parents and had hoped for an opportunity to at least smile at the man while he talked to Titus.

"I've never seen you so attentive to the sermon on a sunny day like this." Mama settled onto the carriage seat across from her and smoothed her dark blue skirt.

Eugenia forced her thoughts from Mr. Stuart to her mother's words. "I'm thinking about what Pastor Bentley said."

The pastor had spoken as if every person on earth was a terrible sinner. She knew some fine people sitting in the church this morning and some equally fine ones who were not there. Papa being an excellent example of the latter. She'd argue with the pastor any day about her father's goodness, but she wouldn't anger Mama by voicing her thoughts.

Perhaps she could manage a ride alone this afternoon and discuss such things with Mr. Stuart. Sad how he listened to her better than her own parents.

"If you have any questions, I'll try to answer them." Mama's eyes sparkled.

"Later, please. I need more time to think."

"Any time, dear." Mama shifted until she could look across the carriage into Eugenia's eyes. "Could you help me understand something?"

"What?" The carriage bounced along a rough spot in the road. Eugenia braced herself. Judging from Mama's solemn expression, her mother's words might jar her more than the bumpy ride.

"Why did you send Jonah away?"

Because he was a boorish dictator in love with her dowry and social position instead of her. "I assume Grace told you about that."

Mama pursed her lips. "She's concerned for you. So am I."

"I'd rather keep my reasons between Jonah and me." She'd had quite enough of her sister's concern.

"I'm praying you give serious thought to reconsidering your actions."

Rather than say something she'd regret, Eugenia replied with a forced smile. Her life had more ruts lately than the rough road they now traveled.

"Don't you think your words to Grace were too sharp?"

Sharp was an understatement for the way her mother's words cut. Being the unpreferred daughter hurt more than she wanted to think about. "Grace must have neglected to mention her words were as harsh as mine. I won't have her running my life."

"The two of you need to talk. You see each other so little. Sisters shouldn't be at odds with each other. Grace has your best interests at heart."

"Yes, Mama." She said nothing more, hoping to put an end to such an unpleasant conversation.

Mama didn't speak again the remainder of the drive home. For some reason, no one said a word about yesterday while they ate lunch. Eugenia suspected she owed her thanks to Papa for such an uneventful meal.

As the family walked from the dining room to the parlor, Gerald took her hand. "Would you read us another story, Aunt Eugenia?"

Bradley's face lit up. "A story?"

"Later, I promise. I'm going for a ride first." She ruffled Gerald's hair.

"I can ride now. Can I come with you?" Gerald stood as straight and tall as he could manage.

"You should ride with Grandpa today." Papa smiled down at his grandsons. "Then Bradley can ride with me on my horse. Your aunt should have some time alone."

"Thank you." Eugenia flashed her father a grateful smile. He understood her so well she didn't have to explain how much she needed some solitude.

"Isn't it hot for a ride today?" Mama fanned herself as she sank onto the couch.

"July is always hot, but I don't get to ride with my grandsons every day." Papa took Bradley's hand. "Let's go tell the groom to saddle the horses while your aunt changes into her riding clothes."

Papa took the boys on a trail in the opposite direction from the one Eugenia chose, allowing her to drink in the peaceful stillness of her solitary surroundings. Only the mockingbirds' calls to each other interrupted the soothing quiet. Sunlight flickering in between the trees made pleasant golden splashes on the ground while easing the tension from her shoulders and neck.

"This is much better, Belle. I wish I could have gone for a ride yesterday. Maybe out here I can think clearly."

* * *

WHILE HE TRIED TO THINK, Paul allowed his horse to take his time going through the woods. If only he could figure out a way to prevent a repeat of this afternoon. He couldn't handle too many more arguments with his father.

Pa had quit trying to understand that Paul needed to make his own decisions the way any grown man should. It hurt something fierce for Pa to yell at him again. Ma didn't see anything wrong with slavery, either, but at least she didn't fight with him about his ideas.

If he had the money, he'd be gone tomorrow. But no matter how hard it was to stay in Tennessee, he wouldn't leave until he had enough money saved up to buy the farm of his dreams.

Maybe between then and now, God would help him and Pa get along again. He'd use the time he had left to do his best to mend his relationship with Pa. He loved his father, no matter how much they disagreed, and hoped Pa still loved him.

"Hello, Mr. Stuart."

He heard Miss Hampton's voice from close behind. She rode up next to him, so he had to say something polite even if he didn't feel like talking. "You must ride out here a lot."

"Yes, especially when I need to think. Things have been perplexing at home lately."

He nodded. She had no idea how hard life at home could get. "That don't sound good."

"It isn't." She sighed. "The woods comfort me."

"I like thinking outside too. I ain't ever talked to my horse about what's bothering me, though."

Unlike the glowing smiles he'd come to expect, this one looked half-hearted. "I'd rather talk with you. You're a better listener than Belle, and you give much better advice."

"I ain't the smartest man, but I guess I can listen." With all the problems he had, God could have picked a different day to send this woman around.

"Thank you for caring."

But he didn't care like she thought he did. He felt cornered—by God, by her, by life in particular right now. If only he could head out for Illinois and his dreams tomorrow.

She let the reins go slack in her hands. He braced himself for a long explanation about whatever was bothering her. Instead of talking for the next twenty minutes, she briefly explained about her problems with her sister and mother.

"Until lately, I had always been certain my mother loved me in spite of my impulsiveness."

The sadness in her voice touched his heart. How could he be so selfish and not listen to her? She must be hurting as badly as he was.

"Ma has told me over and over, just 'cause someone don't understand you don't mean they've quit loving you. Sometimes that's hard to believe, but you still love your ma even though you don't understand her."

The sparkle returned to her eyes. "I never thought of it like that. What an insightful man you are."

"It ain't me—it's God." He needed to listen to what he'd just said as much as she did.

"Just the same, I appreciate your thoughts."

Paul shrugged. Since he didn't like talking about something so similar to his own problems, he changed the subject to the first thing that came to mind. "I still can't figure out why a lady like you wants to talk to me."

They rode through a small clearing. She shaded her eyes from the sun as she looked over at him. "Why do you keep saying things like that? Surely you don't think anything is wrong with a man such as yourself."

"No, but most people like you do."

"Those people are wrong. I told one of my gentleman callers exactly that."

"Telling some man what you think ain't the best way to keep him around." Her pa's money must be the main reason she had any callers at all.

"I don't love the man. And I never shall after he had the audacity to tell me I shouldn't have spoken with you at Titus's wedding, so I sent him away."

His mouth dropped open. Titus had no idea how surprising this woman could be. "You got rid of a man because of me?"

She nodded. "I won't be ordered about by any man, especially when he's wrong."

Picturing the shocked look of her suitor in his mind made him chuckle. "I feel sorry for whoever you marry. That poor planter's son will have his hands full."

Ducking her head to miss a low-hanging tree branch before it knocked off her straw hat, she laughed. "You're probably right. I fully intend to continue thinking for myself, though."

"I can't imagine any man stopping you from doing that."

"You're almost laughing at me the way you did when Belle threw me. Am I that amusing?"

"I ain't ever met a woman like you. You've got more gumption than you need sometimes."

"I've never met a man with such thought-provoking ideas

before. You make me think more than the men I know with a college education." She looked over into his eyes

Unable to think what to say, he stared back at her. He'd never expected a conversation like this with this kind of woman.

The sun splashed through a tree onto her face. "I'm sorry to have to end such an interesting discussion, but I should return home now. As usual, you've given me much to contemplate."

He smiled. "I'll pray for you."

"Thank you. I could use that too." She waved at him before urging her horse toward home.

Wishing she hadn't left, Paul watched her ride off. Ma always said talking with someone was better than moping over your problems alone. He never would have thought that someone would be Miss Eugenia Hampton. For reasons Paul couldn't begin to know, the Lord must have some purpose for putting the lady into his path so much lately. Maybe God was the one laughing at him now.

And maybe she wasn't as spoiled as he'd thought. That idea almost jolted him out of his saddle. Surely he hadn't come to like such a talkative woman. But he had, since he hadn't wanted her to head home so soon.

As comforting as Mr. Stuart's comments had been, Eugenia remained uneasy the rest of the day. Disturbing thoughts still whirled in her mind when she should have been snuffing out her candle and crawling into bed. If one could love someone without completely understanding him or her, why was her mother still so easily perturbed with her daughter? Mr. Stuart accepted her better than Mama did some days.

How she hoped Mama's ever-present fatigue wasn't

another reason for the problems between them. She paced while trying to think of some sort of solution. When she tired of her marching, she sat on her bed. She stared at the Bible on her nightstand. Mama and Clare often spoke of finding answers in the Bible. Mr. Stuart had offered to pray for her. Did God have answers she could find nowhere else?

She picked up the book, with no idea where to begin. She'd paid so little attention to what Mama had tried to tell her. It fell open to the eleventh chapter of the gospel of Matthew. She read the first verse she saw. "Come unto me, all ye that labor and are heavy laden, and I will give you rest."

After reading more, she discovered these to be the words of Jesus. Mr. Stuart lived in poverty, yet he was content. She had countless advantages but no satisfaction. The son of her father's overseer had the kind of peace she yearned for. *Jesus, if You truly do know the answers, please show me how to have such serenity.*

* * *

Eugenia spent the next few days longing for time alone with her mother to discuss the verses in Matthew. Mama and Grace were either off making calls or talking together when they were home.

The words she had read kept echoing in her mind. Perhaps she should ride over to Hopeton and ask Clare to answer her questions, but talking with Mama about the Bible was one of the few things she could do to make her mother feel better. Burning questions or no, she'd wait until Grace left and talk with Mama. Anything that might ease the lines on her mother's fatigued face would be worth the wait.

Early Friday morning, Grace's carriage rolled down the drive to begin the trip back to Nashville. While the puffs of dust from the wheels got farther and farther away, Eugenia rejoiced in silence. Her parents' eyes glistened with tears, while her eyes remained dry.

Mama looked so distraught that Eugenia didn't attempt to talk with her that day. She didn't want her mother to guess how thankful she was to see Grace leave. She and her sister had managed a civil conversation about the day she had sent Jonah away, but things were still strained between them. She doubted she'd ever have a good relationship with Grace.

On Saturday morning, Eugenia saw her mother strolling alone in the flower garden and seized the opportunity. "Is now a good time to talk? Could we sit in the gazebo?"

"Certainly, dear. I know I've neglected time with you, but I see so little of Grace."

"I understand." Eugenia shoved aside thoughts of how well she understood that Mama preferred Grace over her. Perhaps discussing the Bible would help Mama want to be with her younger daughter too.

"I read a few more verses in my Bible the other night. I don't understand what Jesus meant when He said to come to Him. How does one do such a thing?" She seated herself on the wrought iron bench next to her mother.

"By faith."

"Faith?"

Mama nodded. "Faith—believing so strongly that Jesus died for you that you'd give Him the rest of your life."

"It's that simple?" Eugenia shook her head.

"Very simple, but so profound. You're dealing with the almighty God of the universe, Who, for reasons I don't understand, loves us enough to sacrifice the life of His own Son for us." Mama's face glowed.

Somehow, Eugenia knew her mother's words were true

even if she didn't understand completely. "I believe in Jesus as you've said. How do I come to Him in faith?"

"The Bible says faith comes by hearing God's word, so keep studying your Bible. And pray to God. Tell Him what's on your heart."

Mama took Eugenia's hands in hers and guided her through the first sincere prayer of her life. After they finished, Mama hugged her close. Her mother hadn't held her close in so long.

Mama released her just enough to smile through tears.

"I've never been so at peace—as if my cares have been lifted from me."

"You have made this one of the best days of my life." Mama slipped her handkerchief from her sleeve to dab at her eyes.

While Mama talked of other scripture verses, the rest of the morning sped by. Eugenia drank in her mother's attention as well as her knowledge about God. She couldn't remember ever having a more wonderful time with her mother.

Things would be much better between the two of them and between her and God. Now she could talk to God about her problems, especially her worries concerning Mama's health.

Chapter Nine

For the first time she could remember, Eugenia enjoyed going to church on Sunday. The stained glass windows at the front of the building shone brighter. The hymns she'd heard since childhood spoke to her heart. The pastor's sermon made sense. God loved her. Her heart was full.

After the service, her mother waited until the other church members left to guide Eugenia to the back door where the pastor stood to greet everyone. Mama's face glowed as she told him of Eugenia's prayer yesterday.

"Praise God." His warm smile wreathed his face. "Perhaps I could call on you and your mother this week."

"I'd like that." She smiled up at the rotund man, enjoying speaking with him for the first time in her life.

They talked a while longer and agreed the pastor would call on Wednesday. As soon as she could, Eugenia went out to the churchyard to see if Clare had left for home yet. She spied her friend beneath the shade of an oak and hurried over to her. "I have the most wonderful news. I prayed yesterday—a real prayer. I believe Jesus is God's Son, and I'm studying to learn more about Him."

"Oh, Eugenia." Clarisse's eyes filled with tears as she hugged her close. "I have prayed so much for you."

"Thank you. I truly appreciate it."

"We must tell Titus and Jenette." Clarisse grabbed Eugenia's arm and led her over to where Titus and Jenette stood talking with Paul.

"We have marvelous news." Clarisse's words spilled out the second she reached her brother's side. "Eugenia has been praying and studying the Bible."

Titus's broad grin stretched across his face. "I'm very happy for you."

"We both are. " Jenette's warm smile emphasized her words. "We've been praying for you."

"Thank you." Eugenia turned her attention to Paul. "Mr. Stuart, thank you too. Your simple remark about Balaam prompted me to read my Bible for the first time in years."

"I'm proud I could help." For some reason, he looked the happiest of all to hear her news. His eyes sparkled like she'd never seen before.

Mama motioned to her to come to their carriage. In spite of how much she'd like to stay and talk with them more, she bid the other young people goodbye.

"I plan to go for a ride this afternoon. I'd like to talk with you more if you have the time." She kept her fan in front of her face as she whispered to Paul.

His silent nod and beaming smile sent happy shivers through her as she walked toward her mother.

* * *

WHEN HE SAW Eugenia riding toward him that afternoon, Paul couldn't keep himself from grinning. What a change from the days he'd wished he could gallop away before she spotted him on the trail. Today, he could enjoy watching the sun filter through the trees and light up her pretty face.

"Hello." As usual, she spoke first when she rode up to him.

He tipped his hat. "Afternoon."

"I want to tell you again how grateful I am for all the times you've listened to me." Her glowing smile warmed him from head to toe.

"Thank you."

"Could we talk about you for a change? I'd like to know more about you than your vocation and who your father is."

"There ain't a lot to tell about me." He liked the way she looked him in the eyes as if he were her equal, even more so now than the first time they'd met.

"I'm sure you underestimate yourself as usual."

He let his reins go slack, ready for his horse to take his time on the trail. He'd rather visit with Eugenia than rush toward Murfreesboro no matter how hot the afternoon got.

"Would you think me too forward if I allowed you to call me Eugenia? I feel it would be perfectly all right if you called me by my first name."

"I'd like that, and you should use my first name. Calling me Mr. Stuart sounds like you're talking to my pa instead of me." He'd been thinking of her as Eugenia lately, anyway. Being on such personal terms with her felt natural. What a difference a couple of months had made.

She laughed. "Then tell me more about yourself, Paul. How old are you? How did you come to be a wheelwright?"

Sweat trickled down his back. He guided his horse toward a shadier spot. She followed him. "I turned twenty-four last November. I learned my trade in Nashville a few years ago after Pa quit working his own farm. Like everybody else, I'm trying to put a little money away. That's about it." That was all he could say to her, since he couldn't tell anyone why he'd left Nashville so fast.

"I assume you came back to Murfreesboro to be closer to your family."

He nodded. Since he couldn't tell her the truth, better to keep quiet instead of making up an outright lie. He did like being close to his family, except for the times Pa wanted to argue with him about slavery.

"Are you saving for your own business?"

"I want my own farm someday."

"With hard work, a man can prosper, Papa says. You could have your own plantation in the future, and no one would look down on you."

He shook his head. "I ain't planning on a plantation."

"You're not?" She tugged on the reins and stopped her horse while she waited for his answer.

"I surprised you this time by the look on your face." He halted his horse next to hers.

"Yes, you did."

"I hear farming in Illinois is real fine. I'm going to the North someday to buy my farm."

Her eyes got wider. "To the North? Why?"

Tightening his grip on the reins, he took a couple of deep breaths. How he wished she hadn't asked such a question just when he was enjoying his time with her. She'd probably end their friendship here and now, but he had to give her an honest answer. He shifted in his saddle to peer into her eyes.

"I won't own slaves."

She clamped her open mouth shut as she studied him.

Paul swallowed hard several times.

"May I ask why not?" Her tone sounded concerned, not condemning.

He took another deep breath. She didn't appear or sound

angry, but his heart was still pounding at the thought of probably losing her as a friend.

"You really want to know?"

She nodded.

Licking his dry lips, he prayed he wouldn't run her off. The heat had nothing to do with his parched mouth. Giving her an honest answer without saying too much about why he'd come to hate slavery wouldn't be easy.

"The more I've prayed about it, the more I'm sure slavery's wrong. Nobody should own a man like he would a horse. We both know some people whip their slaves or worse. That's wrong too."

Eugenia glanced down and flicked a twig from her skirt. He'd never dreamed she could be quiet so long. Even if he was home in his own bed, he couldn't get comfortable right now.

Chin up, she looked straight at him. "I admit some people do that, but you know our servants are treated well. The Matthews don't mistreat their people, either."

Their people. Talk like that had galled him ever since he'd gotten to know the Quaker preacher in Nashville. His friend had told him too many stories about how badly some people treated their slaves. Many of them, too terrible to mention to a lady.

He tilted his hat back so he could see her better. "Every man should be free to live his own life."

"I hope you keep such unpopular opinions to yourself."

"I sure do." He relaxed his trembling hands. She looked serious but not mad. He prayed she wouldn't gallop her horse away from him. He didn't have any more true friends than she did.

"I'm sure you're as careful about your words as you are about everything else." Her eyes had a teasing sparkle to them.

The knots in his shoulders lessened. He let out the breath

he'd been holding. She really wasn't mad at him. He grinned at her. "It still wouldn't hurt you to be more careful."

"Perhaps, but you know I won't be." She laughed.

He chuckled. "No, especially if I keep telling you to."

Her smile faded. "I hope you're just as sure we can remain friends in spite of our differences."

"You mean that?" He wanted to yell and throw his hat up in the air to celebrate, but he settled for another happy grin instead.

"Yes. I can't imagine severing our friendship because we disagree about owning servants."

"They're slaves, not servants." The words slipped out before he thought.

"I don't wish to argue with you. I have enough conflict to deal with as it is. Could we agree we don't agree and remain friends? I truly value your friendship. Please, Paul." She kept her gaze focused on him.

He swallowed hard. His chest felt tighter than his dry throat. His rash words had worried her, maybe even hurt her. "We're still friends."

"Thank you so much."

"You're welcome. I wish my pa was as reasonable as you are instead of wanting to argue with me all the time." Her bright smile refreshed him as if she'd handed him a glass of cold water straight from a spring.

"Arguing with a parent is quite unpleasant." The sad look in her eyes made him wonder if she understood how he felt from experience.

He nodded. "I have to keep my opinions to myself if I want to be welcome in Pa's house. That's why I'm going North someday, where people will accept me better."

"I'll pray for you, Paul."

"I'd appreciate that." His heart was as light as the white

butterfly that landed on the branch next to his head. She'd pray for him. What a nice change.

"I wish I could talk openly with you this way at church. I feel like a hypocrite ignoring you." She sighed as they rounded a bend in the trail.

"I don't mind. I know how honest you really are."

"Thank you for understanding."

He glanced up through the trees at the sun. "Looks like I'd best be on my way for now. I got a busy day of work ahead of me tomorrow."

"I'm sorry if I delayed you. Perhaps I'll see you next Sunday afternoon."

"Maybe so."

He smiled at her before riding away. He wouldn't fuss if he saw her next week or the week after. Watching her change for the better got more interesting every time he talked to her. This woman accepted him—ideas and all. Good thing he'd listened to God and made friends with her.

In fact, he'd miss her come time to leave for the North.

Chapter Ten

Eugenia reveled in the blessings of her new faith. She had loving friends who prayed for her. Paul had finally accepted her. If she'd known God could give her such peace, she would have prayed to Him much sooner.

She now had common ground with her mother. Mama made regular time for them to discuss Bible passages and to help her grow spiritually. As had become their habit, Eugenia and her mother settled onto an iron bench in the gazebo. Papa didn't care to listen to them discuss the Bible, so they talked outside unless he was gone.

"Mama, I need to ask you something that's been bothering me." Eugenia fanned herself while wishing for a breeze.

"What?" Mama used her handkerchief to wipe the perspiration from her brow.

"Clare tells me a Christian shouldn't marry an unbeliever. Why not?"

"An unbeliever often doesn't understand about faith. Such differences can cause tension in a marriage when the spouses disagree on something so important." Mama's sober expression appeared to indicate she spoke from personal experience.

"Why did you marry Papa?"

"I wasn't a believer when we married. I didn't become a Christian until just before Grace was born."

"Oh." For some reason, she'd assumed Mama had been a Christian much longer. "Papa is a good man, though, isn't he?"

Her mother nodded. "A fine man, and I love him dearly. If you'll look for a Christian man with your papa's kind and understanding ways, you'll find someone wonderful for your husband."

Before Mama had a chance to say anything about possible suitors, Eugenia tried to think of a way to end the discussion on marriage. Luke had started calling on her occasionally, and she had no intentions of encouraging him. "Why doesn't Papa want to discuss spiritual things?"

Mama sighed. "He says he doesn't need God. That he's as good as any other man and lives a more charitable lifestyle than many Christians. Sad to say, but he's correct about some people."

"You pray for Papa often, don't you?"

"Every day." Mama dabbed at misty eyes with her handkerchief.

"I've been praying for Papa too."

"I'm glad to hear that." Mama closed her eyes and leaned against the bench.

As her mother rubbed her temples, Eugenia's heart sped up. "Are you feeling well?"

"I'm fine. Slowing down at fifty-five is quite normal, even if we don't like it." Mama's thin smile didn't look reassuring.

"Perhaps we should go inside."

Mama nodded. "I'd like a glass of water straight from the well as hot as it's getting."

After lunch Eugenia cornered her father as she and her parents walked from the dining room. "Do you have time for a ride, or could I go with you if you need to look at the fields?"

"I'd enjoy your company on my ride to the field this afternoon, dear girl." His warm smile turned up each end of his white mustache.

"Be sure you wear a hat to sufficiently cover your face." Mama's words stopped Eugenia at the foot of the stairs. "You may still ride with your father, but I'll not have my daughter's complexion looking like a field hand's."

"Of course not, Mama."

She kissed her mother's cheek before going upstairs. Any other time, she would have been irritated at how Mama reminded her to get a hat as if she were still a little girl. Today, she had more important concerns about her mother. Papa must know what Mama had said and done this morning.

"Mama isn't feeling well today." Eugenia voiced her worries while she and Papa rode away from the house. "I'm afraid she's in more pain than she wants anyone to know."

"We'll have to watch her more closely. She hasn't said one word to me about hurting or being tired." Papa's bushy white eyebrows knit together.

"Should you send for a doctor?" Her father's worried expression made her stomach lurch. She tightened her hold on the reins.

Papa shook his head. "We both know your mother's opinion of doctors."

Eugenia sighed. Her mother had called doctors foolish men pretending to be wise more times than she could remember. Mama and her herbs tended to the ills of the household—both slave and free. She could barely remember the last time a physician had been summoned to their home. She hoped and prayed Papa was right not to send for a doctor.

* * *

HOPING and praying her mother would get better, Eugenia kept a careful watch over Mama. The once tireless woman now created excuses to nap in the afternoon or retire early. By mid-August, she'd caught Mama rubbing her temples so often that it looked to have become a habit.

"Mama, are you sure you feel well?" Eugenia followed her mother toward the stairs.

"I am quite well. I wish I could convince you and your papa of that." Mama smiled. "I stayed awake praying last night much longer than I should have. I'll rest the hour or so until your papa comes in to change for supper."

Wishing she could swallow the lump in her throat, Eugenia forced a smile. If she knew what worries had kept her mother from sleeping last night, she'd do her best to banish them for her. Mama had made or received calls on Wednesday afternoons as long as she could remember. Staying home today was not right in too many ways.

Lord, please make Mama well again.

She'd lost count of how many times she'd prayed the same prayer in the past month or so. After reading a parable in her Bible about persistent prayer, she had taken God's words quite literally.

She trudged outside to her mother's garden. The colors and scents of flowers in full bloom soothed her. Mama would get better. Eugenia had asked all her friends to pray for her mother. She settled onto her favorite bench in the gazebo and soaked in the serenity until time for Papa to come home.

While walking into the house, she wished she'd thought to gather a bouquet for Mama. The flowers would help Mama's spirits. She'd pick some after supper.

Eugenia spied her father coming in the front door just as

she reached the staircase. "Did you have a good afternoon looking at puppies?"

"I did. I've spoken up for one as soon as it's old enough. Where is your mother?"

"Upstairs resting again," she whispered as they walked toward the staircase. "She's been there since around two. She didn't make a single call today."

Frown lines creased the wrinkles in Papa's brow. "It's time to insist on a visit from the doctor. A two-hour nap is too unlike your mother." He kept his voice low as he reached for the knob of their bedroom door.

Walking toward her room next door, Eugenia heard her father softly say something to her mother. She hoped Mama felt better after her nap.

"Anna! No!" Papa's anguished cry filled the house.

Eugenia dashed into her parents' room. Papa stood over the bed shaking Mama's motionless body. His stricken face told her everything she did not want to know.

"Papa? She's not really dead—is she?" She hurled herself into her father's arms and sobbed. After regaining some control, Eugenia stepped back and stared into Papa's ashen face, wet with tears. "What do we do now?"

"I ..." He shook his head. "I don't know."

She stared into her father's eyes and tried to think of something to say or do. He looked as lost and confused as she was. "I-I'll go for the pastor, if you'd like."

"If he'll be of any help to you, go on. I need to be alone with your mother. Please go."

Eugenia didn't understand his request but left him alone as he asked. Before she trudged half way down the hall, Papa was weeping again. She halted, not sure if she should go to him or leave.

"What am I going to do, Anna? I haven't the slightest idea

how to live without you. Why did you leave me behind?" Sobs choked off the rest of Papa's words.

Unable to bear listening to her father's agony, Eugenia fled down the stairs. Lily and Pansy stood at the bottom. Eugenia almost knocked Lily down in her hurry to run away.

"You cain't run from it, child. Everybody in the house heared the masta. Yo' mama be with Jesus where she'll never hurt again. You and the masta be the ones hurtin' now." Pansy dabbed her moist eyes with her apron.

Tears cascaded down Eugenia's face. *Lord, help me.* She took a deep breath, then another. Nothing helped the ache in her heart. "Have Samson bring the carriage around. I want to go see Brother Bentley. I'll wait in the parlor."

The garish glare of the bright evening sun hurt Eugenia's eyes when she stepped outside to climb into the carriage. Never had she dreamed of not enjoying the summer sun and the glorious scenery while the carriage rolled toward the pastor's house. Her heart ached so that her chest hurt. She slumped against the black leather seat. What was she going to do without Mama? Her sobs came again. The empty carriage closed in around her.

Eugenia found only the pastor's wife home. Brother Bentley was out making calls. His wife assured her the pastor would be by to see her later in the evening. Instead of going home, Eugenia ordered the driver to take her to see Clare. Papa preferred solitude, but she had to talk to someone.

"I must see Miss Clarisse." She stepped inside as soon as the butler opened the door.

"They ain't through with supper yet, Miss Eugenia."

Supper. She'd lost track of the time, but she desperately needed to see her friend. Clare had lost her father two years ago and would understand her grief. "This is an emergency. Get her now. I'll wait in the parlor."

"Yes, miss. I'll go see what she say."

"Go quickly. I'm in no mood to wait." Eugenia didn't care how sharp her voice sounded to the retreating servant.

Clarisse rushed into the parlor moments later. "What is wrong?"

"Mama died this afternoon."

"Oh, no." Clarisse enveloped her in a hug. "I'm so sorry."

"I had to talk to you." Through her tears, Eugenia related the details of her mother's death. The rest of the Matthews family hurried in before she finished.

Clarisse nodded as tears slid down her cheeks. Guiding Eugenia to the sofa, she sat next to her.

"I'm sorry to interrupt your meal." Eugenia's gaze went from her friend to the rest of the family standing around her.

"Don't worry about our supper." Mrs. Matthews dabbed at tears with her handkerchief.

Eugenia kept her time with the Matthews family short. She ached to stay longer and talk with such loving friends who understood her pain, but she should check on Papa. "I need to get home now. The pastor should be there soon, and I don't want to miss seeing him."

By the time Eugenia returned, the house servants had tended to Mama's body and laid her on the large table in Papa's office until another servant could finish building a coffin. Papa refused to eat and insisted on remaining in his office. Eugenia couldn't bear to keep him company in his vigil.

Brother Bentley came to see her, but his words of comfort did little to soothe such raw, fresh pain. The long night dragged by in a painful blur. Once in her bed, Eugenia heard the grandfather clock downstairs strike every hour. When the first rays of sun trickled through her curtained window, she gave up trying to sleep. *Dear God, help me get through today.*

Sitting at the breakfast table with only Papa was like a

living nightmare. How she wished she'd dreamt all of this. "What are your plans today, Papa?" She nibbled at her tasteless eggs.

"We must post letters to Nathan, James, and Grace. I need to see that August finishes the coffin soon ..." His voice trembled. He took a deep breath. "We have other details to tend to for the burial. And I should send some servants around to tell our friends of our loss."

Dropping her fork on her plate, she went over to her father to give him a hug. "We'll survive this awful pain somehow."

Word of Mama's death traveled quickly around the county. Several neighbors called to offer their sympathy and aid that afternoon. Someone dropped by every hour or so until just before dark.

"We shouldn't have anyone else calling this time of night." Papa sighed as he shifted in his chair. He'd spent most of the day in the parlor staring at the coffin holding his wife's body. "Our neighbors have the best intentions, but I need solitude."

The sight of Papa's drooping shoulders added more weight to Eugenia's heavy heart. "Are you all right?"

If only she could ask him something less mundane about his well-being. What—really Who—Papa needed was God, but she dared not mention God again. He hadn't looked happy whenever any of their Christian friends had told him they were praying for him.

"I'm numb, and I feel old—very old. Don't look at me like that, dear girl. I'm not at death's door. I just need time alone."

"Then I'll go upstairs and get ready for bed."

Before he could make any more remarks about feeling old, Eugenia rose, kissed his cheek, then fled. She didn't need anything else distressing to deal with. As she had done the night before, she read her Bible until it dropped from her hands before she could sleep.

* * *

ON FRIDAY AFTERNOON, the scents of flowers and lush green grass mocked Eugenia as she stood in the family cemetery not far from her oldest brother's grave. She gripped her father's shaking hand while clinging to the pastor's words of hope as he read from Philippians.

"For me to live is Christ, and to die is gain."

Mama had gained heaven, but Eugenia had lost her entire world. Perhaps if she'd insisted Papa call a doctor sooner, they'd still have Mama here. Tears streamed down her face as she watched the first shovel of dirt thud over the casket. *Help me, God.*

A few long minutes later, the Matthews family escorted her and Papa back to the house.

"If there is anything we can do, please ask." Mrs. Matthews patted Eugenia's shoulder as they paused near the steps to the front porch.

"We need time alone. I'm sure you understand." Papa's feeble voice sounded as if he'd aged ten years.

Mrs. Matthews nodded. "I understand. We're praying for both of you."

Once inside, Papa collapsed onto a chair in the parlor. Eugenia escaped to her room and the comfort of her Bible. The pastor had given her references to several passages on heaven and the coming resurrection of believers. She read every precious verse before going back to the parlor to check on Papa.

He had not moved from his chair. She bent and kissed his cheek. "How are you doing?"

"I feel as if my heart has been ripped from my chest." His voice cracked as he wiped away tears with the back of his hand.

She laid a hand on his trembling shoulder. "God will help you cope with the pain. He's helping me."

He stiffened the instant she mentioned God. "Go see if Nancy has anything ready to eat."

"All right." She left the room. His curt dismissal pained her, but Papa must be doing a little better if he wanted food. She prayed for ways to help her father as she made her way to the kitchen. Papa would feel so much better if he'd come to church, so she asked the Lord for an opportunity to invite him to come with her tomorrow.

After no such chance presented itself the remainder of the day, Eugenia took a deep breath and prayed while her father opened the door to his room to retire for the night. "I would be honored if you'd come to church with me in the morning."

Papa tightened his hold on the doorknob. "No, but if it helps you, then go."

"But church would help you too."

"Don't argue with me. Go on to bed." He turned his back as he shuffled into his room.

Eugenia stared at the door he'd all but slammed in her face. How Papa needed God's love.

* * *

GOING to church alone the next morning was the hardest thing she'd ever done. The black leather carriage seats matched her bleak mood. She couldn't bear to walk into the white frame church house by herself, so she waited for the Matthews family to arrive.

"May I sit in your pew? I can't bear to sit in ours alone." Her voice cracked. The thought of not sitting in church with Mama threatened to bring tears. She didn't want to cry here.

"Of course." Mrs. Matthews smiled at her.

Before they walked inside, Clarisse gave Eugenia's hand a sympathetic squeeze.

Brother Bentley spoke of the peace that Jesus gives and how it surpasses human understanding. As she thought about her pastor's words, she realized that in spite of her heartache, she did have peace. Poor Papa was still searching for what she already possessed. She'd keep praying for the right words to say to her father. How she longed for Papa to accept God's love and comfort.

Eugenia didn't go for her customary ride after lunch. Instead, she carried her Bible into the parlor and sat in the chair next to her father. He pretended to read whenever she glanced over at him, but never turned a single page of his book.

Laying the book on his lap, Papa sighed. "Aren't you going for a ride? You don't have to sit in this hot musty parlor just to keep me company."

"I don't feel like riding." Battling her grief sapped her energy almost as much as Papa's sadness sapped his.

"We're a fine pair in our misery, aren't we?" His wan smiled didn't reach into his sad eyes.

"I suppose so. God is helping me, though. You should have heard the pastor's sermon this morning."

He raised his hand as if to halt her words. "Don't preach to me."

"Yes, Papa."

Papa's cold demeanor sent chills down her spine in spite of the summer heat. Her father was fighting the very One who could help and comfort him. If only she knew why. She closed her Bible. "I think I'll go for a walk in Mama's garden."

"Go on, dear girl. As I said, don't feel obligated to keep me company."

She rose. At least he'd called her by the special name he'd always used. She made her way to her mother's flower garden.

Memories of Mama were everywhere in this place. Tears blurred the flowers her mother had so enjoyed. If only she could be as at peace as the tranquil garden. She'd read and reread the passages the pastor had suggested. The verses helped, but nothing stopped the pain still squeezing her heart.

* * *

PAUL REINED in his horse on the trail he usually took back to Murfreesboro. Birds chirped. A gray squirrel ran up a nearby tree. The woods were full of normal sights and sounds, but not one sign of Eugenia riding his direction or just ahead of him. He closed his eyes to concentrate better. No sound of Eugenia talking to her horse from somewhere close by. Not another person in sight up or down the trail.

She must not feel like riding today. As awful as she'd looked in her black dress and bonnet this morning at church, he shouldn't be surprised. Her woe-filled eyes made him feel worse than she looked.

If only he could have done more than give her a nod when she walked past his pew. But he'd had a tough time not letting his parents figure out how much he thought of Eugenia when they'd told him last night about her ma. Hiding how much he hurt for her had been harder than pretending he hadn't helped his preacher friend get more slaves headed north than Pa would ever know.

His insides twisted into knots at the thought of not getting a chance to talk to her. To tell her how sorry he was she'd lost her ma. To tell her he'd be praying for her. To tell her ... almost anything and everything the way they'd been doing as often as possible the last couple of months.

No matter how carefully he listened or how hard he

wished, Eugenia didn't ride up to him. He swallowed hard as he urged his horse toward home.

He rode into town a good hour before sunset. He hadn't made it back to Murfreesboro this early on a Sunday for a long time. If he'd had his way, he wouldn't have done it today.

He tipped his hat to a couple of ladies out for a walk. They smiled in his direction but kept going. Good. He was in no mood to talk to anyone.

Well, he was. But only to the one woman he couldn't talk to in public. Since he wasn't some planter's son, riding up to her house and knocking on her front door was out of the question. His father wouldn't understand his friendship with Eugenia. Her father wouldn't accept him for any reason. Being rejected by so many people would change once he got to Illinois and bought his own farm. No one there would look down on him for not owning slaves.

But once he owned his dream, the usually talkative lady he was missing so badly wouldn't be over on the next farm for him to visit. He'd miss her more than he'd realized until he couldn't see her today.

Chapter Eleven

As the long days dragged into September, Eugenia's life settled into an uneasy routine. She ran the household with minimal instructions to the servants. Grace had been appalled when she, Nathan, and James had come a few days after Mama's funeral. But the servants knew their chores well, and she hadn't noticed dust gathering or the quality of the meals suffering.

Papa had become a recluse, rarely going outside except to visit Mama's grave, leaving Eugenia to suffer alone. He hadn't taken the slightest interest in cotton picking. If not for the overseer, the entire plantation might cease to operate.

On this particular Friday, she had to talk to someone who understood her. A ride and a visit to Clare were just what she needed. She had hinted to Papa she'd like company on her ride to see Clare, but he'd ignored her as usual. The grandfather clock in the Matthews' parlor struck three as Clarisse walked into the room.

Clare rushed over to envelope Eugenia in a hug before sitting beside her on the sofa. "I'm sorry I haven't called on you this week, but I'm glad you feel up to calling on me."

Unable to voice how being in a room with sunshine streaming through the windows lifted her spirits, Eugenia nodded. Their house saw little light of any kind these days.

"How has your week gone?" Clarisse handed Eugenia a cup of tea.

Eugenia shrugged. "No different than the other weeks since we lost Mama."

"How is your father?"

"He'd never open the parlor drapes if I didn't insist. I'm worried about him."

Clarisse nodded. "Mama is, too, after I told her he didn't leave his office to greet me the last time I called on you."

Running her hand along the upholstered arm of the sofa, Eugenia sighed. "He's lost weight. He's aged terribly but still refuses to listen to a word about God. I've said little since the day he told me not to preach to him."

"We'll continue praying. Mama says that's the best thing we can do for him until he's ready to listen to God." She squeezed Eugenia's hand.

"I suppose so, but it's so hard not to do something."

Clarisse smiled. "I'm not as good as you are of thinking of a plan of action. I wish I could assist you."

"You help by listening."

Eugenia stayed as long as she dared. If only her home was like Hopeton. She'd wished that much too often lately. Papa preferred solitude to her company or anyone else's companionship. Letters from her sister or brothers were the only communication he relished. She often found him in the cemetery.

* * *

Eugenia's melancholy mood still hovered over her when she walked into church on Sunday. With her thoughts focused on her problems, she barely noticed when the pastor picked up his Bible to begin the sermon.

"I'm reading from Romans, chapter eight, verse twenty-eight. 'And we know that all things work together for good to them who are the called according to his purpose.'" He smiled before continuing. "To some of you, that little verse may not sound sensible, but I'll explain how sensible and right it is."

The curious words from God changed her mood in an instant. How did God work bad things for good for His children? When the pastor looked out at the congregation, it was as if he spoke to her alone. She leaned forward in the pew to better hear Brother Bentley's explanation.

"We often grow more through hard times than we do through good times. The people of Israel called on God when they were in trouble. After they became rich and comfortable, they forgot God." The pastor gripped the edges of the pulpit with his large hands.

The dusty cobwebs cleared from Eugenia's mind. Her spiritual journey paralleled Israel's history. As long as her life had gone well, she'd given God little thought. Frustration and disappointment had spurred her to search the scriptures and listen to God. She'd never read her Bible or prayed as much before her mother died as she did now.

If grief could somehow bring her father to finally accept his need for God, perhaps Mama's death could work for good in spite of the awful pain her family still endured. Her thirsty soul drank in the remainder of the pastor's encouraging words.

After the service ended, Eugenia rushed to be one of the first people to greet Brother Bentley at the back door to the church. "You've helped me more than I can tell you."

"Good. I'm happy to see you smile again. If you have any questions or need to talk, please call on me." He beamed at her.

"I'm thankful you don't tire of my visits or my questions."

"Not at all." The big man patted her shoulder.

With so much to pray and think about, she kept her time outside with Clarisse short. She'd find a way to help Papa realize how much God loved him. As the carriage rolled toward home, she prayed for guidance about how and when to talk to her father.

After lunch, she followed her father into the parlor. He picked up his newspaper. She tried to work on her embroidery, not sure if God wanted her to sit quietly and enjoy Papa's company or use this time to try to talk to him about God. If only she knew more about God's ways. Her thread knotted, then broke. Perhaps she wasn't supposed to do needlework right now.

Setting aside her embroidery, she took a deep breath as she prayed for the right words. "I wish you'd been in church this morning. Brother Bentley's wonderful sermon helped me so much. Did you know God can use bad things for our good?"

An intense frown creased the wrinkles of Papa's forehead. He dropped his paper in his lap. "I do not want or need a lecture about God." His icy tones made her shiver.

"I only want to share something helpful, nothing more." Her heart raced as his expression hardened. Papa had never looked at her like that before. To keep her hands from trembling, she clasped them in her lap.

"I tolerated your mother's religious views only because they made her happy. I want nothing to do with a God who would rob me of my wife even if He does exist."

"He didn't rob you. Mama went to heaven. You'll see her again if you'll listen to God." She leaned toward him. Poor Papa misunderstood so much.

"If your God took my wife to heaven, then He robbed me with that very act."

"No, Papa." She forced herself not to look away from his irate glare. "No matter how much I miss Mama, I wouldn't want her here with us and still hurting so badly."

He pounded the arm of his chair with his fist. Eugenia jumped at such at his uncharacteristic display of anger. "Why didn't your merciful and almighty God heal your mother? You asked Him often enough from what you told me."

She cringed at the sarcastic words he hurled at her. "I don't know why not."

Anger burning in his eyes, he flung his paper onto the carpet. "And yet you dare tell me God loves me!"

She shrank against the back of her chair. Papa had never yelled at her before. "He loves you very much." She whispered her reply, unable to speak in a normal voice.

"If God loves me, He should have healed my dear wife instead of stealing her from me." His lips curled into a sneer.

"I don't understand so many things yet. I don't know what to tell you."

"I'll not hear of your God again!" Gripping the arms of his chair, he shook in his fury.

"Yes, Papa." She stared at her trembling hands in her lap as she blinked back tears. "I-I'm going for a ride."

"That would be a good idea, dear girl." Papa's voice and countenance softened. "I'm sorry to hurt you, but I cannot abide talk of a so-called loving God, who has been anything but loving toward me."

To keep from crying, she took a deep shaky breath. "I'm going upstairs. Please send Lily to help me change into riding clothes."

He nodded before stooping to retrieve his paper.

While her maid helped her change clothes and later as

Samson boosted her up into the saddle, Eugenia managed to maintain a facade of composure. She didn't allow her tears to fall until she neared the end of the long driveway.

"God, what happened?" Choking sobs prevented her from saying more. She prayed in silence, so glad God could hear her unspoken grief and anguish.

* * *

THE INSTANT PAUL saw Eugenia ahead of him on the trail, he smiled to himself. She hadn't felt like riding much the last few weeks, so he hoped this meant she was doing better. He'd missed his talkative friend. The woman had grown on him.

When he heard her crying, he snapped the reins to hurry his horse along.

"What's wrong?" His heart raced as he rode up to her. Peering into her puffy red eyes told him something terrible had happened.

Her lips quivered. "My papa. He's furious with God, and—" A torrent of tears cut off the rest of her words.

"How about if I help you down, and we go for a walk? You ain't in any kind of shape to be riding."

She reined in her horse. He helped her dismount. As she told him about her father's cruel outburst, her words tumbled out one on top of the other.

Rage boiled up inside him. He wanted to shake Mr. Hampton, and he didn't care if the old man's teeth rattled out of his head.

"I feel as if I've lost my papa too." Her voice cracked as more tears ran down her pale cheeks.

"I'm so sorry." Sympathy for her wrapped around his heart and squeezed like a giant fist. Looking into her pain-filled eyes left him speechless. How he wished he could hold her and comfort her instead of just walking next to her.

Hold her? He didn't dare think about that.

"What can I do about Papa?" She sniffed away more tears as she looked up at him.

"I don't know, except pray. I ain't always got answers for you. I'm sorry." Sweat trickled down his back as if it were July instead of September. Good thing he wasn't still wearing his Sunday suit. He clasped his hands behind him to keep from reaching for her.

"I had such hope after the pastor's sermon this morning. Things are not working out for good right now." She dabbed at her eyes with her handkerchief.

"God don't always answer our prayers the way we think He should. Sometimes He does, but He just takes a while to do it." All he wanted was to wipe her tears for her. No. He shouldn't, couldn't think of doing such a thing.

She gulped in a breath of air. "I have so much to learn about God."

So did he, especially concerning her. "My ma says we all keep learning until the day we die, or leastways we should."

"I suppose that's true."

"I wish I could do something to help you besides talk." He shoved his hands into his trouser pockets. What he really wanted, he couldn't do.

"You've helped me more than I can say." Tears still glistened in her eyes, but she sounded a little calmer.

How she managed a weak-looking smile was more than he could imagine. He had to work to put one foot in front of the other as he trudged beside her along the wooded trail. She looked so forlorn in her black hat and black riding habit. Everything inside him ached for her.

He kicked a rock in his path hard enough to make it bounce

off a tree trunk. What she really needed was a hug. He mustered every ounce of strength he had to keep from taking her in his arms.

When had Eugenia's well-being become so important to him? And why did he want to hold her so much it hurt not to do it? Surely he didn't love her. The truth slammed into him so hard it took his breath away. *Lord, help me.*

"You're so kind to always be here for me to talk to." Eugenia ended the silence much too soon.

"I don't mind." He liked talking to her much more than he should. He'd never needed God to show him what to do more than now.

"Is something wrong, Paul? You look pained. Did I say something amiss?"

"Nothing's wrong. I ain't very good with words." He gave her a smile he didn't feel.

"That's not true. Your few words impart so much practical wisdom, and I appreciate the way you share them with me."

"You sound like you're talking about Solomon, not me." If he were as wise as she thought, he wouldn't want her the way he did, and his back wouldn't be soaked with sweat from fighting his wants.

"You underestimate your own understanding of life and especially spiritual things."

She had no idea how little he understood sometimes. Especially now. He took several deep breaths of the pungent forest air, but nothing helped calm him. "I pray a lot. God helps me know what to say." How he needed to pray now.

"But that's why you help me. I feel much better than when we first started talking."

"That's good." He squeezed his damp hands into fists to keep from taking her hand while they walked. She might be feeling better, but his feet and heart felt heavier with every miserable step he managed.

"I should let you go now. I know you need to be on your way to Murfreesboro."

"I ain't in that big of a hurry." But he should be.

"Just the same, I've delayed you. If you need to leave, I'll understand."

"I guess I should go." He walked her back to their horses. Having her foot in his cupped hand made him ache even more to hold her. He boosted her up onto Belle, wishing he never had to worry about the day he'd have to tell her goodbye forever.

The instant Eugenia was out of sight, Paul jerked the reins and galloped his horse toward Hopeton. His feelings tumbled around inside him worse than spoiled food would have done in his stomach. He had to talk to Titus.

"You look worried. What's wrong?" His friend eyed him as they sat in wooden chairs on the front porch.

"A lot." He told Titus about his time with Eugenia. "I'm a fool for falling in love with a woman I can't have." He smacked his open palm on the hard chair arm. Thanks to his aching heart, he barely felt the pain rushing up his arm.

Titus shook his head. "I never thought you'd fall in love with her."

"Me neither. She needs every friend she can get, but I don't know if I can handle talking with her on Sundays anymore. What do I do?"

"Pray." Titus steepled his hands together.

"You better pray hard. I had to fight not to take her into my arms when she looked up at me crying like that. She's hurting real bad, and I sure don't want to cause her more pain." He stared down at his clenched hands.

"You look as if you were kicked by a horse. What about your pain?"

Paul shrugged. "Ain't much I can do but ask God to take those feelings away. At least she don't love me. That's good."

"Yes, it is. That would definitely make things worse."

"I better get going." Paul loosened his grip on the arm of the chair. "Pray about this whole mess for me."

"I will. May I tell Jenette and ask her to pray too?"

"I guess so, as long as she don't tell nobody else."

"You know she won't."

"I know." He stood to leave. "Thanks."

Titus laid his hand on Paul's shoulder. "I wish your love could have a happy ending as mine has."

"We know that's impossible. Her pa would never allow us to be together if she did love me." Paul shook hands with him then left to get his horse.

Talking with Titus didn't ease his mind like he'd hoped. His stomach churned while tying itself in knots all the way back to Murfreesboro. The more he told himself to forget about Eugenia, the tighter the knots got.

Chapter Twelve

Paul's advice helped Eugenia cope. God hadn't forgotten about her, so she'd wait for His guidance as her dear friend suggested. But she wouldn't be upset if God didn't take too much longer to answer her prayers. Especially since September was drawing to an end.

On Friday afternoon while Eugenia read her Bible in the garden, Lily interrupted, "You has a gentleman caller."

"Did he tell you his name?"

"Mista Luke Williams."

Eugenia's heart raced. She grabbed the Bible that almost fell from her lap. "Is he alone?"

"Yes, Miss."

Oh, no. She didn't need or want any man calling on her alone. "Tell him I'll see him in a few minutes. Have Nancy prepare tea and some refreshments. Then come up to my room and see that my hair is still all right." Her hair couldn't be in any form of disarray from sitting and reading in the gazebo, but she'd use any excuse to delay visiting with Luke.

Lily dispatched her duties with Eugenia's hair with her usual swiftness, and Eugenia had no choice but to make her way downstairs. This afternoon could be a severe challenge to her manners. She'd had a hard enough time being polite to Luke when he'd called with his mother after Mama's death. The way he'd watched her told her he'd come to check on more than her welfare. She assumed only his manners and sense of propriety had held his words in check that day.

She trudged into the parlor. "Good afternoon."

When he stood to greet her, she didn't bother with a pretend smile. Let him think she was still downcast from her mother's death instead of being perturbed by his call.

"Good afternoon to you." His eyes never left her face. He nearly tripped over his feet as he stepped back to take the maroon chair across from the sofa she chose.

"I finished work a little early today and decided to come see how you and your father are faring. I trust I didn't interrupt something important."

"I was reading my Bible and praying." She studied him as she waited to see his reaction to her words. His church attendance tended to be sporadic.

"Good. I hope you're doing better."

"Yes, I am." Or she had been. She glanced toward the door. No servant carrying a tray of refreshments was in sight. "How is your father?"

"Much better."

"That's good. Does that mean you'll be able to return to school in the near future?"

He shook his head. "Father isn't strong enough to run a plantation alone. I doubt I'll ever return to college."

"I'm sorry." If only he knew how truly sorry she was that he couldn't resume his studies. "Does this mean you've given up on reading for the law and becoming an attorney?"

His shoulders slumped. "For the foreseeable future, yes."

She clasped her damp hands in her lap while trying to

think of something else to say. As his good friend, she knew how much he wanted to go into law, but her sympathy might be mistaken for more than friendly concern if she said more.

Pansy carried in a tray and spared Eugenia from worrying about conversation for a moment. "Would you care for tea?" She filled a cup for him, grateful for something to occupy her hands.

"Thank you." He smiled over his teacup. "What have you been doing with yourself?"

"Nothing of interest to anyone."

"I assume you're busy after taking over your mother's duties and all."

"I'm doing all right. Our servants are well trained."

She wouldn't tell him how little she still did. Luke didn't need to know how much spare time she had.

"May we change the course of this conversation? I realize you're in mourning, but must we be so impersonal?" He shifted in his chair.

Her tea lost all taste. She knew him well enough to understand every nuance of his subtle hint. She had to find a way to make him realize how unsuitable a match she'd be for him.

His gentle temperament would complement someone like Clare perfectly. She fought back a smile. She should have thought of that sooner. Clare might solve Eugenia's problems with Luke in ways neither of them had dreamed. She'd have to pray about her new idea. Best to be careful concerning matters of the heart, especially so with Clare, who still dearly missed her late fiancé.

"I've told you more than once this summer, I only want your friendship. I truly feel you would be better suited to someone else." Eugenia couldn't resist a little hint.

"I cherish the hope that when circumstances are different,

you'll change your mind." His smile was much too tender as he gazed at her.

"Your aspirations are in vain." She had no problem keeping her voice cool and indifferent.

"Perhaps, but I'm willing to wait and see." His expression reminded her of an expectant child.

"Then don't be hurt or offended when you discover you were wrong about me. I'll warn you of that now."

"Your warning is aptly taken if not received. I'm a much more patient man than Jonah Browning."

She shuddered. His blunt reference to Jonah caused her head to spin enough to make her dizzy. She had to find a way to get him to leave, and soon. "This sort of conversation is too soon—much too soon." She put her hand to her throat as if in distress.

He jumped to his feet so quickly he almost dropped his cup then paused as if not sure what to do next. "You're so pale."

"If I go to my room and lie down a while, I'm sure I'll be better." He had no idea how much better she'd feel the instant he left.

"Do you need assistance? I'll find a servant to help you up the stairs."

She shook her head, but kept her hand close to her throat. "No, thank you."

He nodded. "I apologize for my ill timing. I'll see myself to the door."

While watching Luke trot into the hall, she let out the breath she'd been holding. Her act had worked better and faster than she had anticipated. She'd come much too close to outright lying, but his words were truly unsettling, so she hadn't completely embellished things. She *did* feel dizzy.

Not long after Luke departed, the front door opened. Papa

must be coming in from his walk to the cemetery. She hurried to greet him.

"Did I just see Luke leaving?" Papa hung his hat on the hat tree.

"Yes."

"You don't look or sound overjoyed to see the young man."

"No, I'm not."

"I'd like to hear why after I change clothes." He looked down and brushed dirt from his trousers. "We'll continue our conversation at supper."

She nodded, glad she could postpone telling her father about her caller. Papa probably wouldn't be pleased to hear she'd sent another man away.

As soon as the servants finished serving the meal, Papa resumed their conversation. "Tell me why you think your old friend Luke is so repulsive." He cut up a pork chop as he waited for her answer.

"He wants more between us than I do, and I've told him no more than once." She stabbed a piece of carrot so hard it split.

"You don't think you'll change your mind about him?" He looked over at her.

"No."

"And how can you be so certain?" He took another bite of meat.

"Mama told me to look for someone kind and considerate like you." She didn't mention she'd also insist on a Christian man. No need to antagonize her father during the first real conversation they'd had since Mama's death.

"Has Luke been unkind or inconsiderate?"

"He hinted so strongly about why he was here that he might as well have asked if I'd consider his suit. I couldn't believe how bold he was so soon after Mama's death." She attacked her meat with her knife and fork.

"He knows if he doesn't speak up some other young man will be here in his place, regardless of propriety." Her father's broad smile made her wonder if he sympathized with her feelings at all.

"I still don't appreciate his poor timing."

"Is that the only reason he angered you?" Papa took his time buttering a second piece of bread, a thoughtful look on his face.

"Don't you think if he cares for me that he'd listen to what I tell him instead of ignoring my feelings?"

His eyes took on a more serious expression as he reached for his water goblet. "You have a valid point, dear girl. I assume you sent him away."

"Yes."

"If he's this stubborn, he'll bide his time and try again. I had to work to convince your mother of my good qualities and intentions."

"I won't settle for less than a love match like you and Mama had, no matter who the man is." She hoped Papa's returning grin didn't mean he wished she hadn't sent Luke away. The potatoes she choked down tasted as if they'd been dusted with dirt instead of salt and pepper.

Before he looked down at his plate, she thought she saw tears in his eyes. Papa spent the remainder of their meal discussing the unusually warm October weather. Perhaps she'd made her point.

Eugenia went to bed that night with a happier heart. Luke's unnerving persistence had improved her life in a small way. Papa didn't completely understand her, but he wasn't angry with her for sending Luke away. Best of all, they'd had an honest conversation without an argument. One good thing had come from something bad, just as the verse in Romans stated.

She could hardly wait for Sunday afternoon and a chance to share her news with Paul. How she now prayed for good traveling weather for him on Saturdays and excellent weather for riding with him on Sundays.

* * *

PAPA SMILED at her as they finished lunch on Sunday. "Getting out does you good. I'm glad to see your eyes shining again."

"I'm doing much better today."

Since Papa was trying to live peacefully with her again, she wouldn't risk jeopardizing things by mentioning God was the One who had lifted her spirits. The pastor's sermon encouraged her. Talking with Clare after church helped. Plus, Paul had been in the service with his family. Seeing her dear friend this afternoon would make her day almost perfect.

"If you'll excuse me, I'll go for my usual ride and enjoy this beautiful weather." She walked over and kissed her father's cheek before going to her room to change clothes.

When she reached the end of their driveway, she headed Belle toward the trail Paul usually took. Her pulse quickened when she spied him a few minutes later. If only she were an artist and could capture this wonderful man in a painting. His simple homespun clothes silhouetted against the background of the leaves would make a striking portrait. She doubted any painter could do justice to his warm blue eyes and kind smile.

She guided her horse alongside his mount. "Hello."

"You're smiling. You look and sound happy today." Paul let the reins go slack in his hands.

"I've got good news about Papa, if you have time to listen."

"I got time." He tilted his hat back.

His voice sounded listless, and he had yet to smile at her. She hoped he hadn't argued with his father again. If so, her

113

good news might cheer him. She quickly told him how well she and her father were getting along. "Things are much better between us now."

Before Paul could reply, Papa called out her name from somewhere close behind. She and Paul had been concentrating so completely on their conversation that neither of them had heard him approaching. He rode up beside her while her mind scrambled for the right words to prevent him from guessing how often she and Paul talked.

"If I'd known you wanted to ride with me, Papa. I would have waited for you." Eugenia hoped her face didn't betray her shock.

"I decided you were right about enjoying such a nice day. When I heard voices, I rode this direction. I hadn't expected to see you with anyone." Papa looked down his nose at Paul as if he were a lowly insect he'd like to crush with his boot heel.

"Mr. Stuart happened to be riding by. I don't always get to talk with anyone other than Belle on my Sunday rides." She fought to keep her nervousness from showing in her voice. Thank God her gloves hid her trembling hands.

"I'm sorry to be in such a hurry to get home. Nice to see you, Miss Hampton, Mr. Hampton." Paul tipped his hat to Eugenia before urging his horse into a canter.

"You've seen that man on more than one Sunday afternoon." Papa studied her with solemn eyes.

"Yes, we've greeted each other if our paths have crossed."

He pointed his finger at her. "You've done more than exchange pleasantries. The loving looks that man gave you belie your words."

She gasped. Loving looks from Paul? "No, Papa." Her father had to be imagining such things.

"I know that look. I loved your mother for over thirty-eight years."

Her pulse roared in her ears. Trying to clear her mind, she shook her head. She had to remain calm and hide her anxieties from her father.

"The more you protest, the more you strengthen my supposition." He stared straight into her eyes the way he'd always done when confronting her.

She looked down and brushed a twig from her skirt. "I don't know the man that well." How she hated denying one of the best friends she'd ever had, but for now she couldn't see any other way to remain Paul's friend. She truly hadn't thought about him possibly falling in love with her.

If only Papa would accept Paul for the hardworking man he was. Then, perhaps, she could convince Paul to stay in Tennessee and make his fortune here the way her grandfather did. Papa seemed to have forgotten Grandfather Hampton's humble beginnings as a soldier in General Washington's army. She'd pray for the right time to remind him of his family history and the generous land grant that had allowed the Hamptons to prosper.

She spent the remainder of her extremely long ride pointing out the antics of scurrying squirrels or trying to convince Papa he was wrong about Paul's feelings for her. "I've heard you say for years how respectful your overseer is with you. His son has always treated me with deference if we meet."

"I'll give your protests due consideration, but do be careful of young Stuart."

"Of course, Papa."

She guided her horse toward the barn. After Sampson helped her dismount, she wasted no time going to her room to change clothes. Somehow she'd convince Papa that Paul didn't love her. At least she didn't think Paul loved her. If he did, she had no idea what she'd say or do.

* * *

PAUL GALLOPED his horse toward Hopeton and away from Eugenia and Mr. Hampton. In a few minutes, he pounded on the front door.

"I need to see Titus." He blurted out his words the instant the butler cracked open the front door.

The slave ushered him into the parlor and went to find his master. Unable to sit and wait, Paul still paced in front of the fancy tapestry-print sofa when Titus stepped into the room. "I'm glad you're home. Can we talk out on the porch?"

"If you'd like." Titus's raised eyebrows almost met over his nose as he followed Paul outside.

While Titus took his usual chair, Paul marched up and down the porch. "Eugenia's pa found us riding together."

"That's why you look so upset."

"Yeah." His boots clumping on the porch kept pace with the blood pounding in his temples.

"You've always known Mr. Hampton doesn't want you near his daughter. What's really bothering you?" Titus propped his elbows on the arms of his chair.

"I hope it didn't mess things up between her and her pa. They had just started talking again the other day."

"Sit down. You're like watching a worried fox as the hounds close in on him."

"Sorry." He slumped into the chair next to Titus. "Maybe the Lord answered my prayer about whether I should keep seeing Eugenia. I can't risk causing her more problems with her pa"

"You're bothered about more than trouble between Eugenia and her father." Titus looked him in the eyes.

Paul swallowed hard. "It's tearing my insides up to think about never seeing her again even though I know that's what I have to do for her sake." Voicing his thoughts made him hurt so bad he could hardly breathe. He looked down at his hands clenched in his lap.

"Not seeing her might be best for you too."

Paul jerked up straight. "What?"

"Why prolong your own misery? The sooner you quit talking to her, the sooner you can try to forget her."

"Maybe." Paul slumped back in the chair. There was no maybe. He'd never forget Eugenia, but Titus was right about not drawing out his own pain. "I don't dare risk seeing her again, so how do I tell her that? And how would I convince her it's for the best?"

Titus steepled his hands together. "My sister might tell her for you, if you ask her."

"What do I say? I can't tell her how much I love Eugenia."

"No, but emphasizing the risk of causing trouble between Eugenia and her father should be a good enough reason for Clare to help you."

Paul let out the breath he'd been holding in. "Go find your sister." After Titus disappeared inside the house, he slammed his fist into a chair arm. None of this would be happening if he hadn't been foolish enough to fall in love with Eugenia.

Sooner than he wished, Clarisse stepped out onto the porch. He stood as she walked toward him, sure her bright smile would disappear as soon as he told her what he wanted.

"Titus says you have a favor to ask." The questioning look in her eyes signaled Titus must not have told her much about what he wanted from her.

"Yeah, I do." Paul shoved his hands into his trouser pockets to keep her from seeing them trembling then explained as best he could why he needed her help. He hadn't stretched the truth like this since he'd told his father he'd left Nashville to be closer to family. "Please do this for me. I ain't got any way to talk to Eugenia without chancing her pa seeing us."

With every word he spoke, the flashes of anger in Clarisse's blue eyes intensified. She didn't believe his excuse. But he was out of words to try to explain himself.

"I can't believe you want me to deliver such a message." Her words hissed through gritted teeth as she scowled at him.

He prayed for anything to say to calm her. Good thing her burning eyes couldn't start fires or the whole porch—and maybe the house—would be burning. "You didn't see the way her pa looked at me."

"Why not stop seeing her long enough to convince Mr. Hampton you don't talk so many Sundays?" Clarisse folded her arms in front of her.

Paul shook his head. "What if he saw us again?"

"He won't if you're careful. You can't do this to Eugenia." Her voice cracked.

Searing pain tore at his heart, making it hard for him to focus on the porch floor he was staring at. He couldn't let Clarisse see how much it hurt to know he'd never be with Eugenia again. He sucked in a deep shaky breath. "I have to do this. Please try to understand."

"I don't, and Eugenia won't either. Why are you being so cruel to someone you say you like so much?"

"If I didn't l-like her, I wouldn't care what happened between her and her pa. This is for the best." He barely stopped himself from admitting his love for Eugenia.

She stomped her foot. He jumped. "Not for Eugenia. If it's so good, why won't you even glance at me?"

Paul forced himself to look into her blazing eyes, but couldn't say more without giving away how he really felt about Eugenia.

"Don't be so rough on him, Clare." Titus laid a hand on her shoulder. "I know it's hard, but this is best."

Clarisse jerked away from her brother. "You'll crush her, don't you see that? She's been through so much already." Her voice rose in volume with each word as she glowered up at Paul and Titus. She clenched and unclenched her fists. If she weren't such a lady, she'd probably slap him.

"I'm sorry." Paul fought to keep his voice from cracking and revealing his agony. "I have to go. Titus, try to help your sister understand."

His friend nodded and extended his hand to him. He gripped Titus's hand and then tipped his hat to Clarisse. She scowled at him before he could walk away. One more person who'd like to cut off his head like a poisonous snake.

Paul galloped his horse down the drive, trying to block out Clarisse's angry voice. She'd kept quiet only until he was too far away to make out the heated words she threw at Titus. He'd have to apologize to his friend for putting him in the middle of such a mess.

He was doing the right thing. Better to hurt Eugenia a little now than cause more problems between her and her pa. He'd be gone from here in a few months, so she needed to be on good terms with her pa instead of him.

He groaned. Who was he fooling? Not God or himself. He wanted Eugenia to get along with her father, but really, all he wanted was a woman he couldn't have but couldn't forget.

Chapter Thirteen

Eugenia walked into the parlor with a genuine smile on her face. How wonderful to see Clare instead of an unwanted suitor. Not even the unseasonably cool weather and threatening clouds could dampen her spirits as long as Luke stayed away. She'd take a barrel full of Monday afternoons like this.

"I didn't expect to see you today, but I'm so glad you came." Eugenia seated herself on the couch next to Clare. "Would you care for some tea?

"No, thank you." Clarisse's shoulders drooped.

She hadn't seen her friend look so forlorn or sound so listless in a long time. "Is something wrong?"

"I need to talk to you alone." Clarisse's whispered words were so soft Eugenia had to strain to hear her.

"We can sit in the gazebo if you'd like. The weather is pleasant enough for that today."

Clarisse nodded. "That would be good."

They walked in silence as they made their way to the garden. How unlike Clare to not be chattering away by now.

"What has you so upset?" Eugenia broke the hush after they seated themselves on an iron bench.

Clarisse pulled her shawl tightly around her shoulders as if the cool September breeze chilled her. "Paul came by yesterday after your father found the two of you together. He's afraid to see you again and chance making your father even angrier with you."

Such a cautious reaction from Paul didn't surprise her, but it shouldn't be hard for her and Clare to persuade Paul he had nothing to worry about. "I've always been able to convince Papa to see things my way. Have your brother tell Paul to give me a little time—perhaps two or three weeks—and everything will be fine." She brushed a fallen leaf from her skirt.

"I tried to reason with Paul, but he insisted he can't risk seeing you anymore. My brother agrees with him." Clarisse's voice cracked as she looked away.

Eugenia gasped. Someone might as well have doused her with icy water on the coldest day of winter. She wouldn't have been any more frozen or shocked than she was now. "Never? Not ever?"

Clarisse's lips trembled as she nodded.

"But there won't be any trouble. Papa and I didn't argue yesterday." Eugenia gripped the cold arm of the iron bench. "Did I say or do something wrong? Why doesn't he want to see me again?"

"I'm not sure." Clarisse shifted as if trying to get comfortable.

"Would he talk with me somewhere if he were sure Papa wouldn't find out about it?"

"I don't know." Her friend twisted the fringe on her shawl until the yarn knotted.

"Could you please ask him, or ask your brother to talk to him?"

"I'll try." Clarisse's eyes glistened with tears. "We'll pray. Don't give up hope."

Hope? The sun peeked through the clouds a moment but no amount of sunlight could chase away the chill in Eugenia's heart. "It's hard to remain optimistic when so many bad things keep happening."

Clarisse bit her quivering lip. "I'm so sorry. I can't stay longer." She rose.

"I understand." Her friend shouldn't be Paul's messenger of gloom. He had no idea how such a tender-hearted person hated to hurt anyone. Eugenia patted Clare's arm.

"Thank you for being so kind to the bearer of such awful news." Clarisse blinked away her tears.

"I'd rather hear such things from a caring friend than anyone else." She hugged Clarisse before allowing her to trudge out of the gazebo.

Chilled by a gust of wind, Eugenia gripped her shawl closer, but she remained outside where she could pace and think without Papa watching. She wandered through her mother's fading flower garden, trying to fathom everything her friend had said. Paul was such a special friend—the kind she wasn't sure how she'd manage without.

Her thoughts sounded much like Papa wondering how he'd survive without her mother. She froze. Had she fallen in love with Paul? Could she risk the pain of loving him? Clare's grief over losing her fiancé was awful. Papa might never recover from losing Mama.

Perfect love casteth out fear.

"Oh, dear, Lord. That is so true." She lifted her eyes to the cloudless sky. The verse she'd read in First John last night sailed through her mind and into her heart. No one offered more perfect love than God. With His help, she needn't fear the pain of loving someone or the pain of losing them. God would never forsake her. He'd always be there to comfort her no matter what might happen.

And yes, she loved Paul. She'd risk pain or anything else to be with him. Not being with him would be sheer agony.

* * *

No matter how much time she spent praying that week, Eugenia couldn't understand why Paul wanted to completely sever their friendship. After the church service Sunday, he spoke with Titus while she talked with Clare in the churchyard just a few feet away, but he never so much as glanced at her.

"I hope to talk to Paul and convince him he's wrong not to continue seeing you." Clarisse kept her hand partially over her mouth as she spoke.

"Thank you. I'll leave for home now and give you an opportunity to speak to him."

After lunch, Eugenia followed Papa into the parlor. How she prayed God would change her father's attitude toward Paul because she didn't want to deceive Papa about the man she loved. She longed for the day God answered her prayers, and she could tell her father the truth about everything.

"Would you like to go riding with me today?" She had no desire to sit with her father the way she usually did, so she might as well speak her mind and try to change his perceptions.

Acting as if she hadn't said a word, Papa strolled over to the end table next to his chair and picked up his book. If he was deliberately trying to irritate her, he was accomplishing it well. "I gather you're still trying to persuade me that my conclusions about Mr. Stuart are wrong, since you usually want to ride alone."

"I've enjoyed riding with you since I was a little girl. But you refused so many of my invitations to ride lately that I quit asking." She loosened her grip on the back of the chair in front of her and stroked the soft velvet upholstery, hoping Papa wouldn't notice her anxiety.

He nodded. Eugenia studied him as he seated himself in his favorite chair. He usually loved any mention of their times together. She hoped her reminder would soften his outlook.

"In spite of your invitation, I'm still not sure about that young man's intentions toward you." He rubbed his chin and scrutinized her as if he were testing her.

"Unless Mr. Stuart is standing next to Titus, I don't speak to him at church, after you and Mama got so upset with me. I've greeted him alone only if he crosses my path the way he did last week."

"Is that so?"

"Yes. You may ask any church member you choose—even old Mrs. Crider, who detests me."

Now that she was a Christian, Eugenia knew she needed to stop her old habit of being less than truthful, but she had to see Paul again. God wanted her to marry a Christian man. If God had given her the love she had for such a good man, surely He'd work in Papa's heart and help him accept the Christian man she loved so she wouldn't have to deceive her father. The Lord could yet work this misunderstanding for good.

Papa studied her before opening his book. "If I question someone, and they tell me you don't speak to the young man, perhaps I'll rethink my position."

"Thank you. I'm going to enjoy the sunshine for a while." She kissed his cheek before making her escape from the parlor.

Riding through the woods with no expectation of meeting Paul ruined Eugenia's afternoon, but she couldn't stay home and make her father wonder why she didn't go for her usual ride. She found it hard to pray after the way she'd misled him. She *had* told him the truth, but in a slanted sort of fashion.

"I'm going to talk with Paul again instead of you, Belle. Only God knows how, but I'll see Paul again."

If only she felt as sure as her words sounded. A startled brown rabbit scurried away from her. How tempting to run and hide from her problems like the rabbit had done, but running away wouldn't solve anything. Doing something might help—if she only knew what to do.

* * *

THE NEXT AFTERNOON, Eugenia watched and waited for Clare to come see her. She used every ounce of willpower she possessed not to mention Paul until she and Clare were seated on the front porch out of her father's hearing. "Papa is beginning to believe what I told him about seeing Paul. I think after next Sunday, Paul could meet me as usual."

"Don't expect to see him alone again." Clarisse sighed.

Eugenia gasped. "He still refuses to talk to me?"

"I'm so angry with that man and my brother, I could scream." Clarisse spoke through gritted teeth.

"I should be angry at Paul, too, but I've discovered I love him." Eugenia gripped the arm of her chair.

Clarisse looked directly into Eugenia's eyes. "I know."

"You do? How?"

"You look at Paul the way Jenette looks at Titus, the way Garland looked at me." Clarisse adjusted her shawl around her shoulders.

"I'm afraid Paul doesn't care for me."

"I think he does."

"You do? Why?" Eugenia leaned forward.

"I told my brother I'm sure you love Paul. Titus replied that was even more reason for you not to see each other because both of you would get hurt. When I said Paul must love you if he's hurting, too, Titus refused to confirm or deny my assumption."

A happy laugh welled up inside. Eugenia made no effort to stifle it. "You only thought you had bad news. If Paul loves me, now all we have to do is start praying for God to make a way for us to be together."

Some of the sparkle returned to her friend's eyes. "I thought you were afraid to risk being hurt."

She told Clare how the verse in First John had set her heart free from her fears.

"What if God doesn't want you and Paul to wed?" Clarisse reached over and laid her hand on Eugenia's arm.

A horrible iciness radiated through Eugenia's body. "I hadn't thought of that. We should pray about God's will first." She didn't want to think what she'd do if God didn't want her and Paul together.

"Don't let my brother know I told you Paul loves you."

"Why not?"

"Titus is just as sure as Paul is that your father would never allow you to marry Paul."

"God can work miracles." If only she felt as confident as she sounded.

"We'll pray for a miracle, then, as long as that's God's will." Clarisse's listless tone didn't sound as if she had much hope for a miracle.

* * *

Papa made no mention of Paul the entire week, giving Eugenia hope that her father's concern had lessened. After Clare got a chance to tell him Papa was no longer so upset, Paul would have to see her again.

Eugenia was still holding onto her hope while she and her father ate lunch after church. Clare had promised to talk with Paul again this afternoon, and Papa's relaxed smile at the table gave her more hope for a happy resolution to her problems. Today, she could appreciate the scrumptious smells of the ham and potatoes as the servants brought in the food.

"Getting out today restored you again, judging from your bright smile." Papa's eyes twinkled as he buttered his bread.

"Yes, it did. Would you like to ride with me?"

He shook his head. "Not today. My old bones need a rest after riding the fields so much lately."

"All right, but I'll miss your company." She ignored his unsettling remark about his old bones. She had enough on her mind without being reminded of her father's age.

"There's no need to continue inviting me to ride with you. I questioned more than one friend on more than one supposed ride over my fields, including Mrs. Crider. Everyone confirmed what you've told me. I'm glad you've listened about guarding your reputation."

"Yes, Papa." She ducked her head as she cut up her ham. On the inside, she was jumping up and twirling around the room instead of sitting still.

Not long after they finished their meal, Eugenia left for her ride. She couldn't resist letting Belle gallop some. Perhaps she could soon talk with Paul. She'd do so today if she knew which alternate trail he'd taken back to Murfreesboro to avoid her.

* * *

WHEN SHE WENT to Hopeton on Monday to see Clarisse, Eugenia was still in an exuberant mood as the butler ushered her into the parlor to wait. "Did you talk to Paul?" She blurted out her question the instant Clare walked into the room.

"Yes. He's so stubborn, and Titus supports him." Clarisse's eyes burned with anger.

"Why?"

Clarisse shrugged. "They say they're still worried what would happen if your father saw Paul with you a second time."

"But he won't. Papa rides much less in cooler weather, especially so with October almost here. If I could talk to Paul, I know I could get him to understand."

A servant carried in a tray with refreshments and set it on the table in front of them.

"That will be hard to accomplish." Clarisse busied herself pouring tea.

"I have to do something." Eugenia clenched and unclenched her fists. She wouldn't give up.

"But what?" Clarisse handed Eugenia a cup.

Out of habit, Eugenia sipped the tasteless liquid. "I don't know. I'll think about it." She'd do almost anything if only she knew what to do.

Clarisse laid a hand on her arm. "If you manage to see Paul, be careful what you say to him."

"Why?"

"Don't declare your love. If Titus thinks it's impossible for your father to consent to a marriage with Paul, imagine how Paul must feel about it."

Eugenia nodded. "I'll pray about what to say to him."

"We can both do that. If anyone can devise a scheme to meet Paul, you can." She squeezed Eugenia's hand.

"If I have my way, Paul will find his ride this next Sunday more exciting than he's planned."

Eugenia hoped he would.

Chapter Fourteen

Paul trudged into the barn to saddle his horse for the trip back to Murfreesboro, dreading another afternoon without talking to Eugenia. Three awful Sunday afternoons in a row without talking to her. This first Sunday in October would be the fourth. Telling Clarisse again last Sunday that he still wouldn't see Eugenia again had been the hardest thing he'd ever done. Doing the right thing made his chest hurt from the ache in his heart.

The door creaked open. He turned to see who was behind him. Pa stood, framed in the sunlight filtering through the door. For what felt like an hour, his father remained there and stared before walking toward him.

Pa clenched and unclenched his jaw. He only did that when something was bothering him. "I heard of a good farm for sale that would suit you, son."

They'd finally had a good afternoon together. Until now. If he didn't answer, Pa would accuse him of being disrespectful. If he did answer, only God knew what kind of argument that would start. He swallowed a sigh.

"You know how I feel about farming around here."

Pa grunted. "What would it hurt if you bought one or two Negroes? You'd treat them so good, you'd be doing them a favor."

"No, sir. I can't do that." He'd given up a long time ago ever getting Pa to understand why he hated slavery, but Pa couldn't quit saying aggravating things, no matter how little Paul said.

"If it'll keep you from moving and breaking your ma's heart, you could free them and pretend they're still yours." His father's glare seared Paul's soul.

Paul clamped his open mouth shut. He'd never expected to hear such words coming from a man who had been an overseer for years. "That wouldn't work."

"Why not?" Arms folded across his puffed-out chest, Pa looked about to explode.

"We both know it's illegal for freed men to live in this state."

Red-faced, his father wagged his finger in front of Paul's nose. "If nobody knows what you've done, nobody knows it's against the law."

"It's too dangerous to live a lie like that. For me or any Negro." Paul turned his back and jerked his bridle from a wall peg.

The people he had helped were settled in Canada by now. Pa would disown him if he knew his son had helped a circuit-riding preacher slip a freed man off to the North with his wife after her master refused to sell her to her husband. Yet, he was now suggesting Paul break the law.

"I still ain't got enough money for a farm, so I won't be going anywhere yet." Paul turned toward his horse.

His father's breath whooshed out like someone had knocked the air out of him. Maybe he'd calm down some since Paul couldn't leave for a while longer. At least he didn't say anything else while Paul slipped the bit into the horse's mouth.

Pa cleared his throat. "I got some money saved back. I'd go shares with you or something till you paid me back."

His father would never accept his son's beliefs, but saying that out loud wouldn't cause anything except more trouble. Paul swallowed hard. "Thank you, sir, but no."

If he didn't keep his back turned, his father would see his hands shaking. He couldn't talk to Pa about Noah, the last man he and Pastor Billings had helped. He couldn't say a word to him about Eugenia. His whole world was crashing in hard on top of him, and the man he'd always talked everything over with had no idea how agonizing Paul's life had become.

"Look at me, son." Pa grabbed his arm.

He stared into his father's eyes. The light wasn't good inside the barn or Pa might see the stinging moisture in his son's eyes. "Why are you offering to help me now when you've come close to throwing me out of the house if I mention how I feel about owning slaves?"

"Because no matter what we think about your foolish ideas, your ma and I still don't want our only son moving all the way to Illinois."

His foolish ideas. His own father thought he was a fool. Paul suppressed the groan swelling up in his tight chest. "I'm tired of so many people thinking I'm crazy if I tell them my opinion. If I keep quiet, then people decide I'm for something I think is wrong. I can't live like this much longer."

As if he'd just touched a hot coal, his father jerked his hand from Paul's arm. "I keep hoping you'll change your mind, but I'm about to give up on you when you talk like that."

Such harsh words stung worse than if Pa had taken his razor strop to his back. Paul shook the saddle blanket in his hands and watched the dust moats float off around him. If only his troubles would disappear so easily. "I'm sorry, sir, but I won't change my mind."

"I'm sorry too." Pa's broad shoulders slumped.

His father gave him one last mournful look before trudging out of the barn. Paul picked up his saddle. It was light compared to the painful weight in his heart. He was right about not owning slaves, but he doubted Pa would ever understand that.

He let out a breath. Losing Eugenia was bad enough. Now he'd lost his family too. Pa would have never offered him his savings if Ma hadn't agreed.

His parents and sisters waited for him in the yard when he led his horse from the barn. Ma walked over to him. Her solemn blue eyes were misty. She patted his arm.

"We still love you."

"I love all of you, but I'll be gone as soon as I get enough money." Paul swallowed hard. Only God knew how he managed to keep his voice steady as he spoke.

Ma blinked away tears. "I know." She stood on tiptoes to hug him.

He kissed her cheek. This wasn't a final goodbye, but it was more final than he wanted. Turning down Pa's offer made the split in his family absolute before he actually left.

But he couldn't stay. A man had to stand up for what was right. He wished it didn't hurt so much.

* * *

EUGENIA POSITIONED her horse in a thicket of trees a short distance away from the Stuart house and watched for Paul. Thankful to God for all the times she'd ridden the plantation with Papa so she knew the exact location of the simple frame house the Stuarts called home.

"I hope he hasn't left already." She patted Belle's neck as she whispered to her mare.

Hope warmed her heart as she watched Paul bid his parents and sisters goodbye. After she explained everything to him, he'd surely be willing to resume their visits. He swung up into his saddle. She shadowed him until they were a safe distance into the woods.

"Paul, we must talk." Eugenia rode up from behind him.

He stared at her, a look of despair in his eyes. "We can't take a chance like that." His voice cracked.

"There's no chance to be taken. Papa is completely satisfied that we've only talked briefly if our paths cross."

He shook his head. "How can you be so sure?"

She told him what she had said to her father. "I know I didn't tell him the exact truth, but being friends with you is worth it." He looked much too glum for a man who'd been told such good news.

"What happens if he catches us together again and finds out you didn't tell him the whole truth?"

"He won't. Papa won't be riding much until it warms up in the spring, and I'll be sure to invite him to ride with me if the weather is nice enough to suit him. How will he see us if he tells me to go on alone as usual?"

"What if someone else sees us and tells him?" He gripped the reins as if his horse might spook at any minute.

"You know how unlikely that is. Why do you worry so much about what-ifs?"

"Because I don't want you getting hurt."

His voice sounded thick with emotion. His slumping posture emphasized the misery so evident in his voice and expression. If she didn't know better, she'd think he'd just left the funeral for a loved one instead of bidding his family goodbye.

"Then why won't you talk to me anymore when you know how that pains me?" She shaded her eyes from the sun that shouldn't be shining so brightly on such a gloomy day.

His face blanched. He glanced away. "Didn't you hear a single word I asked Clarisse to tell you?"

"You owe me a face-to-face explanation instead of sending poor Clare to deliver your intentions."

He reigned in his horse. "Can you be gone long enough to walk with me a little bit? If we stay in the thick woods here, maybe nobody will see us."

"I have time to talk." If talking would do her any good. His dour tone and expression didn't give her much hope he'd listen to reason and realize there was no danger of Papa finding them together.

Paul helped her down. As he spanned her waist, she relished feeling the strength in his hands. He held onto her just a little longer than he should, or most likely her imagination wished such a thing.

"Let me tie up the horses, since you think you've got to talk to me." His shoulders drooped while he looped his horse's reins around a mossy log.

She fell into step with him on the narrow trail. The woods were so thick here that her skirt almost brushed his trousers. No one could possibly see them.

Paul halted and looked down at her. "I won't be the reason you and your pa quit getting along. Believe me—you can lose someone even if they don't die."

She was thankful she'd spent time praying and thinking about what to say to his incessant argument concerning her father. She had a reply ready before the words left his mouth. "Then why do you continue to visit with Titus? Mrs. Matthews still doesn't like you. Aren't you worried about causing problems between that good friend and his mother?"

"It ain't the same." He shoved his hands into the pockets of his trousers then marched away.

"Why not?" She dodged a fallen branch in her path as she rushed after him.

"Titus is a man running his own place. What his ma thinks can't hurt him so much."

"What do you mean?"

"What would you do, where would you go if your pa got so mad he disowned you?" He stopped in front of her and looked deep into her eyes.

"I ... I don't know."

She hadn't anticipated such a disturbing question. While trying to think what to say, she ducked her head and smoothed her skirt. "You're not being fair by using those what-ifs again. Papa would never turn me out of the house."

"I won't risk you being wrong about that."

Without thinking, she grabbed his shirt sleeve and then released it. "I will."

"I ain't worth that." He kicked at a rock in his path so hard that it banged against a tree trunk and bounced back toward them.

"Yes, you are. Your friendship means that much to me." She quickly added the last sentence to prevent herself from blurting out how much she loved him.

He stared slack-jawed at her.

"How would you feel if Titus avoided you the way you've avoided me? What would you do without his friendship?"

"I wouldn't want to lose my best friend." He looked away, but not before she saw the anguish in his eyes.

"Can't you understand how I feel then?"

He nodded.

"But you still don't want to see me. You wish I hadn't cornered you, don't you?"

"I didn't say that."

He might as well have the way he refused to look at her, much less barely speak to her. No good would come from this conversation no matter how hard she'd prayed. "I can't force you to talk with me, or to be my friend. I'm sorry to have inconvenienced you."

She whirled and strode toward the horses, scattering the fallen leaves in her path. If she stayed much longer, the tears stinging her eyes would escape and slip down her cheeks. When she started to mount Belle, Paul's strong hands assisted her. She took the reins then gazed down at him. For the first time since they'd met, she had no idea what to say.

"I'm sorry, Eugenia."

"So am I."

Were there tears in his sad eyes? Had she imagined his longing gaze as he spoke? He looked away too quickly for her to be sure. She snapped the reins but didn't allow herself to cry until she was well out of his sight.

Oh, God, this pain is terrible. Please help me. Where is the good in this situation? What are You going to do?

While attempting to make sense of what had happened, she rode aimlessly. Her idea to force a face-to-face meeting had been disastrous. She'd lost Paul for good.

Chapter Fifteen

Paul watched smoke rising from chimneys as he led his horse toward the blacksmith's shop early the next morning. Not many people out and about yet. That was fine. He didn't feel like talking to anybody.

As if yesterday afternoon hadn't been bad enough, his horse had thrown a shoe not far from Murfreesboro. He'd walked Rusty the rest of the way home. Then Eugenia's woeful face had haunted him every time he'd shut his eyes last night, robbing him of sleep. He couldn't remember ever being so bone tired. His heart ached worse than his exhausted body.

"Good morning, Mr. Stuart."

He jumped at the sound of the blacksmith's daughter's voice. He'd just passed their house, but where had Lydia Preston come from? He'd been so deep in his own thoughts he hadn't noticed her soon enough to dodge her the way he usually did. And that wasn't good. The whole town knew she had her cap set for him and that the Prestons were more than ready to marry off the last of their four daughters.

"Morning, Miss Preston." He tipped his hat to her.

"Good morning." Her long dark lashes fluttered as she smiled up at him. "I see your horse is limping."

He nodded. "Rusty threw a shoe."

"So that means you're heading to my pa and brother?" Her face lit up in an ear-to-ear grin.

"Sure am."

"I'm on my way to see about Mrs. Allen so I can only walk with you a little bit."

If only she knew how long a little bit with her was to him. He'd walk forever listening to Eugenia chatter about anything, but Lydia's voice sounded about as sweet as a scolding blue jay chasing after him.

"Some of Ma's biscuits and apple butter should help that poor widow feel better." She patted the cloth-covered basket she carried.

The tempting smells from Lydia's basket made his stomach growl. With his appetite gone, he hadn't fixed anything but coffee this morning. He ducked his head, studying the dusty street while he kept walking. The way Lydia talked and talked he doubted she heard his noisy stomach.

"I hope your horse is the only thing that has you looking so worried."

His head jerked up. He didn't want this woman paying so much attention to him any day, especially not this one when he wanted to be around people about as much as he wanted to catch the measles. "I care about my horse."

"Any man worth his salt should take care of his livestock, so that's one more good thing about you, especially as far as Pa's concerned." Lydia's saucy grin made him shudder.

How much her pa liked him didn't matter. He stared down the narrow street with its small collection of businesses. She'd have to turn off soon to go to the widow's cabin.

"Ma keeps telling me not everyone has to like talking as

much as me, but I declare you're too quiet for your own good. How's a body supposed to get to know you?" Her brown eyes sparkled when he looked down at her.

This yappy female couldn't have picked a worse time to corner him. Paul gripped the reins in his hand.

"I'd best go see to Mrs. Allen." She paused and looked up at him. "If Pa's too busy for you to wait, I could stop by the smithy later and bring your horse to you after he's shod. Then you wouldn't have to leave your own work."

"Uh, no. If need be, I'll come get Rusty so I can pay your pa."

"Pa and Rueben would trust you to pay them later."

Her adoring gaze made his skin prickle. He'd better be real careful around this woman. "Thanks, but I pay my debts when I make them." Paul jerked the reins toward the blacksmith's. "I got work to do. Good day, Miss Preston."

"Good day." Her eyes were full of questions he didn't intend to answer.

Paul left the little flirt staring after him as he marched toward her father's place. If only Murfreesboro were big enough to need more than the Prestons for blacksmiths. But it wasn't, so he'd have to figure out what to do about the blacksmith's daughter. And why she'd stuck with him this morning. God worked in mysterious ways, but he had too many other things on his mind to figure out why the Lord had allowed Lydia to aggravate him today.

The woman he didn't want looked like she might have him in a heartbeat. The woman he wanted couldn't be his if he had a hundred years to work for her. He had to let go of his love for Eugenia, but how was more than he could imagine. Just thinking such a thing made it hard for him to breathe.

He gulped in the crisp morning air. *Lord, help me.*

By the time Paul finished the wheel he'd promised, he was

fighting to stay awake. He slammed his shop door shut as he stepped outside. Good thing he worked alone and didn't have to explain to anyone why he was so out of sorts.

Trudging down the street toward the blacksmith, he tipped his hat to a couple of the local ladies, glad everyone else looked to be in a hurry to get home for supper. He'd better hurry on so the blacksmith could get to his family. So he could get to bed sooner and maybe sleep tonight.

Matthew Preston grinned as Paul walked into the smithy. "Evening, Paul."

"Good evening, sir." Paul halted just inside the door while his eyes adjusted to the dim interior. He dug into his pocket for the money to pay for his horse. "I'll settle up with you so you can close."

Matthew led Rusty over to him. "The wife figures you had enough troubles with your horse yesterday that you'd appreciate not having to cook for yourself tonight. She said I should tell you you're welcome to come to our house."

Gripping the coins in his hand, he shook his head. "I appreciate the offer, but I'm worn out from getting home so late yesterday. Thank you anyway."

"Then maybe some other time."

"Maybe." He paid his bill and left as quickly as he could without being rude. He had no idea why Lydia and her family liked him so much. This wasn't the first invitation he'd turned down. Lately, Lydia hadn't tried to disguise her high opinion of him.

"Ain't no maybe about getting anywhere near that woman," he muttered to himself once he was away from the smithy. Head down, he rode to his own place as quickly as possible. He'd be sure to stay clear of Lydia Preston and her family.

Or should he? Where'd that crazy question come from? His

lack of sleep had muddled his mind. He shook his head as he finished tending to Rusty. If he got any lonelier, he'd be talking to his horse like Eugenia did to hers. She was rubbing off on him.

He groaned. He could still see Eugenia's tear-filled eyes looking down at him after he'd helped her mount Belle. Yesterday felt like ten years ago. *Stop thinking about her.* But his heart wouldn't listen to his mind.

The cool night air and reality hit him in the face as he walked toward his cabin. As hard as he'd been working to avoid Lydia Preston, had God shoved her in front of him for a reason? Maybe turning his attention to another woman would help him forget Eugenia. No, he'd never forget such a wonderful lady. But he'd be foolish to ever think he could have her, so he needed to figure out a way to go on without her.

Finding another woman would be the sensible thing to do. Lydia liked him. She was easy on the eyes and had a reputation as a kind soul. Maybe that wasn't so bad. He groaned as he strode into his cabin, flinging his hat onto his bed. All four walls closed in on him at once. Waiting for next spring and the best time to leave for a new start in Illinois could be the longest five months of his life.

THE MISERABLE WEEK DRAGGED ON. Paul prayed for guidance and peace. A cold October rain started Saturday afternoon, forcing him to stay home instead of riding to his folks' house. Preventing him from trying to get a glimpse of Eugenia on Sunday. Which he shouldn't do, anyway. On top of that, Pa might not want to see him any more than he wanted to see his father for a while.

The doubts wouldn't leave him alone at night any better

than they did during the day. He tossed on his cornhusk mattress as he'd done all week.

Sunday morning dawned clear and beautiful in spite of being a little chilly. Paul choked down his breakfast of porridge. He almost cut his chin while shaving. He had to get hold of himself. Even when life got rough, a man faced things head on. He'd walk into the little Murfreesboro church straight past wherever the Preston family sat and worship like he should on the Lord's Day.

Paul prayed during his entire walk to church, paying little attention to the cabins and houses he passed. He slipped inside the back of the church just before the service started, praying to hear the Lord's voice.

If only God's voice had been the only one he'd heard as soon as the service ended.

"Glad to see you here." Matthew Preston pumped Paul's hand before he could escape from the churchyard. Mrs. Preston and Lydia grinned like happy possums as they stood beside Mr. Preston.

"Thank you." Paul pulled his hand away as soon as he could manage. Anybody watching would think he was some kind of long-lost relative come home the way the whole family looked.

"Since I never met a man who cooked a lot for himself, you're more than welcome to come to our house for lunch." Mrs. Preston's motherly smile said so much more than her words.

His own mother would be downright happy, too, if she knew he was thinking about seeing a good woman like Lydia. "I couldn't impose on you like that, ma'am."

Lydia shook her head. "You could never impose on us. Ma always fixes extra in case the preacher doesn't get asked to anybody else's house."

"Then I guess I'll take you up on your offer. Thank you, ma'am." Paul looked straight at Mrs. Preston while trying to ignore the happy sparkle in Lydia's eyes.

Mr. and Mrs. Preston started toward their house. Lydia fell into step with Paul.

"I'm glad the weather's nice today. I so like a walk on Sunday afternoons." Her gaze reminded him of an adoring puppy. How she kept from tripping when she hardly took her eyes off him was beyond him. But thankfully, she did. If he'd had to catch her, she'd have taken that so wrong.

Paul shoved his hands into his suit coat pockets, wishing he could focus on the dirt street beneath his shoes instead of his companion. His mind told him not to ignore her hint about going for a walk later, but his aching heart made it hard for him to force any words from his tight throat. "Today's a sight better than yesterday."

Her smile didn't dim. She chattered all the way to the house, all the way up the porch steps, and into the door he held open for her.

What should have been a delicious meal of ham and sweet potatoes tasted like the wood shavings on his shop floor. Paul had to take a drink of water after almost every bite. He wasn't sure how he managed to clean his plate.

"We're glad you came. Always good to get to know another businessman better." Mr. Preston grinned from his place at the head of the long family-size table.

"Yes, sir." Paul turned his attention to Mrs. Preston. "Everything was delicious. Thank you, ma'am."

"You're more than welcome." She rose. "Lydia and I'll get these dishes taken care of, and you men can talk for a spell."

Paul followed Mr. Preston into the small front room. The two story house was nothing fancy, but it was nicer than any place he'd ever owned. Lydia had to be used to better things than a man like him could offer her for a long time. If God meant for him to find another woman, he should have been invited to eat with a family living in a cabin like his. Maybe he wasn't where God wanted him. And maybe he was. If so, he'd sure like to be happier about it.

Before taking the wooden chair closest to the fireplace, Mr. Preston reached for his pipe sitting on the mantle. Paul took the other chair. "The whole town's been glad to have a good wheelwright these last few months. You should have a nice business going in no time."

"Thank you." Paul wondered if Mr. Preston was glad to see a wheelwright and good customer for the tires he made come to town or happier to see another prospect for a son-in-law.

Mr. Preston lit his pipe and leaned back. "We're growing good now. As long as Old Hickory gets reelected, we'll all be just fine around here."

Paul shifted. He wouldn't vote for Andrew Jackson or any other slaveholder, but he knew to keep that to himself. If only winter wasn't coming on, and he had the money to leave for Illinois tomorrow.

"I don't expect Henry Clay can beat General Jackson, so you shouldn't have anything to worry about." The older man grinned as he puffed on his pipe. Paul relaxed a little since Mr. Preston looked happy with his opinion of Clay.

"I imagine your pa's real happy to have you closer to home now."

"Yes, sir. Him and Ma both."

"Family's important. It's real nice at my age to have my son working with me and all my children and grandchildren close by. I expect your folks feel the same." Mr. Preston's brown eyes almost looked holes through Paul.

Paul's chair felt harder than a jagged rock. Mr. Preston had been in Murfreesboro for years and knew nearly everyone in the county. He had to know Paul's parents had no grandchildren, so talking about such things didn't make sense.

"Well, I guess they would, but they don't talk much about grandchildren after my sister and her baby died last year."

"No, I don't suppose they do." Mr. Preston puffed on his pipe.

The silence eased a few of the knots in Paul's shoulders. The tobacco smell reminded him of his pa. He might have felt at home here if not for Mr. Preston's mention of grandchildren. If the man hinted like that to all of Lydia's callers, no wonder she was still unattached. And Paul hadn't even come calling. He was scouting out God's will, nothing else.

Mr. Preston had turned the conversation back to what was happening in Murfreesboro not long before the ladies walked in.

Lydia fanned the air around her with her hand. "I don't guess I'll ever get used to tobacco smoke as long as I live. I'll go for a walk while Pa enjoys his pipe." She stared straight at Paul, so did her mother.

Paul recognized this hint. But he was here to see what God wanted, so he might as well give it a try. He forced himself to stand. "I'd like a walk, too, if you don't mind company."

Her face lit up like a kid with two new tops. "I'd enjoy your company, Mr. Stuart."

After she put on her bonnet and grabbed a shawl, he escorted Lydia out the front door. Since the Prestons lived on the edge of town, he hoped no one would see him walking in the yard with this woman. Good thing they weren't well enough acquainted to walk too far from the house together.

If only he could stroll with Eugenia in public and not worry about what would happen. His tight chest squeezed his heart. His one good suit felt mighty tight. He shoved his hands into his trouser pockets. Stop thinking about the woman you can't have and try finding something good about the one walking next to you. Especially if God might be the One sending her around.

"What a wonderful day. It's not too hot, not too cold. The clouds are gone. It's perfect." Lydia lifted her face to the sun.

Looking down at her, she wasn't the least bit ugly. Her green wool dress made her look real nice. Her warm brown eyes suggested a smart caring woman. "Best enjoy a day like this when October can change so quick."

She laughed. "And I do, especially since I like spring and all the pretty flowers so much better than the brown grass and leafless trees we'll have soon."

Eugenia also loved spring. Too bad Lydia couldn't enjoy a different season so everything she said wouldn't remind him of the woman he loved. Enduring their walk was harder than he could have ever imagined. He fought not to stare off at the neighbor's house in the distance as they walked. She talked so much, he didn't have to worry about what to say. A sudden gust of wind swirled the dust around them. She gripped her shawl closer around her narrow shoulders.

"You'd best get inside the way this wind's picked up." Paul turned to walk back to the house without giving her a chance to protest. "I wouldn't want you to catch a chill."

"I had no idea you're such a thoughtful man." Her adoring smile made him cringe.

If only he could take back the words she'd taken the wrong way. He'd wanted a way to end this too long short walk, not dig himself deeper into trouble.

After returning Lydia to her house, Paul said his goodbyes as fast as he could then rushed home so quickly, the people he passed by probably wondered why he was in such a hurry. He slumped into the chair beside his small homemade table, leaning forward with his head in his hands. Trying to figure out God's will shouldn't make a man so miserable.

Show me what to do, Lord. Then give me the strength to do it.

* * *

Paul lost count of how many times he prayed the same desperate prayer for guidance and strength. He hoped God didn't mind hearing those words over and over for a whole week. He'd had enough work that he could dodge the Preston family without any trouble. But that hadn't kept his insides from squirming every time he thought about Lydia. The more he tried to convince himself to be sensible, the more his heart rebelled.

He finished work early enough on Saturday to go for a ride. Rusty needed exercise, and he had to do something besides stare at the four walls of his cabin. With no particular place to go, Paul gave Rusty his head and let him trot toward the outside of town at the edge of the woods. He prayed for the strength not to turn his horse onto the trail toward his folks' house. Nothing but trouble waited for him there or at his parents' church—Eugenia's church.

"Hello, Mr. Stuart." Another sort of trouble waved and called his name at the edge of the Preston's property. "I didn't expect to run across you this time of day."

Paul halted his horse and looked down at Lydia. "I finished work a little early."

"And I'm just getting back from buying the thread Ma needs." She flashed him a radiant smile. "I haven't seen you all week."

"I've been busy." Really busy, staying away from any place she might be, but he couldn't tell her that.

As she gazed up at him, she shaded her eyes from the evening sun. "And now you're going to see your folks?"

He shook his head. "Not today, but Rusty needs a good run." So did he.

"Then I suppose we'll see you in church tomorrow?" Her grin spread ear to ear.

"I imagine so." His grip tightened on the reins.

"Then you must plan on lunch with us again. Ma would be furious with me if I didn't ask you to come." Her giggle made her sound more like a schoolgirl than a grown woman.

Paul choked back a groan. "Thank you. I'll be there."

Rusty snorted and shook his head. His horse wasn't the only one ready to move on. He tipped his hat to her. "I need to get going so I'm home before dark."

"I'll bake an applesauce cake just for you." She waved as he rode off.

He forced himself to wave back. Maybe another Sunday afternoon with Lydia might put him one step closer to figuring out God's will about the woman God kept shoving in front of him.

Except he felt as if he'd just set up his own hanging.

Chapter Sixteen

Paul's shop door creaked open. "Be with you shortly."

Rather than risk looking at whoever had walked in, he kept his eyes on the wheel he was building. He hoped the intruder wasn't Lydia come to pick up her mother's empty plate. Mrs. Preston had insisted on sending the rest of the cake home with Paul after church yesterday.

Not that he hadn't enjoyed the last piece of the treat Lydia had baked for him, but he wanted to see her right now about as much as he'd welcome a visit from a bounty hunter looking for runaway slaves. Lydia adored him, and he wouldn't miss her a single minute if he could leave for Illinois tomorrow.

"I'm glad to see you're all right." At the sound of Titus' voice, Paul almost dropped his plane.

Paul grinned and walked over to Titus. Before shaking with him, he wiped his hands on his apron. "It's real good to see you here."

"How are you?" His friend's intense expression said he wanted to know more than if Paul felt good or not.

"I've been better."

Titus's eyes widened. "Have you been ill?"

Paul shook his head. "I've been praying and trying to sort a few things out."

"That's what I assumed. Eugenia told Clare about forcing you to talk to her and how badly that went Sunday you were home. Now Eugenia is worried about you. We all are."

Painful memories he'd worked hard not to think about rushed back through Paul's mind. "I can't talk here where someone could walk in and hear us. You got time for coffee in my cabin?"

Titus nodded.

"I didn't promise my customer I'd finish this today." He glanced at his unfinished job. Rather than turn down a chance to talk to the one person who tried to understand him, he'd leave early without putting his tools away.

Neither of them spoke as Titus led his horse while walking down the dusty street beside Paul. Sure was nice to have a friend who understood when a man didn't want to talk. Especially as they passed other people and the other shops. The weather was almost perfect with no need for a jacket, but he couldn't enjoy the bright sunshine and clear blue sky.

He hadn't intended to worry so many people by staying in Murfreesboro two Sundays in a row. Hoping he wouldn't have to deal with another kind of worry right now, he kept a watch out for Lydia until they left the main part of town

"Is someone following you or are you looking for someone? I've lost track how many times you looked over your shoulder or checked around a corner of a building." Titus followed Paul inside the cabin and hung his stove pipe hat on a peg near the door.

"Neither. More like glad not to see a certain person." Paul stirred the banked coals in his fireplace to heat the coffee.

"Are you in trouble? Is that why we haven't seen you in two weeks?" Titus seated himself at the small table in the corner.

While they waited for the coffee to boil, Paul set two tin cups on the table "I guess you could call it trouble." He did his best to explain why he'd been seeing Lydia and how she might be the answer to his prayers concerning his problems with Eugenia.

Placing his elbows on the table, his friend stared straight into Paul's eyes. "I've never seen a man look so wretched while trying to find God's will."

Paul shrugged. He got up, filled both cups then slumped into his chair again. Taking a deep breath, he stared at the mug in his hand. Maybe he could taste the coffee after it cooled enough to drink. "If only I hadn't been fool enough to fall in love with Eugenia."

"But you did." Titus blew on his coffee.

"Lydia's a good woman. A lot of people don't marry for love the way you and Jenette did." Paul choked back a groan. Talking out loud about things he'd been thinking the last few days cut his insides worse than if he'd let a chisel slip and gouged his hand.

"True." Titus's grim tone echoed Paul's morose mood.

"Then why can't I even think about being sensible without feeling like I've been whipped? Especially since I'm doing the right thing." Paul took a big gulp of coffee. The scalding liquid burned all the way down. Hearing Titus agree with his thoughts made his heart hurt worse than his throat.

"Have you considered God might intend for you to wait until you get to Illinois to find a wife?" Titus tilted back in his chair until the front legs left the floor.

"Then why did God let Lydia come along?" Paul laid his arms on the table and stared at him.

"Are you certain God sent her?"

"What do you mean?" He gripped his cup as he waited for Titus to take a drink.

"Isn't she the one you've mentioned before who's had her eyes on you since you came to Murfreesboro?"

Paul nodded. "Her and her folks."

"Many parents would deem you a good match for their daughter." Titus grinned.

"A poor wheelwright like me?" Paul jerked up straight. His friend wasn't making any sense.

"A hard-working man like you could be quite successful one day, especially if his father-in-law is the blacksmith who makes the iron tires to go around your wheel rims. An alliance like that could be lucrative for both of you."

Paul shook his head. Maybe Titus had hit on why Matthew Preston was so interested in a wheelwright's business. "Yeah, but I hope money ain't the only reason they like me."

"Granted, I don't know the Prestons and could be wrong, but money is more than enough motivation for a lot of people."

"Not for me." Paul shoved his cup. Good thing it wasn't full or he'd have coffee all over himself and the table.

"Then perhaps you should go back to concentrating on saving money and leaving for Illinois." Titus leaned toward him.

"You think so?" Paul blew on his coffee before taking another sip. The more he thought about Titus's words, the better his drink tasted.

If he hadn't been so out of sorts the last couple of weeks, he might have thought about the very things Titus mentioned. Maybe not getting a good night's sleep for so long had made him short-sighted.

Titus walked over to the fire place and refilled his cup. "May I tell Clare she can assure Eugenia that you're all right?"

"Just be sure she understands I still won't risk seeing her." Paul leaned back in his chair.

Titus seated himself again. "If I tell my sister you're visiting a lady in town, Eugenia would be less apt to expect to see you."

"But I probably won't see Lydia anymore unless God changes my mind, especially if you're right about the money part."

"Clare and Eugenia don't need to know that." Titus's eyes twinkled.

Paul shook his head. "I don't like deceiving anybody, but Eugenia might feel better about me not seeing her if she knew about Lydia."

"I won't lie or hint at anything serious between you and Miss Preston, but I'll not mention you're already thinking about not seeing the woman again." Titus stood. "I should start for home."

"Thanks for standing by me." Paul clapped his hand on Titus's shoulder.

"You're welcome."

Paul spent the rest of the day thinking and praying about Titus's words. His friend's idea made a lot of sense. Maybe he had misunderstood God about Lydia, especially if Titus's suspicions about his future income were right.

Just because she was a good woman, didn't mean she was the woman God meant for him. He ate an early supper and went to bed. If God would hurry up and show him what to do about Lydia and everything else, maybe he could sleep well again.

THE NEXT AFTERNOON, Paul's shop door scraped open. He looked up from the wheel he was repairing to see Lydia framed in the doorway. Just the woman he didn't want to see. Maybe Titus was right about God not sending Lydia since he felt anything but peaceful every time she showed up.

"Looks like you've got plenty of work." Her eyes sparkled as she stepped inside and closed the door. She took a deep breath. "I like the wood smells in here so much better than the horses and hot metal at the smithy."

She'd soon have wood shavings on the hem of her skirt if she didn't take her eyes off him and watch where she was going. Paul set his work aside. He strode over to a bench near the door where he'd laid her mother's dish. No use letting Lydia and her swishing skirt get any closer to his work area.

"I got your ma's plate."

"If I'd been thinking straight the other day, I'd have told you to bring it back this Sunday." She grinned up at him.

As he handed her the plate, her fingers inched close enough to his he could have touched her hand if he'd wanted. "I'm going to see my folks Saturday if the weather's nice."

Disappointment clouded her eyes. "Oh. Ma says you're welcome to come any Sunday."

"I appreciate that, but I don't want to wear out my welcome."

She shook her head. "You could never do that."

"Oh, I might. You still don't know much about me." If she'd talk less, she'd know more. But maybe that was for the best, considering all the things he still needed to think about.

"What I do know is good, and I'd be happy to find out more." Her long dark lashes fluttered.

"Maybe. I need to get back to work. I got things promised."

She nodded. "Remember you're welcome at our house any Sunday you're in town."

"Thank you."

He opened the door for her. She waved to him, took three or four steps, and waved again. He nodded and forced himself to smile at her and then shut the door as quickly as possible. Closing his eyes, he slumped against a wall. The rough boards jabbed into his shoulders.

If God hadn't sent Lydia, then he had to figure out a way for her to realize that. He'd run from Eugenia only to create a worse misunderstanding with a different woman. His business and the means to save money for his Illinois farm could be hurt if he made the blacksmith mad by slighting his daughter.

Traveling to Nashville for tires would be inconvenient and expensive—it could also be dangerous. One too many people there suspected he'd helped Noah and his wife disappear. *Help me, Lord.*

Trying to get comfortable in the side chair by her bed, Eugenia grabbed her Bible from the nightstand. She'd rather sit in an upholstered parlor chair, but Papa had hinted yesterday that she'd been spending too much time reading and should get more exercise. She couldn't explain to him she'd been hunting for guidance, answers—any shred of hope since her plan to force Paul to talk to her three weeks ago had gone so badly.

If only she could find the right verses ...

A light knock on the door frame interrupted her thoughts. "Miss Eugenia, Joseph say Miss Clarisse come to call."

"Wonderful. Tell Nancy we'll have tea and refreshments." This Wednesday afternoon would be a pleasant one.

"I done that already."

"Good. You may go now." Eugenia closed her Bible then hurried down the stairs. No need to have Lily check her hair or appearance for Clare. Thankfully, Luke hadn't returned after she'd sent him away. She hoped and prayed he'd never come again.

"I'm so glad you're here." She seated herself on the couch next to Clare.

"Thank you." Clarisse's solemn expression held no hint of a smile.

"Papa went to visit Mama's grave while the weather is still nice, so I'm happy to have someone to visit with."

Eugenia quickly let Clare know she could speak without fear of Papa hearing them. But looking into her friend's serious eyes made her wonder if she wanted to hear what she had to say.

"Titus rode to Murfreesboro Monday to check on Paul." Clarisse lowered her voice as she ducked her head and smoothed the folds of her red wool dress. "Paul is well."

Every word Clare left unsaid spoke much too loudly. "But he hasn't changed his mind about seeing me again, has he?"

She kept her own words too soft for any servant to overhear. Joseph was so loyal to Papa he might report anything he thought was wrong.

Clarisse shook her head. "I wish that was the only thing my brother learned. Paul has been visiting with a young lady in Murfreesboro."

Eugenia gasped. Her friend might as well have slapped her. She stared at the blurred oil paintings of her parents hanging above the fireplace mantle. "You said he loves *me*."

"I'm sure he still does, but we both know what a practical man he is." Clarisse squeezed Eugenia's hand. "I'm so sorry."

Lily arrived with refreshments, interrupting their conversation. As she served Clare tea, Eugenia fought to control her emotions. She left her own cup untouched on the silver tray on the table in front of her.

"Why did God allow Paul and me to fall in love if He doesn't intend to work the miracles necessary for us to marry?"

"I don't know." Clarisse looked down as she stirred her tea.

To prevent her stinging tears from dampening her cheeks, Eugenia squeezed her eyes shut. She took a deep breath. "Mama told me walking by faith and not by sight can be a difficult journey."

"We can continue praying." Clarisse patted Eugenia's arm.

"Yes, we can." Except Eugenia feared this could be another time God chose not to answer her prayers the way she hoped.

Chapter Seventeen

The sunshine and light breeze reminded Paul more of spring than fall as he rode toward his folks' house on Saturday afternoon. Rusty was as frisky as a colt. His horse must be as happy to get out of town as he was. He still didn't know what to say to Lydia now that he'd decided God might not be the one who had put her in his path, but that could wait a while. So, for now, he'd ride from one set of problems into a whole passel of other troubles.

When his parents' house came into view, his grip tightened on the reins. The dog barked, announcing his coming. He swallowed hard. Only God knew if Paul was still welcome here. Might as well ride up to the house and find out.

"Paul!" His youngest sister, Sarah, bounded out the door toward him, her red braids bouncing behind her.

Ma, Leah, and Mary followed close behind Sarah. As soon as he dismounted, all three sisters tossed questions at him while trying to hug him all at once.

"We missed you. You missed us, too, didn't you?"

"Why didn't you come home last week when the weather was so pretty?"

"Let your brother catch his breath." Ma laughed.

Paul untangled himself from three sets of arms to accept his mother's hug.

"We've all wished you'd come home sooner." Ma beamed as she stepped back from him.

"Me too." He spotted Pa standing on the small front porch, arms folded across his chest, watching everything. He hoped his father had missed him too.

"I waited supper, hoping you'd come today." Ma rubbed her hands up and down on her apron.

His mother only did that when she was nervous. Maybe Pa didn't want him home.

"I appreciate that."

"Go tend to your horse so we can eat." Ma gave him a gentle nudge.

"Yes, ma'am." Paul stooped to pick up the reins.

"I helped make the biscuits." Sarah gave him a gap-toothed grin, displaying another missing tooth.

"Then I'll be sure and eat extra."

"You always eat extra." Mary's blue eyes twinkled.

"I sure do." He tugged on one of Mary's brown braids before leading his horse to the barn.

After quickly taking care of Rusty, Paul let his nose guide him back to the house. The smells of biscuits, ham, and potatoes made his stomach rumble before he opened the back door.

He took his usual chair at the table next to Leah and across from the two younger girls. Ma and his sisters acted as if everything was fine, but he wondered about his silent father. Pa nodded Paul's direction and smiled after he said the blessing. This might be the first meal that tasted good in quite a while.

"How are things in Murfreesboro? Have you had plenty of work?" Ma passed the biscuits to him.

He winked at Sarah and grabbed two biscuits. His nine-year-old sister's face lit up. "I've had enough work."

"That's good." Pa cut up a piece of ham.

Paul paused to butter a biscuit and give himself a moment to think about what else he should say. If he didn't mention Lydia, his parents would hear about her from someone else the next time they came into town. From what people had told him, Lydia hadn't wasted any time letting all of Murfreesboro know he was seeing her. "I've visited some with Lydia Preston after church the last two Sundays."

Everyone looked at Paul. Ma's face glowed. Pa grinned. Sixteen-year-old Leah giggled. All of them probably hoped being interested in a local lady might keep him from moving to Illinois.

"I ain't sure if I'll see her again."

"Why not? I hear she's a fine young lady." Ma's sunny face clouded.

Paul took his time chewing up his biscuit while trying to figure out what to say that wouldn't cause him more problems. Mentioning his suspicions about the Prestons liking him for his business wouldn't be right when he didn't know the truth himself. Telling them any woman would have to be willing to go to Illinois with him wouldn't be a good idea for keeping the peace in his family. "Because I've been praying about the whole situation, and I ain't certain what God wants me to do."

"Always be sure about the Lord's will first. It keeps us all from making serious mistakes." Pa shoved a fork full of potatoes into his mouth.

His father's words were probably a caution about more than just asking God about a woman, but at least Pa wasn't arguing with him at the table. Better enjoy tonight while he could. He still dreaded going to church tomorrow and seeing Eugenia when he had no chance of riding with her ever again.

PAUL TRUDGED into the small church building with his family the next morning. If only he could be somewhere else. Sitting through the service would be rough, especially if Eugenia gave him her usual discreet smile while she and Clarisse walked past him to sit in the Matthews' pew. Too bad his normal spot was closest to the aisle, but if he'd tried to change places, his whole family would wonder why.

Straightening his shoulders, he focused his attention on the stained-glass windows at the front of the church. Someone cleared their throat as they walked by his pew. Without thinking, he looked toward the sound. Clarisse glared at him. Eugenia gave him a quick, mournful glance as she passed by. His chest ached so much he couldn't take a breath for a moment or two. Doing what was right shouldn't hurt so bad. But it did.

The pastor stood. He smiled at the congregation before raising his large hands toward heaven. "Let us pray and thank God for another wonderful day."

Giving thanks for today would take more strength than he could muster right now. If he so much as glanced away from the preacher or the windows, he could see Eugenia's slumping shoulders ahead of him in the Matthews' pew.

Maybe he should have stayed in Murfreesboro again and figured out what to do with Lydia and her family. Except he didn't know what that would be. And he couldn't keep worrying his family by staying in town. He'd never stand a chance to solve his problems with his father if he never came home. Last night had been good. He still prayed he could somehow be on better terms with his parents before he left for Illinois.

He bowed his head, hoping for peace and answers. None came.

"Turn to the gospel of John, chapter thirteen, verses thirty-four and thirty-five. The Lord has impressed me to preach on loving one another." Brother Bentley beamed as he picked up his Bible from the pulpit in front of him.

To keep from groaning out loud, Paul clenched his jaw and gritted his teeth.

"'By this shall all men know that ye are my disciples, if ye have love one to another.'" The pastor looked right at Paul as he read the verse.

Paul ducked his head. Love had caused him nothing but pain. He'd had to run from Nashville after helping Noah and his wife escape to Canada. Loving Eugenia hurt something fierce. If loving someone was so right, why did God let him fall in love with a woman he couldn't have? No matter how hard he prayed, he still couldn't get any answers to his questions.

"In conclusion, I need to add one more observation about love." The pastor's words interrupted Paul's gloomy musings.

He forced his thoughts away from his agony. God might give him some answers if he listened to his pastor the way he should have been.

"Loving people can be costly. Jesus left the splendor of heaven and gave up His life for us. How dare we not risk loving someone because the cost is too dear?"

Brother Bentley's simple words slammed into his soul. Not that Paul didn't care about causing trouble between Eugenia and her pa—what he really dreaded was his own misery every time he saw her. The last two Sundays he'd run from that pain and caused himself more problems.

Eugenia needed him, and all he'd done was hurt her.

She'd asked only for his friendship. He'd rejected her. If God treated him the way he'd done Eugenia, he'd be in a lot worse trouble than he was now. Maybe he was wrong to think God didn't want him to see Eugenia again. Maybe he was only thinking about himself. He bowed his head and prayed.

* * *

Eugenia took her Bible and followed her father into the parlor after lunch. She was in no mood for a ride after the disastrous turn things had taken when she'd forced Paul to talk to her a few weeks ago. Seeing him in church this morning had been more painful than ripping the scab from an unhealed wound.

"Aren't you going for your customary outing?" Papa's eyebrows shot up when Eugenia took the chair next to his.

"No."

A log crackled in the fireplace while Papa studied her. "It can't be good for you to sit and read every spare minute. The air is crisper than I prefer, but should do a young lady good if you dress for it."

Another solitary ride with no chance of seeing Paul would be more like torture than pleasure, but worrying her father wouldn't be good, either. She closed her Bible. "Perhaps I have spent too much time reading." She left to change clothes.

Going down her favorite trail alone brought back bittersweet memories of past times with Paul. She should have chosen a different way. Her heart was as lifeless and trampled upon as the dead leaves carpeting the ground.

"I'm back to talking to you on my rides, Belle." She bit her lip to stop her tears. The horse continued down the trail with little guidance.

"I hope your mare still don't answer you," Paul called out

before riding up beside her. "I wouldn't have known you were here if I hadn't heard you talking to your horse."

She clamped her open mouth shut as she stared at him. "Why are you here?"

He took a deep breath. "I thought God didn't want me to see you anymore, but I was wrong."

"Clare told me you're seeing a woman in Murfreesboro, so why are you here, talking to me?"

He shifted in his saddle, reminding her of a squirming child caught taking a forbidden extra slice of pie. No wonder. No lady she knew would be happy if the man calling on her was also talking with someone else in secret. But she and Paul were only friends unless God still planned to work more than one miracle and allow them to admit their love to each other.

"I ain't courting the woman, and we don't have any kind of understanding."

"Clare never hinted at that." While her heart silently shouted for joy, Eugenia fought to keep her elation from showing on her face. His quick and fervent denial of any serious involvement with the other woman sent happy shivers up and down her spine.

He looked toward the clearing a few feet ahead of them. "I … uh … thought God was telling me not to talk to you after your pa found us together."

"I see." She didn't see, since she completely disagreed with his interpretation of that afternoon. But she hoped to somehow keep the quiet man talking.

Gazing into her eyes, he swallowed hard. "Like the pastor said this morning, a real friend wouldn't hurt someone the way I hurt you. I'm sorry for how I talked to you the last time. Just because I was upset with my pa didn't mean I should have been so rough on you."

For someone intent on doing God's bidding, the man

looked quite dejected. His eyes held no hint of their usual sparkle. She wished she could remind him the pastor's sermon concerned love not friendship, but she'd best settle for a safer topic instead. "Did you and your father have another misunderstanding?"

His shoulders slumped as he told her about his father's offer to loan him money for a farm. "I think his real reason was because he still hopes to change my mind about slaves someday if he can get me to stay."

If only he knew how much she wished he'd change his ideas about owning servants. Perhaps they could discuss such things another time. For now, she'd rejoice there would be other times to talk if Paul didn't look so gloomy. "We both know too well what it's like to disagree with our fathers."

He nodded. "How are you and your pa doing?"

"We're speaking to each other, but I can't share anything about God with him. I pray for him every day."

"I'll pray for him too." His voice still sounded strained.

Paul's kind offer warmed her more than the sun that had come out from behind the clouds. "Thank you and I'll pray for you and your father."

They visited as long as Eugenia dared. "I should be going. Papa won't expect me to stay out much longer, especially the way the wind has picked up."

"Then you'd best go."

"Yes, I should." She peered into his gentle eyes, full of unspoken love for her. How she wished they could be honest with each other. "I'll see you next Sunday if the weather is agreeable. Goodbye."

"Goodbye. Don't gallop your horse since you're in a hurry. That way you should get there in one piece." His eyes twinkled.

His gentle teasing lifted her spirits. Finally, he looked and sounded more like the warm, caring man she knew. "I'll take your words of caution into consideration." She grinned then waved at him before riding away.

She thanked God for the small miracle of this afternoon all the way home. Now, if only Paul would quit seeing the other woman and declare his love for her. She'd worry about their differences over servants later. If God put the two of them together, He'd surely help them find a workable solution about whether or not to own servants.

Chapter Eighteen

ugenia kept a watchful eye from the parlor window, praying Papa rode up soon. If not for the chilly November weather, she'd have been thrilled for him to leave the house and ride off to see anyone, anywhere. He'd been a recluse much too long. But the rain that started a short while ago got heavier by the minute. Papa had ridden to Hopeton earlier. He'd shown signs of a cold since Tuesday. She prayed he hadn't started for home and been caught in this downpour.

She paced the floor. The rain came down so hard, she had a difficult time seeing past the front porch for a while. *Stop it!* Wearing a hole in the carpet wouldn't do one bit of good. Mama said worrying never helped anyone or anything. But her nerves wouldn't cooperate with her mind. Her pacing resumed.

When Eugenia spied her father galloping his horse up the drive, she ran out to the porch. "Don't ride to the barn in this deluge. I'll have a servant see to your horse."

"I intended that, dear girl."

She marched inside. "Joseph, come see to Papa. He'll need

out of those wet clothes quickly. And send someone to tend to Papa's horse."

Joseph met Papa coming in the front door. A servant scampered out to get the groom.

"I'll have Nancy fix you some tea while you get into dry clothes," Eugenia called to her father while he and Joseph proceeded toward the stairs.

After Papa returned to the parlor, Eugenia looked him over. His thinning white hair was still damp. While he took the tea Pansy brought, Eugenia chose the maroon chair next to his. He should be standing by the fire.

"You don't have to hover over me. I'm fine." He smiled before taking another sip of tea.

"But if riding in chilly weather makes your bones ache, how will getting drenched affect you? You haven't admitted it, but you've had a cold the last two days."

"Only a slight cold. I'm dry, and I'll soon be warm again. I've been caught in worse storms."

Joseph put another log on the fire. The day had barely been warm enough for riding before the rain came. Thankfully, the weather had been better Sunday when she'd finally seen Paul again.

"Just the same, you should have had Titus come here. He could withstand being soaked better than you."

He shook his head. "I've stared at these walls too long. Your mother would expect me to go on living and not sit like a cold stone in this house."

"You still didn't need to get sopping wet."

She kept a careful watch on Papa the rest of the evening. By the time they stood in the upstairs hall to bid each other good night, he looked none the worse for his soaking

"Don't lose sleep over me. Your papa can survive a storm." He patted her hand.

* * *

THE NEXT MORNING, Papa took so long to come downstairs that Eugenia was already seated at the table when he walked into the dining room. His flushed face made her pulse race. How she wanted to jump up and touch him to see how warm he might be.

"You look as if you have a fever. Should you have come downstairs?"

"I stood closer to the fire than necessary while I was dressing." His smile was more like a grimace as he seated himself across from her. "Joseph, start serving now. I don't want a cold breakfast."

Eugenia clasped her trembling hands in her lap. She bowed her head and said a silent prayer for her father before asking a quick blessing for the meal. Papa must remain healthy. Watching her father eat every bite of his eggs and bacon would have eased her mind if he hadn't coughed several times during their meal. He placed his napkin on the table before pushing his chair back.

"I'll be in my office. I have paperwork to do."

"Yes, Papa." She'd argue with him about working today, but he wouldn't listen.

She rushed through assigning the servants their tasks for the day then went to her room to get her Bible off her nightstand. She clasped the book to her heart as she sat on her bed, wondering where to search for comfort this morning.

Lord, please watch over Papa. Please don't let anything happen to him.

No matter how much she needed God's guidance and reassurance, she couldn't concentrate on the words. Her gaze fell on her neglected needlework scattered on the chest near the foot of her bed. What a fine excuse to go downstairs. She could stitch in the parlor and be just across the hall from her father's office. When she walked by the closed office door, her father's cough informed her he was still inside.

While the clock slowly ticked away the minutes, Papa's coughs became more frequent. If not for her thimble, her finger would have been full of needle pricks. The clock finally struck twelve times. Papa would leave his papers to eat. She rushed into the hall the instant she heard him slide his office door open.

Papa shook his head at her. "I'll rest after lunch just to make you happy."

"That's good." She hoped her fake smile hid her anxiety.

Papa rested a short time before returning to his office. He'd neglected his paperwork long enough he had a lot to catch up on, but Eugenia feared he hid in his office to keep her from checking on him.

He shuffled into the dining room for supper, looking as if he'd worked the fields all day. One quick glance at his red face, took Eugenia's breath away. "Papa, you look as if you should be in bed."

A cough prevented him from replying as he took his chair. "I'll retire early. But I won't take my dinner in bed like an invalid."

"Yes, Papa."

By the time Papa agreed to go to bed, Joseph had to help him up the stairs. Eugenia summoned Pansy. She'd assisted Mama for years with illnesses and would know what to do for Papa. A short time later, Eugenia moved a chair beside the bed to better watch over him. Pansy washed his face while Eugenia sent up frantic silent prayers.

"Masta goin' to be fine. I can tell this ain't no bad fever." Pansy grinned at her before dipping the rag back into the water basin. "The missus's poultice will have him well in no time."

"You continue talking so sensibly, Pansy." Papa kept his eyes closed. "Listen to her, Eugenia."

"I am." As she watched Pansy work to get Papa's fever down, she continued praying

"Both of you leave and let me rest. I'll sleep much better without someone fussing over me." Papa allowed them to stay only until normal bedtime.

"But, Papa—"

"I'm not dying." He raised his head. His stern expression told her his patience had waned.

"I know, but—"

"Go to bed and—" A cough prevented him from saying more.

Eugenia rose then kissed his warm wrinkled cheek. "Call for me if you need anything."

She dismissed Lily as soon as she was ready for bed, but didn't snuff out her candle. Wrapping her arms around herself, she paced beside her bed and prayed.

Papa had to recover. He was not ready to die. God knew all about her fears, but she couldn't stand still. If Papa were a believer, she wouldn't be so anxious. She repeated her plea for God to watch over her father more times than she could count. She prayed and read her Bible until she could barely keep her eyes open long enough to snuff out her light.

Her fitful sleep brought little rest. She awoke early and summoned her maid. "Just tie my hair back for now, Lily. I have more important things to worry about." She marched downstairs to the dining room. "Pansy, go tell Nancy to fix Papa a tray for breakfast. And be quick about it. I'll take it up to him before he has a chance to come down here."

"Yes, miss." Pansy hurried off to the detached kitchen.

A short time later with a tray in hand, Eugenia tapped on Papa's bedroom door. "Are you awake?"

"Yes, I've stayed in bed a little later than usual, but I'll be up and about soon."

"May I come in?"

"I'm fine, but come in if it will make you feel better."

Eugenia set the tray against the door frame and opened the door. The room felt more like an August afternoon with no breeze. Papa had had Joseph build a roaring fire.

"I brought your breakfast. This way you don't have to worry about going downstairs."

Papa shook his head as he rolled onto one elbow. "I told you I am not dying."

"You look better this morning, but you should rest to get over this fever." She hoped her forced smile masked her fears.

He sat up in the bed and propped himself with a pillow behind his back. "I suppose I have no choice but to allow you to take charge of my recovery." He wagged his finger at her. "But I'll permit it just this morning."

"Yes, Papa." She set the tray in his lap, glad he felt good enough to argue with her.

His eyes twinkled as he covered his nightshirt with his napkin. "You're too much like me. I pity the man who has to deal with your determined spirit one day."

Eugenia grinned back at him as she fluffed the pillow behind him. "You're the one who taught me to take action instead of sitting back and merely wishing for something to happen."

"Yes, but you may be too independent for many young men's liking." He took a bite of his buttered biscuit.

Papa shouldn't be worried about her marriage prospects at a time like this. She shivered in spite of the oppressive warmth. "Someone will accept me and love me as I am." If only Papa would accept the man who loved her. She patted her father's shoulder. "Enjoy your breakfast. I'll send someone for the tray and dishes later. I'm not going to church today."

* * *

GERALD CONTINUED RECOVERING from his cold just as he'd assured Eugenia he would. He'd been as frightened as she was for the day or so his fever had crept up, but he had no intention of telling his daughter such things. Uncertainty for Eugenia's future scared him more than his own well-being. He wouldn't always be here to see to her. His willful daughter needed a husband to care for her, whether she wanted one or not.

On Thursday morning he ordered the carriage around to take him to Murfreesboro.

"Are you sure you're up to such a long drive today? Can't you send a servant to post the letter to your factor?" Eugenia and her questions followed him onto the porch, still too intent on watching over him. He could and should be the one to look after her no matter how she felt about it.

He took a deep breath of the crisp air. "I'm fine. I need to see my attorney. Don't be worried if I'm not back until late in the afternoon." At least she was so concerned about his health that she hadn't thought to ask why he needed to speak to his attorney as he'd let that slip. He'd keep that business to himself for now.

"All right." She kissed his cheek before she allowed him to walk off the porch. "Be careful not to do too much too soon."

"I will." He doffed his stovepipe hat to her before climbing into the black carriage.

Leaving the confines of his house made him feel like a new man. He needed fresh air and sunshine. His overseer had run the plantation since Anna's death, seeing to harvesting the cotton with little help from him. Autumn had come and almost gone, and he'd barely noticed. Anna would not have wanted him to hibernate like a bear. And it was especially not good for a young woman like Eugenia.

Upon his arrival in Murfreesboro, he posted his letter. A red-haired man talking to a young woman caught his attention as his driver helped him back up into the carriage. The man had to be Paul Stuart. He looked too much like his father not to be. Gerald couldn't help but grin at the adoring looks the lady showered upon young Stuart. What a wonderful confirmation that Eugenia had told him the truth about his overseer's son. This one sight was worth his entire trip.

His steps were much lighter when he opened the door to his attorney's office. "I'm here to see Mr. Glynne," he told the clerk.

"He's with another client, Mr. Hampton, but you're welcome to take a chair and wait. He shouldn't be much longer."

"Thank you."

Gerald settled into the worn leather-upholstered chair to wait. A man as successful as Adam Glynne should have an office that reflected his achievement. Unlike the shiny floors in his own house, this one hadn't seen polish in quite a while. A good-sized cobweb hung near the front door. The clerk's desk was the only well-kept spot in the room.

The door to Adam's office opened. The attorney bid his other client goodbye before turning his attention to Gerald. "Good to see you."

Gerald shook the attorney's outstretched hand. "I apologize for coming in with no notice, but I was ill last week and uncertain about setting up a time to meet with you."

Adam's brow furrowed. "I trust you're well now."

"Oh, yes." Gerald answered quickly after noting the

concern in his friend's eyes. "That youngest daughter of mine would hear of nothing but a complete recovery."

"I suppose so." Adam's eyes twinkled. "What brings you here today?"

"I'd like your advice if you have the time."

"I'm free until after lunch. I'm always glad to help an old friend."

"Old friend indeed." Gerald followed the attorney into his office. "I've been too much reminded about the old part of late."

"That doesn't sound good. How are you doing?" Adam studied Gerald while he stacked a pile of papers lying on his cluttered oak desk.

"Better lately." Gerald took the chair in front of his friend's desk. "I'm learning to cope with losing my beloved Anna. I must do that for Eugenia's sake."

"Oh, is she struggling to deal with her mother's death?"

"She has handled our loss better than I have. I still worry about her, though. My short illness made me wonder what would happen to Eugenia if I died."

"Wouldn't either of your sons watch over her?"

"Not the same way George would have done if he'd lived to inherit the plantation as I'd always assumed. Nathan and James are almost like strangers to her. And, as we've discussed before, neither of them has ever shown much interest in cotton."

Adam nodded.

Gerald took a deep breath, hoping Adam wouldn't think his client had gone daft as soon as he heard Gerald's reason for coming to see him. "I've decided I'd like to see Eugenia happily married soon."

"Your daughter has a serious suitor?" Adam grinned as he leaned back in his creaking chair.

Gerald shook his head. "She will once I convince her to accept any one of the good prospects she's shown no interest in."

"That could be difficult. Speaking as one father to another, I'd dread having to force my daughter into marriage, even for her own good."

"That's why I'd like to discuss a possible incentive with you. What if I left the plantation to Eugenia once she has a husband to care for the place for her?" Gerald rubbed his damp palms on his trousers. He'd much rather use enticements than force with his precious girl.

Adam jerked up straight. "It would be highly unusual to leave the plantation to the youngest daughter."

"I had houses built for both sons and helped them get their businesses started in Nashville. I built a house for Grace when she and David married. I want the assurance of the same security for Eugenia. Especially so, since my other sons would rather sell my plantation than bother with seeing to it from Nashville. If I continue to prosper, I'll leave the others a monetary inheritance."

"You've given this much thought, I assume." Adam leaned his elbows on his desk and looked Gerald in the eyes.

"Yes." Lying in bed with a fever had focused his thoughts on little other than Eugenia's future.

"I would advise you to ask your other children about such an arrangement. A contested will can be a terrible thing to deal with."

Gerald hadn't thought about such possibilities. "If my other children agree to my idea, would you write it into my will?"

"Of course."

"Thank you." Gerald leaned back and ran his fingers along the wooden chair arm. "If only I can convince Eugenia to consider marriage while she is still in mourning. She's sent one young man on his way for hinting about courting her at this time."

Adam chuckled. "I have a new client coming in this afternoon who might have the solution to your problem with your daughter."

"Oh?"

"Come home with me for lunch. I'll explain."

Gerald shook his head. "I couldn't impose on you like that."

"I bring clients home often enough that my wife has our cook prepare extra." Adam stood then motioned for Gerald to precede him out of the office as if his invitation had already been accepted.

Too intrigued by Adam's comments to say no, Gerald took his hat off the brass hat rack and walked out the door. "Tell me about this new client." He ushered his friend into his waiting carriage.

Adam settled onto the leather seat across from Gerald. "My new client acquired the Hall plantation, not too far from your own. I was impressed with the man's eldest son."

"Good, so tell me about the young man." Gerald hadn't felt this light-hearted in quite a while. He might accomplish more today than he'd dreamed possible.

"Such a striking man should appeal to any young woman's eye. He has a quick mind and asked some astute business questions during our first meeting."

"I'd like to meet my interesting neighbor this afternoon. Titus Matthews mentioned someone new to me a few days ago, but I paid little attention to what he said."

"Perhaps the man will come in with his father as he did the first time."

After an agreeable lunch, Gerald and Adam returned to the office to await the arrival of the neighbors. To Gerald's delight, father and son walked in together. Their spotless black boots shone like mirrors. They wore coats in the latest cut-away style, revealing buff-colored trousers of very good quality. Both had the appearance of being accustomed to success. Quite impressive.

"Good afternoon, sirs." Adam shook the father's hand and then the son's. "May I introduce you to one of your neighbors? This is my esteemed friend, Gerald Hampton. Gerald, Walter Parker and his son, Alton."

"I'm pleased to meet you and your son." Gerald extended his hand to the father. He liked the man's firm handshake and warm smile.

"Likewise, Mr. Hampton."

"I apologize for not knowing you moved to our area, but my daughter and I have been recluses since the death of my wife."

"I'm sorry about your wife."

"Thank you." Gerald turned his gaze to Alton Parker.

"I'm pleased to meet you, sir." Alton looked directly into Gerald's eyes as they shook hands.

"The pleasure is mine." Gerald's hopes soared as he studied his young neighbor. Surely Eugenia would be taken in with the charming smile that sparkled into his deep brown eyes. His full cheekbones and narrow chin gave him the look of a subject for a painting. She should also like the thick chestnut brown hair hanging almost to his shoulders.

He talked a few minutes longer with his new neighbors. That they hailed from his native Virginia and didn't say one word about religion made everything even more pleasant. Before taking his leave, he extended an invitation for the entire Parker family to dine with them on Saturday night. The sooner he could begin implementing his plan to find a suitor for Eugenia, the better.

The carriage hadn't come to a complete stop before his daughter rushed down the front porch steps. By the time Gerald stepped out, she stood in the yard waiting to greet him.

"Your happy smile looks wonderful. I hope it's not my imagination about how spry your steps were when you left the carriage."

"I had an enjoyable visit with Mr. Glynne. I also met some new neighbors at his office. How did we both miss knowing someone had moved to the Hall plantation?" He extended his arm to her as they walked toward the front porch.

"I remember Clarisse mentioning them. I think Titus is the only one in the Matthews family who has met any of them."

"They've been settling in since October. We've isolated ourselves far too long when we don't know of new neighbors until November." He opened the door for her and then followed her into the house.

"I call on Clarisse or Pastor Bentley quite often, so I'm not isolated."

Gerald handed his coat and hat to Joseph. "That's a pitiful social life for a young lady."

"I don't want a social life yet."

Her words made him cringe. "More social contacts wouldn't hurt either of us, so I invited the Parker family for dinner Saturday evening."

Her hands fluttered to her cheeks as she gasped. "This Saturday?"

He nodded. "Our servants are quite capable of handling dinner guests on short notice."

"But Papa, we're still in mourning."

Her perplexed expression convinced him how right he'd been to ask the Parkers to come. "A simple meal with neighbors isn't improper. I have no plans for a ball or anything such as that."

"I suppose a quiet dinner would be all right."

"I'm sure it will be." He patted her shoulder. Her obvious reluctance to resume her social life concerned him.

"How many people did you invite?"

"Mr. and Mrs. Parker and their four children."

"Four children?" Her hands dropped back to her sides. The worry lines on her face eased. "I do enjoy children."

"I believe the two older ones, a son and a daughter, might be considered young adults, if I recall our conversation correctly."

He omitted any details about Alton Parker, glad she was too rattled to ask which members of the Parker family he'd met today. She'd forget about the conventions of mourning as soon as she met a dashing man like Alton.

"How old is the daughter? I wouldn't mind another friend."

"Mr. Parker didn't mention exact ages." He must remedy her lack of interest in a young man soon, especially since a man as impressive as Alton Parker could be the end to all his concerns about his daughter's future.

Her uneasy expression returned. "Then we'll wait for Saturday evening to discover more. I'll need to talk with Nancy about everything."

"You should have time to make mention of it now while she's still cooking supper. While you're doing that, I intend to write a few letters."

"I'm glad you enjoyed your trip. I'll give Nancy as much warning as possible." She kissed his cheek before heading toward the back of the house.

"One more thing." Gerald halted her steps.

Eugenia turned to look at him. "What?"

"I saw Paul Stuart in earnest conversation with a fetching young lady. I appreciate knowing my daughter is telling me the truth about him."

"Of course. I must talk to Nancy while there's still time." She hurried off.

His daughter's abrupt departure and undue concern over a few dinner guests left no doubt he'd done the right thing today.

* * *

THEIR COOK BUSTLED about the warm brick kitchen in full stride when Eugenia walked inside. "Nancy, I need to talk with you. Papa invited guests to supper on Saturday. Since you're busy, I'll speak with you after supper."

"This Saturday be in two days, miss." Nancy looked up from the potatoes she was slicing, a look of wide-eyed disbelief on her face.

"Yes. We'll discuss it later since you're busy."

Nancy ducked her head, but not in time to hide her scowl as she sliced a potato with swift cuts from the sharp knife. Eugenia made a hasty escape, happy to let Nancy take out her frustrations on the potato. She dared not upset the cook when she had no idea how to plan a meal for six extra people, even if she had twenty years to prepare instead of two days.

In spite of her worries over the upcoming dinner, Eugenia's mind was still on Papa's remark about Paul when she walked into the dining room a while later. Paul could have changed his mind about the lady in Murfreesboro and not told anyone. He'd never lied to her, yet her father wouldn't have mentioned it if he hadn't seen the event he described.

Watching the servants tend to their food returned her thoughts to Saturday. She had no more experience being a hostess than planning a meal.

"What has you so perplexed that you are just shy of a

frown?" Papa cut up his pork chop while he waited for her answer.

"I have no idea how to plan for our guests. If only I'd paid more attention to Mama's instructions."

"Decide what to serve. Nancy knows the proper ingredients and proportions. As friendly as you are, you'll be a gracious hostess."

She cut up her first bite of tasteless meat. Papa's sudden turnaround made no sense. "What shall I serve?"

"You know I've always been partial to ham."

"I'll have Nancy fix your favorites." The second bite of pork chop tasted no better than the first. If only playing hostess would be as simple as deciding on the menu. And if only Papa hadn't seen Paul talking with another woman.

Papa's eyes sparkled while he reached for his water goblet. "Saturday night will be splendid. Wait and see."

Her father's glee tied the knots in her shoulders tighter. She couldn't recall him ever inviting so many guests with such little notice. Mama would have had a fit with only two days to plan such a dinner. She couldn't imagine anything that could happen during one trip to town that would explain his sudden change in behavior or his almost childlike glee over entertaining new neighbors.

Chapter Nineteen

Eugenia spent the next two days trying her best to arrange for the unexpected guests. In truth, she told Nancy and Joseph of Papa's invitation and let them take care of the preparations. Despite such well-trained people, she barely tasted her breakfast coffee on Saturday morning. She was so deep in her own thoughts it took her a while to notice Papa studying her.

"Your dear mother wouldn't want us to continue the solitary lifestyle we've adopted these last few months."

"We're having guests tonight." She grabbed her water goblet to wash down the bite of biscuit she'd popped into her mouth. Papa's sudden concern over their quiet lifestyle still didn't make sense.

"Yes, but something else occurred to me just now. You should add some white lace to your dress collar and perhaps at the cuffs of the sleeves."

Her fork stopped in midair. "White lace?"

He shrugged. "It's time for a small step."

"I'll have to think about it."

She concentrated on the tasteless eggs on her plate while

puzzling over her father's request. His vague explanation about the lace had not sounded truthful. Two weeks ago, she couldn't get him to think about seeing anyone. Now, he was as excited about dinner guests as he'd be if her sister or brothers were coming.

After breakfast, Eugenia set the servants about their varied tasks. She consulted with Nancy to see that everything was all right in the kitchen then fled outside. She preferred walking down paths surrounded by bare trees and bushes to staying inside and dealing with Papa's inexplicable enthusiasm for the people coming tonight. She pulled her shawl more tightly around her shoulders. The brisk breeze didn't cause her shivers. Only God knew how she'd manage tonight.

She filled her time with as many monotonous tasks as possible to get through her dreaded day. Time to be ready for visitors came sooner than she wished. Lily was so good at doing her hair that she wasn't a moment late coming down the stairs. Papa stood in the parlor near the window, looking as happy as if he were watching for his grandchildren's arrival.

"I see you decided against any lace for now."

"For now." Her pulse quickened as she watched Papa's countenance fall. He shouldn't be thinking about something as scandalous as white lace while they were still in mourning.

A strange carriage rolled up the drive. Eugenia watched from the window as the family stepped out. Even through the shadows of dusk, she could see the last person to exit was no child, but a man who looked to be close to Paul's age. Did Papa know more than he'd said about this oldest son? She feared her father's excitement answered her question.

"Are you ready to greet our new neighbors?" Papa's warm smile sent chills down her spine and back up her neck.

She nodded, following him out of the room. Before the butler could get to the door, Papa reached for the knob.

"Good to see you again." Papa beamed as Mr. Parker ushered his wife inside.

"It's good to see you too. May I introduce my wife, Emily?"

"My pleasure, madam." Papa bowed to her.

"Likewise, Mr. Hampton, and thank you for the invitation."

"You're most welcome. This young lady beside me is my daughter, Eugenia."

"I'm pleased to meet you both." Eugenia forced the words from her dry throat.

The rest of the family followed Mr. and Mrs. Parker. The eldest son bowed to her without introducing himself to her father, which made her suspect Papa hadn't mentioned he'd met the elder and younger Mr. Parkers in Murfreesboro.

"Alton Parker at your service, Miss Hampton. I'm very happy to meet you."

His leering smile set every nerve on edge. No need to guess why he'd come, yet the man's forward manner and gaze didn't appear to bother Papa in the least.

"And I'm Marissa. I'm so glad to meet you." Alton's sister had to push past her brother to introduce herself.

"I'm pleased to meet you." She returned Marissa's glowing smile with one of her own.

"And these are my brothers, Derrick and Dylan."

Papa soon ushered the guests into the dining room. Eugenia felt a twinge of sadness, taking her mother's place at the table, but how wonderful to be the hostess in charge of seating everyone. After the way Alton greeted her, she placed him to her father's left with his parents to Papa's right. She seated his sister to her left. By putting the twin boys in between the adults, she had several chairs between herself and Alton.

The meal progressed better than she had feared. Marissa and Mrs. Parker were wonderful conversationalists, and no one appeared to notice how little Eugenia said. If the after-dinner talk went as well, she might survive tonight.

"Gerald, I'd like to ask your ideas on planting cotton here if I could." Mr. Parker made his request as he and Papa walked with the ladies out of the dining room.

"I'd be happy to help."

Papa's fading smile said otherwise, but Eugenia knew his impeccable manners wouldn't allow him to reject a guest's question.

"Follow me down the hall into my office, and we can discuss crops without bothering the ladies."

Mr. Parker grinned and motioned to his son before falling into step with Papa. "Alton and I have been talking about the differences between Virginia and Tennessee. I'd welcome advice from another native Virginian."

Eugenia hoped she didn't look too pleased when Alton tore his gaze away from her and trudged behind Papa and Mr. Parker.

"We can visit while the men discuss business." Eugenia guided the ladies and the twins into the parlor. "I'm sorry we have no one the age of Derrick and Dylan. Papa has a chessboard in here."

"They'll be happy with each other's company tonight." Mrs. Parker chose a comfortable maroon chair.

The twins walked over to the chessboard in the corner. Eugenia sat next to Marissa on the couch. Eugenia and her visitors were involved in a lively conversation about current fashions when the men came into the parlor. The business discussion in the office had taken up much of the evening. Eugenia had only to make a few polite remarks to Alton before Mr. and Mrs. Parker decided they should return home.

"Thank you for your gracious hospitality." Mr. Parker shook Papa's hand while everyone stood in the hall.

"You're more than welcome. Please feel free to come again." Papa looked straight at Alton.

"We'll soon be settled enough to return your favor," Mrs. Parker said.

"We'll look forward to that time, madam."

Alton lingered in the hallway after his family stepped outside. He bowed to her while taking in much more than her face. "I hope to see you again. Please accept my apology for discussing business so long with your father."

"Papa loves nothing better than talking about his crops. You have been an excellent guest."

She smothered a laugh. He looked so taken aback that she hadn't missed his company tonight. If only he knew what she truly thought of him. A man so full of himself couldn't compare to Paul. And the man she loved had never looked at her in such a lascivious manner as this man had all night.

"I'll look forward to seeing you another time." He stood as if his feet were rooted to the floor.

"I don't get out much since we're still in mourning. It might be a while before our paths cross again, sir." She forced her lips to turn up. If fake smiles caused one's face to crack, she'd be broken into a hundred pieces after tonight.

"I hope that won't be the case. Good night, Miss Hampton, Mr. Hampton."

"Good night, Alton. Do come again." Papa grinned at him before the man finally took his leave.

The knots in Eugenia's shoulders loosened. "I'm going to bed. If I stay up much later, I'll oversleep and miss church. Good night."

She gave her father a quick kiss on his cheek before scurrying up the stairs. Papa's open admiration for Alton disturbed her. She couldn't help wondering if the men discussed more than crops tonight, especially since Papa appeared to be so taken with Alton. Why, she wasn't sure she wanted to know.

* * *

EUGENIA WALKED into church the next morning, still going over last night's disturbing events. She could hardly wait for the end of the service and time to visit outside with Clare. She thanked God for a clear, sunshiny day.

"Could I call on you soon?" Eugenia cast covert glances toward Paul and Titus as she and Clare strolled together, waiting for Mrs. Matthews to finish her conversation with another neighbor.

"Of course. Come tomorrow, if you'd like."

"Thank you. I shall." Eugenia looked around to be sure no one stood near enough to overhear her. "Has Paul said anything more to your brother about the woman he's seeing?"

Clarisse shook her head. "Why?"

"I'll discuss that and more with you tomorrow. I should go home now. Papa will be waiting for me."

Not long after lunch, Eugenia guided Belle down the trail where she usually met Paul. If her father's observations about him and the lady in Murfreesboro were correct, she'd be doomed to riding alone again. She strained to hear or see any sign of the man she loved. Her heart did a happy flutter when she spied him waiting for her around the next bend. If he was serious about the other woman, such a sincere man wouldn't be watching for her.

"I figured you'd be by this way on such a nice day." His countenance shone with unspoken love as she rode up beside him.

"I had to visit with one of my best friends." How she

wished she could stop pretending to be nothing more than his friend.

He looked away from her, but not before she saw the longing look in his eyes. "Titus says your pa was sick. I hope he's all right now."

"He's well."

"Good. We all prayed for him."

"Thank you. Seeing him so ill terrified me since he isn't ready to die." Her voice cracked. The gust of wind rattling through the bare branches couldn't chill her like the thoughts she'd just voiced.

He nodded. "I can understand that."

"Could we talk of something more pleasant? Papa invited guests for supper last night. We met the people who purchased the Hall plantation."

"Are they nice folks?"

"Except for the too-friendly son, who appears to about your age." She gave him a sidelong glance to check his reaction to her mention of the son.

"Uh, a son?" He swallowed hard as he tightened his grip on the reins.

"Three sons, actually, but the twins are twelve and too young to be a problem. I liked Marissa, the daughter."

"But not the eldest son?" He stared straight ahead toward the bend in the trail.

"No."

She suppressed a chuckle while watching relief wash over his tense features. Perhaps she should make it a habit to mention other men. His jealousy might prod him to declare his love to her. She'd be sorely tempted to tell him she loved him if she thought he was serious about another woman.

"I'm afraid it could be hard for me to dismiss this man. Papa adores him."

Paul cleared his throat. "Maybe he ain't as bad as you think."

"Perhaps, but no one in the family said one word about God. I will not become involved with an unbelieving man."

"That's good." He guided his horse around a fallen log.

"Pray about it, please. I don't want to anger Papa once I manage to send the man on his way."

When he glanced at her, the adoration in his eyes said so much more than the words he wouldn't speak. "I don't mind praying for you."

"I know." The words each left unsaid could fill a library full of books.

He looked toward a squirrel chattering in a nearby tree. "Uh ... I'm sorry to be rude and not talk more, but I got a busy day already planned tomorrow. I'd better get going."

"I understand." If only she could tell him how much she understood. "I appreciate you talking with me this short time."

"Thanks. I'd visit longer if I could."

"As would I. Goodbye, Paul."

She waved before he urged his horse into a trot. What an odd conversation they'd just had, each of them measuring each syllable before speaking. Again she prayed for the day they could tell each other their true feelings.

Eugenia was still musing about Paul when she walked into the house. Papa stepped out of the parlor as the heavy oak front door closed behind her.

He helped her remove her cape. "Your ride agreed with you judging by your rosy cheeks and shining eyes."

"I needed time outdoors after spending so many hours inside getting ready for last night." She hung her top hat on the hat rack, wishing she could find a way to postpone further conversation about the dinner party.

"Why don't we go into the parlor and talk?"

"Before I change from my riding clothes?

"I'd rather talk now instead of later at the table with the servants around us." His serious expression filled Eugenia with dread.

She followed him into the parlor and sat beside him on the couch.

"We need to discuss something." He patted her arm.

"What do you want to talk about?" She hadn't enjoyed most of their serious conversations lately. Since Papa didn't want the servants overhearing this discussion, she assumed he wanted to tell her something important.

"I had a lot of time to think while I was recuperating from my fever. Dear girl, what would you do if something happened to me?"

She stared at the oil paintings of her parents hanging over the fireplace. "I-I don't know."

"That's the same conclusion I arrived at, but I'll tell you what I'd like."

"What?" She looked into his eyes, afraid she didn't want to hear his answer after his behavior toward Alton Parker last night.

"I want to see you find a good, capable husband. Then I'd leave this plantation to you, knowing you would be cared for the rest of your life. I've already written letters to your siblings asking for their approval."

Eugenia stifled a gasp. She clasped and unclasped her hands in her lap to keep them from trembling while sending up a frantic prayer for help. With all that had happened last night, she wondered what else Papa might be planning for her future. But voicing such thoughts couldn't be good at this moment. "Your generosity has left me speechless."

He smiled. "I assume you're amenable to my ideas."

Of course not, unless he'd accept Paul as her husband, and

Paul would agree to be master of a plantation. The grandfather clock ticked-tocked several times while she struggled to think of a reply. "I've always loved this place, but I hope and pray your plan won't be necessary for a long time, especially since I have no idea who I'll marry one day."

"If you could forgive Luke for being so forward too soon, he would be a good prospect. Alton Parker should also receive your consideration."

His words made it hard to breathe. She understood his favorable opinion of a long-time family friend like Luke, but she couldn't begin to fathom how he could be so enamored with an almost stranger like Alton Parker. They had to have discussed more than cotton last night.

"I ... uh ... I hadn't given either of them any thought."

He smiled. "You don't have to make up your mind this instant. I didn't intend to shock you so. I love you, and I want nothing but the best for you."

"I do appreciate your offer. I should change for supper. Please send Lily up." She rose before her father could protest and left him standing in the parlor.

The family oil paintings lining the stairway blurred as she fled upstairs to the sanctuary of her room. Spending the rest of her life here in her beloved home with any man other than Paul would be like enduring a never-ending nightmare. A nightmare her father seemed too eager to implement.

Chapter Twenty

Paul slumped into his chair and groaned as the pouring rain roared outside his cabin walls. He wouldn't be going to his folks' house in this weather. The entire Preston family would expect him to eat with them after church tomorrow. Too bad he hadn't finished work in time to leave before the storm came in.

Over a month of praying hadn't brought him any closer to solving the problems he'd created concerning Lydia. He didn't love her. If the Lord wanted him and Lydia together, he figured God would have changed his heart by now so he at least liked the woman. Dodging Lydia got harder by the day. He had to pick up his mail, go to the general store, and such. If she didn't catch him then, she stopped by his shop while running an errand for her ma.

The looks she gave him whenever she cornered him made his stomach burn. Money possibilities or not, she adored him —or she was sure good at pretending. He didn't want to hurt her or make her look foolish to the rest of the town. Anybody in Murfreesboro would have to be blind and deaf not to know that Lydia Preston had her cap set for the local wheelwright.

The rain let up later that night. Tired of tossing on a mattress that felt like he'd stuffed it with rocks, Paul threw a blanket around his shoulders and sat in front of his window, watching the sun rise. He'd be old before his time if he didn't start sleeping better soon.

Not a wisp of a cloud moved across the yellow and orange sky at dawn. Perfect weather for walking to church. After another desperate prayer for help and guidance, he rose and dragged the chair over to the corner table where it belonged. He laid the blanket across his bed before lighting a fire. This late November morning chilled his bones all the way through to his heart.

He drank coffee and ate cold biscuits. No use going to much trouble for breakfast. Mrs. Preston would have a feast fixed for lunch and be expecting him there after all the rain. Too bad he probably wouldn't taste a bite of whatever he'd force down.

Paul picked his way around puddles as he walked to church. If it stayed this cold, Lydia would have to settle for talking to him on her porch out of the wind instead of going for a walk and showing him off to the whole town. He thanked God for that one small favor.

He did his absolute best to listen to the preacher, but couldn't have told anyone what the man said once the service ended. He'd spent the entire time thinking and praying about his own problems. Jesus said God's house was a house of prayer, so he hoped the Lord understood if he prayed about something besides the sermon.

The Prestons surrounded Paul as he walked outside.

"I fixed plenty for lunch, and you're more than welcome to come to our house." Mrs. Preston's grin stretched across her round face.

"Thank you, ma'am." Paul hoped he looked happy on the outside.

"I'm sure that means, yes, you'll come." Lydia laughed as she stood much too close to him.

Paul nodded. Mr. and Mrs. Preston turned to walk home. Lydia fell into step with him. He stuffed his hands into his coat pockets after her gloved hand brushed his sleeve the second time.

Maybe she wouldn't slap him after she heard what he needed to say later. He had to be truthful with her. Only God knew how he'd manage that, but a man did what was right by a lady instead of giving her false hope. And since God hadn't given him good traveling weather yesterday, he figured the Lord was pushing him to be honest with Lydia.

"Since we dried so many peaches this year, I baked a pie." Lydia beamed up at him.

"That sounds good." Except Paul doubted he'd taste one of his favorite desserts with so many problems tying his stomach in knots.

Lunch dragged by worse than listening to a long-winded preacher on the hottest day in August. Somehow he managed to nod and say a few words. Lydia's perfect-looking pie almost choked him while he fought to keep pretending he was as fine as could be.

He then trudged into the front room with Lydia's father. Mr. Preston barely had time to start enjoying his pipe before Lydia and her mother walked in.

"It don't take much time to clean up from a simple stew and a pie I baked yesterday." Lydia waved her hands in her usual show of disapproval over the smoke. "Mr. Stuart, could we sit on the porch while Pa enjoys his pipe?"

"That would be fine with me." *Hypocrite.* Nothing about being around her was fine with him.

After helping her with her cape, Paul slipped his coat on, and then opened the door for her. He might as well get this over with. "I can scoot the chairs over in the corner where we're out of the wind. We should be warm enough in the sunshine."

"You're such a gentleman." Lydia seated herself as soon as he moved the chairs.

Her words took him back to the first time Eugenia had insisted he was a gentleman. He swallowed hard as he took the chair beside Lydia. Today was bad enough without reminding him about something the woman he loved kept telling him.

Lydia sighed. "I wish we could have walked down to the river today."

"Why?" He liked walking along the Stones River, too, but he wasn't about to tell her that and have her interrupt him in one of his favorite places to think.

"The running water blocks out the other sounds and makes it feel quiet and peaceful." Her adoring gaze left no doubt she was thinking of much more than an enjoyable walk with him.

Paul couldn't imagine Lydia liking any place quiet but knew better than to say such a thing. "It is pretty around the river."

"Don't you have somewhere special to go when you want to be alone?" She placed her hand on the arm of her chair closest to Paul's.

"Not really." He shifted. Sitting on pine cones would be more comfortable. He couldn't mention the favorite trail he rode on with Eugenia.

She studied him with way too much concentration. "You have to be the quietest man I've ever met."

Paul shrugged. Eugenia didn't mind him being a quiet man. Something else he couldn't say.

"But I truly don't mind." She cocked her head. "I have another place I wish we could walk to."

"Where's that?"

"I so enjoy going by Dr. Maney's house." Her eyes sparkled.

"Why?" Paul watched a gray squirrel scamper up the tree not far from the porch railing. Too bad he couldn't join the animal. A squirrel could jump from one tree to the other and be quite a ways from here in no time.

She turned to look into his eyes. "Because I like to dream. Don't you?"

"Yeah. I imagine everyone does." Her intense expression puzzled him. Walking past a fancy house was no reason to get so serious.

"I love to imagine living in a nice two-story house like that with Pa and Ma sitting on the porch watching their grandchildren playing on the lawn."

Paul stared at her. At least she had the decency to blush a little while making such a forward statement. He had to put an end to her dreaming. He searched for the words and courage to tell her the truth.

She laughed. "Can't you picture someday having a home like that, maybe even bigger, with servants and coming down a grand staircase to greet guests when they arrive?"

Icy shivers ran through him. Her dream would be his nightmare. This definitely wasn't the woman for him. "No."

"But you said you have dreams. What do you wish for?" Her saucy smile signaled she had no idea how much this discussion disturbed him.

"Nothing that big. Maybe a farm of my own someday."

Her eyes clouded. "That's all?"

"That's pretty much it." At least all he could tell her. No one in Murfreesboro needed to know their prized wheelwright planned to leave in the early spring—and especially not why.

"But if you want to farm, why not dream of a prosperous plantation someday? A man with your talent could buy whatever he wants one day, the way Pa says your business is growing."

Paul looked her in the eyes. Titus was right. Lydia and her family thought way too much of his money possibilities. "I don't have plans like that."

She stared at him, her eyes full of bewilderment. This had to be the first time he'd seen her so quiet. "I don't understand you. Pa's done better than his pa, and he's proud of it. He expects his children to do better than he has."

He shook his head. His ideas about better didn't match hers at all. "I don't want or need a fancy house or servants."

"But I do." Her lip quivered as she gripped the arms of her chair. She struggled to her feet as if some sort of heavy load made it hard for her to stand.

Paul rose. He looked down at her to wait and see what she'd say or do next. He'd seen people leaving a funeral who looked happier.

She placed a gloved hand lightly on his coat sleeve. "I wish we'd talked like this much sooner. I'm sorry, but we don't have any hope of a future together except as friends. Goodbye, Mr. Stuart."

He tipped his hat to her. "I'd best head home then."

Tears stuck to her lashes as she gazed up at him.

Paul turned and walked off the porch. He sure didn't feel like crying. Instead of whooping for joy and throwing his hat in the air, he settled for a silent prayer of thanks as he walked away from the Preston's house. Being free of worries over Lydia felt good. Real good.

But he hoped she meant what she said about staying friends. If not, he had one big problem solved and another big problem only God could handle if he had to find another place to buy his iron tires.

* * *

DESPITE HIS WORRIES, Paul enjoyed the most peaceful week he'd had the last couple of months. Work kept him busy enough that he'd barely had time to leave to pick up his mail. Not having Lydia waylay him anywhere along the way felt fine. Fine enough that he was willing to see what God would do to solve his possible problem about where to buy his tires.

The door creaked open. Matthew Preston's large frame filled the entryway. Paul's throat tightened up as if he'd swallowed half the wood shavings on his floor.

"Evening, Paul."

"Good evening, sir." Paul took his time leaning the wheel against the wall before walking toward the blacksmith.

Mr. Preston stuck out his hand. Paul shook it. The man didn't look happy, but he wasn't glaring at him. Maybe that was good.

"Lydia finally told me what the two of you talked about Sunday. Can't say I blame you for being spooked when a woman you ain't officially courting starts talking like that." Mr. Preston looked away as he shoved his hands in his trouser pockets.

Paul stared at the man. The way Mr. Preston had talked about grandchildren the first time he'd been to his house, the man shouldn't be bothered by his daughter's words. Unless he was trying to patch things up between Paul and Lydia. "We came to a real clear understanding of what each of us wants, so it all worked out for the best." That is if the blacksmith wasn't going to tell Paul to buy his tires someplace else.

Mr. Preston stroked his beard. "Lydia's young and don't always think about what she's saying before she says it. Maybe you'd consider seeing my daughter again?"

Why? Paul clamped his mouth shut to keep from asking his

question out loud. He'd best be careful what he said and how he said it until he could figure out what this man really wanted. "Lydia will be a fine wife for some man, but not me." Paul picked up a chisel and set it on his workbench, hoping the honest truth wouldn't make Mr. Preston mad.

"You're sure about that?"

Paul nodded. His heart thudded, but he had to be honest in the nicest way he could. "A good woman like her deserves a man who would make her happy and give her what she wants. I ain't that man. I'd only disappoint her."

The blacksmith ducked his head and shifted his weight from one foot to the other. "I hope that don't mean you'll be buying your tires from somebody else."

"No, sir. Not if you still want my business."

Mr. Preston looked him in the eyes and grinned. "I'm much obliged. I been worrying I'd lost one of my best customers. Can't be doing that when so many people around here have their own Negro blacksmiths."

"I understand, sir."

The man grabbed Paul's hand and pumped it like a politician looking for votes. "Me and Reuben appreciate it."

"You're welcome."

"Thank you, young man." Mr. Preston grinned as he opened the door and stepped outside.

Paul stood rooted to his spot on the floor. What a strange conversation. Titus's suspicions about the Prestons wanting a good financial alliance looked to be right. He had good news to tell Titus after church tomorrow Thankfully, Mr. Preston needed Paul's business too much to be angry with him. He hoped and prayed the blacksmith didn't change his mind or become busy enough he didn't need Paul's money.

Chapter Twenty-One

Ma reached up to give Paul one last hug before he left to go back to Murfreesboro. "I'm sorry for the way that young lady treated you, but keep trusting the Lord."

"Like I said, it's for the best." Paul swung up on his horse as soon as his mother let go of him.

Ma was still trying to smooth things over after Pa spoke his mind last night. His father couldn't see anything wrong with Lydia's ideas, but found plenty to say against his own son's dreams since they had probably cost him a marriage with a woman like Lydia Preston. Paul waved to his sisters and parents before riding off.

No matter who disagreed with him, Paul knew deep down how wrong slavery was. He sighed as he guided Rusty onto the trail toward Murfreesboro. The bleak-looking bare trees didn't help his mood. Come spring, he'd put all this behind him and start over where people understood him.

Eugenia waved to him. "I've been waiting for you. I was afraid I'd missed you."

Looking into her sparkling eyes made the trip home worth

every one of the troubles he'd had with Pa. "I took a little longer leaving my folks' house today."

Her smile faded as she studied him. "You look upset. Did you have words with your father again?"

She'd learned him as well as Titus had if she could tell this easily when something was bothering him. "Pa's upset I parted ways with the lady in Murfreesboro because she sees nothing wrong with owning slaves one day."

"Oh." Eugenia looked down and smoothed her cape. "I'm sorry to hear that."

He couldn't miss seeing her pretty face light up before she ducked her head. She wasn't sorry at all. In fact she looked happier at his news than someone who was only a friend should. Surely a lady like her couldn't love him the way he loved her. She'd better not.

Eugenia looked up at him with a serious expression. "For all their differences, our fathers are alike in some ways. Both of them say they want what's best for us, but Papa refuses to listen to me just as your father won't listen to you."

Paul guided his horse around a low branch. Eugenia followed behind him until the trail widened enough for her to ride beside him again.

"I admire a man like you who holds to his convictions regardless of the consequences."

Her praise warmed him inside and out. As usual, she made him sound like a much better man than he was.

She took a deep breath then gazed into his eyes. "How did you decide owning servants is so wrong you'd go against your own father?"

He clamped his open mouth shut. No one else had ever cared to ask him why he hated slavery. "You really want to know?"

"Please. I can only pray I'd have the strength to defend my beliefs to Papa the way you do with your father."

No words came to mind at first. He'd never expected such a request from her, and wasn't sure if he should answer. If he made her mad, she might quit talking to him. But not telling her the truth would be wrong. "Making friends with a preacher in Nashville who helped slaves started me thinking."

"How so?" She halted her horse in the clearing.

Paul guided his horse next to her. Since he'd started his story, he might as well tell her what he could about it. "Everybody says Negroes ain't smart, and they need us to take care of them. I met a man named Noah. He's one of the best blacksmiths anyone could know. Smart with his money and his business—better than some white men." He wouldn't tell her how Pastor Billings had pretended to own Noah for a while.

The reins went slack in her hands. "I've never thought of such things."

"I hadn't either 'til I saw the way Noah trusted God no matter what. He ain't any different than you and me. The more I prayed about it, the more I decided how wrong slavery is."

He left out the part about how unfair it was for such a good man not to be able to buy his wife's freedom or to have to pretend to still be a slave to stay in Tennessee. Some things he'd keep between him and God. So far, her thoughtful look wasn't any different than any other time they talked about something serious. He prayed she wouldn't get mad at him and ride off for good.

She looked straight at him. "But the Bible tells slaves to obey their masters. Brother Bentley owns house servants."

"I know." Paul's hands shook. If they kept talking like this, he'd soon have one less friend. But he couldn't go against what he knew was right even for Eugenia. "Noah's my brother in

Christ. How could it be right for me to own my brother the same as I would a horse?"

Eugenia shook her head but surprised him by keeping quiet.

"I decided to become Jesus's servant because He loves me so much. Shouldn't a Negro be able to choose for himself who he serves?" Paul held his breath as he waited for some kind of answer from her. The moment or two she toyed with the reins in her hands dragged by like an hour.

"As usual, you've given me much to think about. And I still admire you for daring to stand up for your convictions." Her lips trembled as if she was fighting tears. "Could we remain friends even if I don't change my mind about servants?"

Relief flooded through his entire body, as he sucked in a deep breath. "Sure we can."

"Good, because I don't know what I'd do if I lost your friendship." She blinked as she lifted her face to the sun. "I should go. I don't want Papa worrying about how long I've been gone."

"No, you don't want trouble with your pa."

She nodded. "I'll hope and pray for good weather next Sunday."

Paul watched her ride off as he'd done so many afternoons. One day, he'd do that for the last time. He hoped today wasn't that day in spite of how much she said she wanted to stay friends. She might change her mind after she'd had time to think about everything he'd told her.

Eugenia's conversation with Paul haunted her the rest of the week. She spent considerable time praying and thinking about his ideas, but still couldn't agree with him. He had some strong arguments, yet the Bible didn't condemn slavery. If she never changed her opinions, and Paul never changed his … If he were thinking about their conversation half as much as she was, would he be watching for her on their favorite trail next Sunday or not?

The week dragged its way to Saturday. Instead of counting the stitches for a sampler, she counted the hours until she hoped to see Paul on Sunday. Eugenia looked out her bedroom window as she tied a knot in her thread. She'd embroider another afternoon. Today could pass for October instead of almost December. She should relax and enjoy a walk outside while she could.

Lily knocked on her open door before stepping into the room. "Mr. Parker and his sister be here to see you."

"They are? Oh, dear." She stood so quickly her embroidery hoop crashed to the floor. "How does my hair look?"

"It's fine, miss." Lily stooped to pick up the scattered needlework and set it on the nightstand.

Eugenia smoothed her skirt, wishing she could stay in her room or, better yet, fly out the window like a bird.

"They's dressed for a ride, miss."

"Oh. Then send word for Samson to saddle Belle before you lay out my riding clothes. I'll greet my callers and be back in a few minutes to change."

Half an hour or so later, Eugenia and her unwanted guests guided their horses down one of her favorite trails. Her mood was as bleak as the brown barren trees looked since Marissa hadn't come alone. Tomorrow. Tomorrow would be so much better as soon as she could see Paul. If she saw Paul. She refused to dwell on such a dire possibility and prayed he loved her enough to continue seeing her in spite of their differing opinions.

"I'm so glad for such wonderful weather." Marissa lifted

her face toward the sun. "I could become quite fond of Tennessee winters."

"This isn't normal for December, but even when it snows, it usually doesn't last too long. And wait until you see our spectacular spring with all the flowers in bloom."

Eugenia hoped her prattling bored Alton enough to make him wish he'd stayed home. The more annoying she could be, the better. She'd take full advantage of not having Papa around.

Alton guided his horse alongside hers when the path widened. "I'd say you enjoy riding regardless of the season."

"Yes, I do." She gripped her reins, wishing she and Belle could gallop far away.

A lone rider rounded the bend ahead of them. Eugenia waved the instant she recognized Luke. She hated to encourage the man, but she welcomed any chance to discourage Alton.

Luke returned her wave as he rode toward them. "Good afternoon, Eugenia. I don't believe I've met your companions." He smiled at Marissa and Alton.

"These are new neighbors, Luke. May I present Miss Marissa Parker and her brother, Mr. Alton Parker? Their father recently purchased the Hall plantation." She hoped Mr. Parker noticed that she and Luke were good enough friends to be on a first-name basis.

"Pleased to meet you, Miss Parker, Alton. I'm Luke Williams." He tipped his hat to Marissa, but hardly took his eyes off Eugenia.

She must think of a way to get him to notice how beautiful Marissa looked in her deep blue riding habit, which brought out her sapphire blue eyes.

"We're very pleased to meet you, Mr. Williams." Marissa's sparkling smile left no doubt how happy she was to see Luke.

"I'm likewise pleased." Alton's cool tone and solemn expression contradicted his words. He appeared as pleased to see Luke as he would to see a skunk amble onto the trail.

Luke gave him a quick glance before returning his attention to Eugenia. "I'm glad to see you resuming your social life."

"My social life is still limited. I won't defame Mama's memory."

Luke nodded. "I admire such loyalty."

"Thank you." She gave Mr. Parker a discreet sidelong glance. His tense jaw and stiff posture signaled his displeasure. "If you're not going anywhere in particular, you're welcome to enjoy the sunshine with us, Luke."

"I'd like that, if I'm not intruding."

"You're not intruding at all." Marissa batted her lashes.

"Then I thank you ladies for your invitation." Luke's gaze included both women this time.

A chattering gray squirrel scolded them from a nearby tree. The raucous animal was more pleasant to listen to than the empty bantering going on around her. If only she could jump so nimbly from limb to limb and disappear like the startled animal did when they rode too close.

Eugenia prayed for patience and endurance during the remainder of the ride while allowing her companions to supply the conversation. Luke and Alton's exchanges were more like spoken jabs, interrupted by Marissa's inane comments aimed toward Luke. The whole scene would have been entertaining if the men's verbal jousting wasn't over her. She shouted for joy on the inside when they rode up to the beginning of her driveway.

Luke tipped his hat to the ladies. "I'll bid you all good day. Thank you for a pleasant afternoon."

"You're quite welcome." Marissa's face still glowed when

she returned her attention to Eugenia. "We must do this again."

"If the weather allows. But never on a Sunday. I won't break the Sabbath or profane Mama's memory by doing so." Eugenia turned Belle onto the driveway. "I don't want to worry Papa since he wasn't expecting me to go anywhere this afternoon. Good day."

Alton tipped his hat to her. "I'll look forward to seeing you again."

She didn't bother with the slightest nod before urging Belle forward. With any luck, her terrible manners would discourage Alton enough to focus his attention elsewhere. She wasn't the only unmarried woman in the county with a sizeable dowry. His fascination with her made no sense.

Papa stepped out of his office and into the main hall as Eugenia walked inside. "Lily tells me you went for a ride with Alton and Marissa Parker."

"Yes, and we came upon Luke, so he joined us."

Papa's broad grin turned up both ends of his mustache and crinkled his eyes. "Wonderful. Rest assured your mother would not object to the way you are doing things."

Eugenia nodded rather than voice her true thoughts about how worrisome two possible suitors would be. How sad she and Papa were more like strangers now. She'd continue to pray for the day she could be honest with him. How she hoped God never tired of hearing the same prayer.

The weather turned cooler the next day, but Eugenia had no intentions of missing a chance to be with Paul. She glanced at him while she and Clare walked past his family's pew. He looked her way, but never changed his expression. After their conversation about servants last week, she couldn't tell if he was being cautious in case someone was watching him or had changed his mind about their friendship. She prayed she'd see him on the trail this afternoon.

After lunch, Eugenia walked with Papa to the parlor but couldn't manage to sit for even a few minutes. "I think I'll go for another ride and enjoy this pleasant sunshine while I can."

"Go on, dear girl. Tomorrow could be too cold and blustery to step away from the fireplace. If I were younger, I'd join you."

"You're welcome to do that any time."

"I'd rather be like an old cat and soak up the sunshine from inside on such a brisk day." He picked up his newspaper and settled into the chair closest to the window.

She kissed his cheek before going up to her room to change, thankful to God for another beautiful day, especially on a Sunday. At least she hoped she'd still be thankful after her ride.

Her hands shook as she guided her horse onto the trail she and Paul usually took. She strained for any sight of him as she rode. "I wish I had your good hearing, Belle."

Paul's chuckle floated from somewhere behind her. "I figured you'd be out and talking to your horse on a nice day like this."

His voice had to be one of the sweetest sounds she'd ever heard. She halted Belle and waited for him to catch up. "I couldn't resist getting out even though I spent much of yesterday afternoon riding with other friends." What she couldn't resist was the chance to see him. How she wished she could speak her true thoughts.

His eyes widened. "I thought you didn't do much of anything like that yet."

"I'm making friends with Marissa Parker. She talks as much as I do." She laughed.

He grinned. "That's hard to imagine. I don't mean that in a bad way, but I ain't ever met anybody else like you."

"I suppose I should be glad for that." Her spirit soared. How wonderful he didn't think she had an equal. "I didn't enjoy my other companions. Marissa's brother came with her, and Luke Williams joined us later."

He swallowed so hard she could see his Adam's apple bobble. If only he'd speak what was really on his mind.

"I rode with the gentlemen only because Papa wants me to socialize again. I must do what I can to keep the peace with my father." She had to ease his mind no matter how much she wished his jealousy might force him to declare his love. Seeing him look so unhappy made her miserable.

"It's good to keep your pa happy." His listless tone signaled his discomfort concerning their topic.

"We get along if I don't mention God. It's a good thing he didn't hear what I told Mr. Parker and his sister about why I'd never ride with them on a Sunday."

Paul's jaw dropped as he looked at her in alarm. She quickly repeated what she'd told the Parkers about not breaking the Sabbath or profaning her mother's memory.

He brushed a strand of red hair from his face. She gripped her reins to still her hands instead of reaching over to straighten his hair for him.

"If it was any place for a lady, you should be in one of them plays on a fancy stage as easy as you can think of what to say."

If only he knew how adept she had become at acting with him and everyone else. Too much of her life was nothing more than a charade. She couldn't tell her father or the man she loved the truth without the risk of losing them both. How she prayed for the day she could be honest with everyone. "I'll do whatever is necessary to prevent someone from seeing us talking. You and Clare are still the best friends I have."

He shook his head. "I've known you seven months, but I

still can't figure out why you want to be friends with someone like me."

Seven months? He remembers how long we've known each other. She wanted to shout for joy. Instead, she looked down to brush a twig from her cape lest he see her elation. "I enjoy being friends with a gentleman like you."

His laughter echoed through the woods. He sobered as he looked over at her. "You know I ain't a gentleman and never will be."

She smiled. "Your assessment of yourself is wrong."

"Is that so?" He let the reins go slack in his hands.

How nice to see him relax. "Yes, it is. I know you better than you know yourself, concerning some things."

Paul's face lost all color as Eugenia swallowed her gasp of surprise at the unintended words that tumbled out on their own. He'd understood every syllable she'd spoken as well as every word she'd left unsaid. She dug through her mind for something to say to undo the message of her misspoken but true words. "For instance, I doubt you realize how often you shake your head when I puzzle you. I imagine you've learned enough of my ways to tell how I feel before I say anything too."

"Yeah, I guess so." His face regained some of its color.

"Then I'd say we're good friends, wouldn't you?" More truly spoken words with a deeper meaning she couldn't say aloud without making him uneasy.

He nodded. His yearning look spoke of so much more than friendship. His thin, stiff smile never reached his eyes. "It ain't all that hard to learn about you when you've been telling me nearly everything since the first time we met."

"That's because I've been comfortable with you from the day you rescued me."

"Yeah." He cleared his throat. "I ... uh ... I got a lot of work to do tomorrow. I should get going."

"I understand. Lord willing, I'll see you next Sunday."

Her words haunted her as she watched him ride away. Lord willing, her life of charades would end soon. But if Papa had his way, she'd never see Paul again. The way her father had been behaving lately she had no idea what to expect from one day to the next.

Chapter Twenty-Two

Eugenia and Papa settled into their respective chairs in the parlor to enjoy the Saturday afternoon when the brass knocker resounded on the front door. Every inch of her neck and shoulders tensed. Since Clare had called on her yesterday, she suspected she wouldn't want to see the visitor at the door.

Papa cocked his head toward the sound. "Are you expecting anyone, dear girl?"

"No. I was about to ask you the same question."

Joseph appeared in the doorway. "Mista Luke Williams be here to see Miss Eugenia."

A broad grin spread across Papa's face. "Send him in and tell Nancy we'll have some coffee."

"Yes, sir." Joseph bowed and exited the room.

Eugenia fought to hide her displeasure. How she needed a fan to hide behind, but December wouldn't afford her such a luxury.

Luke beamed at her as he strolled into the parlor. "Good afternoon, Mr. Hampton, Eugenia. I hope you don't find my call presumptuous without an invitation, but—"

"Nonsense." Papa waved his hand toward Luke. "Our families have been friends too many years for you to need a formal invitation. Please be seated." Papa's eyes sparkled.

Luke chose a maroon chair across from the couch where Eugenia sat. "I enjoyed riding with you and the Parkers so much that I decided I should visit with you again."

She hoped her fake smile disguised her annoyance. "I trust your father is well."

"Yes, he is. Thank you."

Eugenia chattered on about Luke's family until Pansy brought in the coffee and interrupted the vapid conversation.

"Now that my cup is empty, I'll go to my office and let you two young people visit." Papa stood and kissed her cheek before leaving the room.

Luke set his cup and saucer on the end table by his chair. "I came to apologize for trying to court you while you're still in mourning."

"Your apology is accepted." She busied her hands by adding cream and sugar to the beverage she no longer wanted.

"For now, I'll enjoy your friendship and nothing more unless you tell me you're comfortable considering other options." His adoring gaze told her he wanted much more than friendship from her.

"Would you like more coffee?" She'd ask him to leave if Papa wasn't across the hall. For all she knew, her father might be standing with his ear pressed against the door, straining to hear every word she said.

"Please." He handed her his cup. "I should have remembered how headstrong you've always been. I don't recall many times, even as a child, when you could be swayed from your opinions."

She used both hands to pour Luke's coffee. Only God knew how she kept from spilling everything. "I have no intention of changing." There, she'd spoken her mind as kindly and clearly as possible. Yet this man remained sitting across from her.

"I wouldn't expect you to." He took a sip of his drink. "Your impetuous style makes life interesting for everyone around you."

Eugenia cast about in her mind for anything to say that would convince him to leave for home. But no words came to her.

His eyes twinkled. "Has my willingness to accommodate your wishes taken you by surprise? You're not normally this quiet."

"Uh ... yes."

"You gave me a lot of time to think. A man can and should learn from his mistakes, don't you think?"

"Well, I suppose so." The tender look in his blue eyes rattled her so much that she couldn't think of a more fitting reply. She looked down as she added more sugar to her coffee. She'd have syrup soon, but that was the least of her concerns at the moment.

She spent the next hour rummaging through her mind for words. She'd been honest with Luke but not so honest that he'd left. She dare not tell anyone the man she truly loved. Yet he had to bear some of the responsibility for putting his heart at risk by ignoring her straightforward words. If she dared anger Papa, she'd send Luke away again and not worry about such misgivings. How she prayed for God to change Papa's mind about Paul soon so she could cease living such a duplicitous life.

Yet she'd rather deal with Luke than endure a visit from Alton Parker. She hoped and prayed the man would reconsider calling on her since she'd treated him so rudely every time he'd seen her.

* * *

THE NEXT FEW days came and went with no sign of Mr. Parker. Perhaps she'd managed to irritate him as much as she hoped. Eugenia chose the chair closest to the parlor window and picked up her needlework. Papa had secluded himself in his office. She'd enjoy an afternoon to herself for a change.

"Miss Eugenia, Mistah Alton Parker be here to see you." Joseph stepped into the parlor.

She stabbed her needle into the cloth so quickly she missed her thimble and pricked her finger. If only she'd drawn blood and could run to her room to tend to her finger. "Show him in, and have Nancy fix some coffee."

"Yes, miss."

Eugenia set her embroidery on the end table as Alton stepped into the room. She didn't bother to try to smile.

"Good afternoon. I hope I'm not intruding or interrupting." As usual, his intense gaze took in much more than her face.

Of course he was intruding and interrupting. This man was more stubborn and more obtuse than Luke, the way he ignored her obvious disdain for him. Luke truly admired her, but this man's obsession with her made no sense.

"I'm surprised to see you out in this weather. Papa thinks we could have snow tonight."

He took the chair next to her. "The light in your eyes and the warmth of your smile will do me better than the coziest fire at home."

Every ridiculous word of his speech made her cringe. He sounded as if he'd come courting. "You'll be disappointed once you become better acquainted with me." Hands clasped in her lap, she kept her back rigid as she stared him down.

"I doubt that." His thin smile never reached his eyes.

If he knew her thoughts, he'd have no doubts. While she

struggled to think of something else to say, she wondered why her father hadn't come to greet the man he liked so well. She knew their voices could be heard in his office. Papa always greeted visitors. And where was the coffee the servants were supposed to be bringing?

The two hours spent with Mr. Parker dragged by like two hundred years. She talked about Marissa, horses, and anything else she could think of while he did his best to keep the conversation on a much too personal level. How she longed to send him away.

Papa didn't make an appearance until Eugenia escorted Mr. Parker to the door. "I must have been concentrating on my ledgers more than I realized, Alton. I didn't hear you until now. Do come again any time." His glowing smile was broad enough to turn up both ends of his mustache.

"I'll do that, sir." Alton grinned at her father before returning his attention to Eugenia. "Thank you for a wonderful time."

"You're welcome, sir."

He made a slight bow before ambling outside. Eugenia battled the urge to lock the door behind him lest he change his mind and return.

"I assume you've had an enjoyable afternoon." Papa looked happier than she'd seen him in months.

"It has been interesting." She ducked her head to smooth her brown wool skirt, hoping Papa wouldn't say more about Mr. Parker.

"You should have invited such an interesting guest to supper. It would have been the polite thing to do."

Her head jerked up. "That wouldn't be proper only four months after Mama's death."

Papa's smile disappeared. "Before your mother's demise,

you cast off any convention of society you deemed cumbersome. I don't like this change in you."

A sigh escaped before Eugenia could contain it. "I'll think about what you've said."

"I'm glad to hear that." He patted her arm. "If I were still being so dreary, you'd be concerned for me, wouldn't you?"

"Yes, Papa."

"We should both freshen up for supper now. We'll talk of more pleasant topics while we eat." He smiled before heading up to his room.

The only pleasant topic she'd like to discuss, Papa wouldn't hear. He'd consider Paul Stuart a quite unpleasant subject. Eugenia trudged up the stairs. Papa's disregard for their time of mourning made her wonder how much he wanted to see she had a proper suitor, perhaps even a serious suitor. Surely he wouldn't force her to marry just to see her cared for by a husband.

Or would he? She gripped the top of the banister as panic seized her. The man who had so often indulged her now acted quite determined to have his way in this matter. God's word said not to wed an unbeliever, but also commanded her to obey her father. What should she do?

As soon as the weather allowed, she'd go for a ride or call on Clare. Even better, she prayed for nice weather so she could ride with Paul. She'd rather talk to him than anyone.

On Saturday the weather finally cooperated with Eugenia's need for a ride. "Belle, I can't describe how absolutely glorious the sunshine looks today. And I can hardly wait to arrive at Hopeton."

Visiting with Clare was like a tonic. Her friend was sympathetic when she voiced her concerns over her father's attitude. With her spirits lifted, the ride home was more enjoyable than the trip to Hopeton had been.

Papa greeted her as soon as she walked in the front door. "I've been waiting for you to return. I had no idea you'd ride this long."

Eugenia's lighthearted mood turned to gloom at the sight of her father's sparkling eyes and glowing smile. Lately, anything that thrilled Papa filled her with dread. She braced herself for what might come next.

"I called on Clare while I was out."

"If I'd known this letter was coming today, I'd have ridden for it myself instead of sending Samuel for the mail." He waved a page in the air, grinning like an excited child at Christmas. "Come into the parlor, and I'll share Nathan's letter."

He thrust the paper into her hands the instant she settled onto the couch with him. Again, he wanted to show her something before she changed from her riding clothes. She skimmed her brother's letter. He spoke for James and Grace as well as himself. All three of her siblings endorsed their father's idea of leaving the plantation to Eugenia if she found a suitable husband. She stared unseeing at the paper in her hands and pretended to read the rest of the letter.

"What do you think, dear girl?"

She shook her head. What did she think? Her whole family was conspiring against her. "I'm ... uh ... not sure. I'm shocked my siblings would all agree to your proposition. This is their home too."

"They've had their own households for years. Since George's untimely death, you're the only one of my children who still views this as your home. Now it can remain that way." He beamed at her when she handed the letter back to him.

"I can't find the words to express my feelings."

He patted her shoulder. "No words are needed."

"I should change clothes now. I'm sure Lily is already

laying out a dress for me." She forced herself to slowly rise and kiss her father's cheek instead of running to the sanctuary of her room. How she wished she could stay there alone for a while.

Papa's eyes hadn't lost their happy glimmer when she walked into the dining room for supper. "If this nice weather holds, I'll go see Mr. Glynne next week and have him rewrite my will."

She slid into the chair Joseph held for her. "Don't rush. I hope and pray you don't need a will for a long time."

By the time she could shut herself in her room, her head pounded from pretending to be as happy as her father was. If Paul could see her tonight he would indeed think her an accomplished actress.

* * *

PAUL CLAMPED his hat down tighter on his head. He didn't like riding on such a chilly day in spite of the sunshine. If he'd known the weather would turn this cool, he'd have stayed in Murfreesboro instead of coming home yesterday. But he'd do almost anything to lay eyes on Eugenia for even a few minutes. Since he'd seen her in church this morning, he hoped and prayed she wouldn't stay home.

He spotted her on their trail a few minutes later and rode up to her. "Usually you're talking to your horse, and I hear you before I see you." One look at her drooping shoulders and sad eyes told him she was too quiet for a reason.

She gave him a thin smile. "I've been thinking about something Papa said yesterday."

"I'll listen if you want to think out loud with someone."

"I'd like that." Her face brightened just a moment or two before her eyes again took on a somber look. "Papa surprised me again. He wants to leave the plantation to me, and my siblings agree with him."

"He does?" He barely ducked a low-hanging branch in time. "Why aren't you happy about that?"

"Because my inheritance hinges on me having a suitable husband to run the place before Papa dies."

"Oh." The air left his chest as if someone had knocked him to the ground. It hurt something fierce to think of Eugenia marrying another man. She didn't look any happier than he felt.

"Papa is much too fond of Alton Parker, but I've never heard Mr. Parker utter one word about God."

"That ain't good." He gripped the reins so hard his fingers cramped.

"No, it isn't. I fear my father is much too serious about me marrying, and he prefers Mr. Parker. How can I obey my father when he's wrong?" Her voice cracked.

Paul swallowed the lump in his aching throat. She wasn't the only one who was afraid. Her words terrified him. Eugenia couldn't marry an unbeliever. God's word was plain on that, but he had no idea what to tell her about obeying her pa. He prayed for the right words. "There's a story close to the beginning of Acts about Peter and John. The Jewish leaders told them more than once not to preach about Jesus. The disciples told the leaders they had to obey God instead of men. So they kept preaching no matter how much the Jews threatened them."

Eugenia looked much too serious as she nodded. "I'll find those verses and read them. I hope Papa doesn't start threatening me."

"You know I'll pray for you." If only she were his and he could protect her the way he wanted, but he couldn't. He balled his gloved hands into fists to keep from reaching for her.

"You always help me and cheer me up." Her sad eyes told him she didn't feel that much better.

"I'm glad." Too bad no one was around to help him feel better.

A strong gust of wind tore at his hat. Eugenia gripped the hood of her cape. "I should start home now. Papa cautioned me not to stay out too long in this weather."

"Your pa's right."

"Yes, and I shouldn't delay your return to your own fire in Murfreesboro. I'll pray for more pleasant weather next Sunday."

"Yeah. It never hurts to pray about the weather."

If only that were all he had to pray about. Paul swallowed hard as he watched her ride off. He might have helped Eugenia to keep from marrying an unbelieving man, but what could he do to prevent her from marrying a good Christian planter? Nothing.

His tight chest made it hard for him to breathe. Handling the pain of hiding his love for Eugenia got harder every time he saw her. He was crazy to keep doing this to himself. Eugenia would never be his. Continuing to see her made less sense than trying to visit Lydia again.

Unless God told him something different, he might have seen Eugenia for the last time.

Chapter Twenty-Three

Eugenia welcomed the continuing whirl of Christmas activities she couldn't participate in. Luke and Alton were so occupied with social invitations that she saw little of either man. How nice to be only days from Christmas and not have to worry about callers. But after Christmas, there would be no parties to interfere with someone coming to see her. What kind of excuse could she use to discourage Luke or Alton in January?

"It's just the two of us again tonight." Papa settled into his favorite chair as Eugenia brought her needlework into the parlor and sat near the fireplace.

"The Williams are hosting a ball." A log crackled in the fireplace as Eugenia set her scissors in her lap.

Papa shook his head. "It's a shame to see you sitting here alone like this."

"I don't mind." She concentrated on threading her needle to postpone glancing at him. There had to be something she could say to make Papa understand why she didn't want a social life right now.

"Your attitude bothers me more all the time."

She looked away from her stitching and forced a grin. "Mama always wished I weren't so impetuous. It's been difficult, but I'm finally growing up."

"Your craving for isolation troubles me. I fear you're receiving calls from Luke or Alton only because I insist." A deep frown creased Papa's forehead.

She tugged so hard on her thread it broke. She hadn't fooled her father at all. How to get him not to insist she should accept gentleman callers? He'd understood her, taken her side from the time she was small, granted the favors she asked for. Perhaps she should try explaining herself again.

"Being alone soothes me and helps me cope with losing Mama the same way it helps you to visit her grave and talk to her. It's hard to explain such deep feelings, but I'm truly trying to honor Mama's memory. Indulge me for a while longer, please."

The clock ticked by a minute or two as Papa looked toward the paintings above the fireplace. His gaze appeared to lock on his wife's portrait. Perhaps she shouldn't have mentioned his frequent trips to Mama's grave before asking him to treat her the way he'd always done before.

"Indulge you?" He returned his attention to her. "I've done that since the day you were born. I suppose I can manage to do so for a while longer, especially for the sake of your mother's memory."

"Thank you, Papa." She dared not reply more enthusiastically and give away her elation at possibly winning him over for a while.

When she made her way upstairs to get ready for bed, Eugenia's heart was lighter than it had been in weeks. She'd found a way to keep Papa from worrying about her. Perhaps she wouldn't have to entertain her callers so often now. She laughed to herself while she turned the knob on her bedroom door.

"You must be real happy tonight, miss." Lily straightened up from adding a log to the fireplace.

"Papa and I had a most delightful conversation." She said no more. Her maid needed no explanation. Whatever Lily was wondering, she would keep to herself.

Paul's words about Negroes being equal to everyone else intruded into her mind. She'd taught Lily to read years ago rather than endure studying boring lessons from her tutor alone. But that didn't make Lily her equal. Or did it? Lily had caught on very quickly. She shoved her troublesome thoughts aside. Even if Lily were free, a maid should know when to speak and when to keep quiet.

Plus, Eugenia had more important and happier things to consider. How nice to have Papa sounding more like the tolerant father she'd always known. Now she could look forward to Christmas and enjoy this time with no gentleman callers to worry her.

* * *

She awoke on Christmas morning and stretched leisurely in her bed while watching her maid stir the embers in the fireplace. "Good morning, Lily. It's going to be a very nice day."

"I hopes it's a real fine day, miss."

"I think I heard Papa stirring a few minutes ago, so I suppose I should hurry to get dressed."

When she made her way downstairs, Papa stood outside the dining room, waiting for her. As he seated her, she noticed a small box by her plate. "What's this?"

"The Christmas present I couldn't wait to give you." He

beamed at her as he took his seat at the table. "Please open it now."

Eugenia picked up the shiny hinged mahogany box and lifted the lid. "Oh, Papa ..." Words eluded her while she stared at the simple drop pearl necklace and matching earrings nestled inside the box. Papa shouldn't be giving her jewelry she couldn't wear yet. "I'm not sure what to say. It's simply—"

"Exquisite." Papa's eyes sparkled. "Exquisite in the simplicity of design. I asked my factor to locate something suitable, yet elegant, for you to wear at this time. He did an admirable job, don't you think?"

"Uh ... yes, he did."

The servants brought in the meal and created a welcome interruption. She stared in silence at the gift, wishing she could snap the box shut and shove it away. The man who was so concerned about her reputation when she'd spoken to Paul now wanted her to wear jewelry before their mourning period ended. She hoped this gift didn't signal the end of Papa's short-lived patient indulgence. If so, she dreaded discovering why he'd changed his mind.

Shivers radiated down her spine as she recalled the carriage ride home from Clare's house a few days ago. Alton had waved to her as he passed by. She'd leaned back from the window and pretended not to see him. She had no idea where the man had been, but now she wondered if he'd talked with Papa while she was calling on Clare. If so, the coming New Year and the end of the party season might not bode well for her.

Chapter Twenty-Four

The next several days were blessedly uneventful. Eugenia hoped the blustery wind would continue to keep her unwanted callers close by their own warm fires this first Monday of January. She walked with Papa into the parlor after supper. Taking the chair next to her father, she picked up her embroidery.

Papa grabbed his book but didn't open it. "Have you thought how you'd like to celebrate your birthday?"

She shrugged before threading her needle. "I suppose I'll have Nancy make my favorite dishes."

"Is that all the festivities you've considered?"

"Grace can't travel now in her delicate condition, and I don't expect Nathan or James to leave their businesses simply to celebrate my birthday. I assumed we'd have another wonderful evening with the two of us."

"I was thinking of a less solitary time than that."

"Oh?" Her needle slipped from her fingers. She bent over to retrieve it. Papa's serious expression caused her heart to speed up.

"A young lady shouldn't celebrate her nineteenth birthday

with only her old father for company. We'd be well within bounds to invite a few friends over for dinner."

Papa would invite the Williams or the Parkers if she didn't say something quickly. She hoped the fake smile she flashed him looked natural. "We should ask the Matthews family. They've all been so kind, and celebrating with my best friend would be nice."

"The Matthews family is a good choice. We should also invite the Williams and Parkers."

She shook her head. "I could never be a hostess for such a crowd."

He reached over and patted her arm. "Don't underestimate yourself so."

If only a lack of confidence in her abilities was what really worried her. But refusing to comply with Papa's idea might make him more concerned about her reluctance to socialize. Might give him an excuse to try more drastic measures than insisting she entertain gentleman callers occasionally.

Eugenia concentrated on her embroidery. Her shoulders had more knots than her tangled thread. "I'll try, Papa."

"Then I'll send a servant round with the invitations tomorrow." Papa looked as gleeful as a child with a room full of new toys.

She ducked her head and pretended to stitch on her needlework. Even if Joseph had built a bonfire in the fireplace, the chill she felt wouldn't be warded off. Something—or worse, possibly someone—had changed Papa's mind about indulging her.

The next afternoon, she bundled into her warmest clothes and cape to deliver the invitation to the Matthews household in person, even though her birthday was two weeks away. She couldn't risk Clare making other plans.

"I don't know what I would have done if you'd said you

couldn't come." Eugenia shifted on the couch she occupied with Clare.

"No one in my family would think of missing your birthday, especially when I explain the situation."

"Thank you. I'm sure the Parkers and Williams will accept their invitations." Eugenia sighed. "I don't understand why God is allowing all this turmoil in my life."

Clarisse squeezed her hand. "I don't either, but God still cares."

The grandfather clock struck four times, an unwelcome signal that Eugenia should end her visit. She dreaded leaving this comforting place for the house that no longer felt like home. For all she knew, she'd return to discover Papa had come up with another scheme to see her married soon. "I should go. Thank you for being such a wonderful friend."

"You're more than welcome." Clarisse stood and walked with her to the door.

* * *

THE WEATHER LEADING up to her birthday did nothing to lessen Eugenia's apprehension over the special dinner and the guests coming. Bitter cold and a dusting of snow prevented her from enjoying so much as a short walk outdoors. Sunday was too cold to even think about standing outside after church and talking with Clare. Since she hadn't seen Paul during the service, she assumed the weather had forced him to remain in Murfreesboro.

Eugenia awoke the morning of her birthday wishing this particular Thursday was already done. If only the snow from last week had lingered through today and made traveling impossible. She stretched as she watched Lily stir the embers in her fireplace. No one who knew her would expect her to get out of her bed until the room was warmer.

By the time she wandered downstairs, Papa waited for her in the dining room. "I was beginning to wonder if you'd overslept."

"It was hard to get out of a warm bed this morning."

He kissed her cheek before Joseph seated her at the table. "Happy birthday, dear girl."

"Thank you." Her tension eased when she saw no sign of a present lying on the table as there had been Christmas morning. She hoped Papa wouldn't surprise her with more jewelry later.

Eugenia welcomed the effort and time needed to be ready for so many guests coming. As many trips as she made to the kitchen, she hoped Nancy didn't tire of seeing her. But staying busy helped her fret less about the night she dreaded.

"Don't you think you'd better take time for yourself?" Papa stopped her in the entry hall before she could escape to the kitchen one more time. "Have Lily take a little extra time to do your hair. There's nothing wrong with indulging yourself on your birthday."

"I need to check on the food once more. Tell Lily I'll be in my room soon."

She darted toward the back door before Papa could protest. Their cook needed no further instructions, but walking outside to the kitchen made a welcome diversion. When Eugenia trudged upstairs, Papa stood in the hall outside his room. His warm smile sent shivers of dread through her body. If Papa was this happy, something had to be wrong.

"I waited for you to be sure you allowed enough time for Lily to do your hair properly."

She opened the door to her room and gasped. A pale gold

satin dress lay on her bed, shimmering in the sunlight filtering through her window.

"Happy birthday, dear girl. Please indulge me and try it on. Also put on the pearls I gave you for Christmas. They should complement the dress nicely. I'll wait here in the hall to see everything."

Eugenia forced herself not to slam the door. She slumped against the wall and stared at the dress. Another present she couldn't yet wear. Why? Her maid watched in silence as Eugenia took in several shaky breaths. "Lily, help me try this dress on for Papa then get out my black satin for tonight."

"Yes, miss."

While Lily finished buttoning the dress, Eugenia blinked at her image in the cheval mirror. She'd become so accustomed to wearing only black that her image looked more like a stranger to her. The dress was gorgeous. The puffed gigot sleeves tapered beautifully down to her wrists. It fit as if she'd met with the dressmaker in person.

But she couldn't treat herself to such a wonderful gown tonight. Papa wouldn't dream of her doing something so improper—or he shouldn't. Her mouth went dry.

"Missy, you looks so pretty in that gold that it almost hurts my eyes. The masta sho knows how to pick out dresses."

Lily's words grated on her ears, but she dared not voice her true feelings with her father standing just outside her door. "Papa has always had good taste."

"He sho has."

When Eugenia stepped into the hall, Papa's glowing smile indicated his unabashed approval. "You are an absolute vision. We must write Grace soon and tell her how perfect the entire ensemble is."

"Why should we do that?"

"I wrote her saying you deserved something special. She

suggested a new dress, and I agreed. She took your measurements to her seamstress in Nashville and did the rest for me."

Eugenia fingered the soft skirt. "I'll enjoy wearing such a beautiful gown later."

"I see no harm in wearing it tonight. Your accepted mourning time for a parent will end next month. It's not too soon to indulge yourself."

She gripped the door frame to keep from losing her balance. "Tonight?" The way Papa was counting down the time for her mourning period to end couldn't bode well for her.

"You shouldn't look like a dreary crow on your birthday."

"But I'd be the talk of the entire county!" Papa, of all people, should be concerned about her reputation.

He patted her shoulder. "Our dear friends would never start gossip like that. I'll be sure to inform everyone you are indulging your old father tonight."

Eugenia shook her head. He'd planned every detail much too well, leaving her with no way to argue with him. "All right. I'll have Lily fix my hair. That way I'll be downstairs in plenty of time to help you greet our guests."

"Excellent."

She whirled and then fled inside her room. If only she could lock and bar the door, but her problems couldn't be solved so easily. "Be careful and take your time with my hair, Lily."

She wondered if her maid could hear her pounding heart as she seated herself on the stool in front of her dresser mirror. Lily was such an expert hairdresser that every curl would soon be done to perfection, leaving her no excuse to delay going downstairs.

"Miss Eugenia, if you don't be still, I ain't going to ever get your hair fixed up right or any other way."

"I'm too nervous to sit still, so do the best you can." She clasped her hands in her lap, hoping to stop them from trembling.

Much too soon, Eugenia peeked out the parlor window to see a carriage coming up the drive. Relief flooded through her when she recognized the Matthews' coach. They had come early as Eugenia had requested. She would have a few allies tonight.

"Shall we greet our first guests?" Papa sprinted toward the front door as spryly as a much younger man.

To their credit, none of the Matthews family said anything when they saw Eugenia's dress. Their raised eyebrows or wide eyes spoke more than enough. How she wished she had the courage to run upstairs and change clothes.

"What do you think of the gown I gave Eugenia for her birthday?" Papa's face glowed.

"It's beautiful." Mrs. Matthews' solemn expression didn't match her words.

"My daughter is indulging her old father by wearing it for me tonight."

"Tonight only," Eugenia added her thoughts while other people were present. Papa's good manners would prevent him from disagreeing with her for now.

"It's quite becoming." Clarisse's thin smile signaled she understood her friend's predicament.

Playing hostess gave Eugenia some relief at dinner. She seated the entire Matthews family and Marissa at her end of the table with Luke's family in the middle and the Parker family at the other end by Papa. Luke and Alton spent so much time staring at her or glaring at each other she doubted either of them would remember what they'd eaten.

An eternity later, she stood in the hallway telling everyone goodbye. Alton and Luke lingered by the door while their families stepped out to their carriages.

"I hope you've had a wonderful birthday, Eugenia." Luke's smile looked smug as he bowed to her. He probably relished that he'd used her first name and Alton hadn't.

"I've always enjoyed dinners with friends."

His smile dimmed. "I'll bid you and your father good night before my parents leave without me."

"As should I, Miss Hampton." Alton bowed to her and planted a quick kiss on her bare hand before Luke was out the door.

She jerked away from him and thrust both hands behind her back. Papa should be tossing this audacious cad out the door, never to return.

Instead his eyes twinkled as indulgently as they did when he grinned at one of his grandchildren. "Good night, Alton. Please come again and often."

"I'll do that. Good night." He gave Eugenia one final glance over his shoulder before stepping outside and closing the door behind him.

"I'm tired from such a busy day. Good night, Papa." She scurried to her room rather than give her father a chance to respond or mention Mr. Parker. Judging by Papa's behavior, she feared he'd chosen Alton over Luke.

Papa should have reprimanded any man as forward as Alton Parker. Only someone confident of his status as a serious suitor would dare behave in such a manner in front of a woman's father. Her beloved papa had turned on her.

* * *

Eugenia did her best not to squirm while Lily checked her hair. She'd done little during the day, but wanted her hair to look

238

nice for the afternoon call she planned to make. The sooner her maid finished, the sooner she could leave to visit Clare. Her friend wouldn't know what to do about last night, but talking with someone who cared might help ease her tattered emotions.

A tap on her door interrupted Lily's efforts.

"Mista Williams be here to see you, miss." Pansy's voice drifted into the room.

Eugenia groaned. "Tell him I'll be down soon. And have Nancy fix refreshments."

"I cain't finish if you don't sit still," Lily gave her usual admonition while adding another pin to Eugenia's hair.

"I don't care if you never finish."

Lily shook her head at Eugenia's reflection in the mirror. "You don't like this man, either?"

"No. And worse, he just thwarted my plans for a visit with my best friend."

The irony of the differences between her and her maid's situations galled Eugenia. Papa had allowed Lily and her beloved Sampson to jump the broom and marry, but he wouldn't permit his daughter to choose the man she loved.

She trudged down the stairs a few minutes later. If she didn't know Papa was in the house, she'd have told Pansy she didn't want any callers. Luke couldn't have a valid reason for returning so soon. He'd gawked at her enough last night.

Luke rose the instant she stepped into the parlor. "Good afternoon." His customary smile was missing.

"Good afternoon. I sent for coffee." She chose the chair close to the end table a few feet across from the chair he had taken.

"You looked lovely in that gown last night. It was perfect for you." The warm glow in his eyes chilled her to the bone.

"I indulged Papa last night only."

"I understand." He shifted before saying more. "I have an important reason for calling, but I'm not certain how to broach the subject I need to talk about."

"Oh?" Her heart raced. She didn't want any more unwelcome announcements from anyone. The serious look in his eyes made her wonder what kind of errand he was on.

He gripped each chair arm as if trying to hold the piece of furniture on the floor. "Because of our past misunderstandings I don't want you to misinterpret my words."

"Please speak your mind. You know I don't like to be kept in suspense."

A log crackled in the fireplace. Luke jumped.

A servant carried in the tray with coffee and refreshments. Eugenia poured coffee for Luke then herself.

"Is your father in his office?" His voice was so low she had to listen carefully to hear him.

What a strange question. The man looked as nervous as a cat treed by a pack of hounds. "Yes. Why?"

He leaned forward in his chair. "I'd rather speak to you in private if I may."

Eugenia strained to hear his whispered plea.

"I realize my words sound like nonsense, but please go for a walk with me." Luke's grip tightened on the cup. "Since it's sunny with no wind, it should be warm enough."

"All right." She set her cup on the serving tray. "If you don't mind, I'll get my cape."

He nodded. "I'd also prefer to talk first."

Luke rose and walked with her to the entry way. Neither of them spoke as he helped her don her cape before he slipped into his coat. He shut the door behind them. "Thank you for being so cooperative without an explanation."

"I expect one very soon." She prayed for strength and tried to brace herself for whatever unknown might assail her today.

They walked in silence until they were out of sight from the part of the yard visible from Papa's office window.

Luke halted. "How well do you know Alton Parker?"

"Not well. Why?" She pulled her cape more tightly around her. The mere mention of that man's name caused unwelcome shivers.

He took several deep breaths as he stared at some point beyond her. "I enjoy a game of chance once in a while as much as any man, but Alton has a problem with his gambling. His losses are mounting and could cause him trouble in the near future."

"How do you know about Mr. Parker's predicament, and why should I be the least bit concerned about him or his vice?" She didn't bother to hide the irritation in her voice. She didn't want anyone thinking she cared one whit for Alton Parker or his predicament.

"Because it concerns you." He clenched and unclenched his jaw as he gazed down at her.

"Because you're jealous of Mr. Parker?" Eugenia balled her gloved hands into fists lest she pound his arm. If he kept talking in such riddles, she might not be able to restrain herself.

"Yes, I'm jealous. That's why I've hesitated to tell you what I've heard. I assumed you wouldn't believe me." He reached for her arm. "Eugenia, please hear me out. This involves your future."

She stared into the solemn eyes of her childhood friend. The kind of friend who wouldn't toy with her. "All right. Tell me."

"He owes me and several other men money. Someone has pressed Alton to pay his debts." Luke shoved his hands into his coat pockets. "Parker assured my friend he had nothing to worry about. He bragged that taking you for a wife will soon solve his money problems, thanks to your generous father. ”

Eugenia gasped. “Why didn’t you tell me this sooner?”

“Until last night I assumed his words were empty bluster. Your father wouldn’t have smiled at me if I dared kiss your hand the way he did.”

Luke’s words cut through her like an icy wind. No amount of afternoon sun could warm her after such chilling news. “Mr. Parker is really talking about marrying me?”

“He’s taunted me about winning you and one day owning two of the best plantations in the county.”

“How dare he!” A lady couldn’t say what she truly thought of such a horrible man.

“I’m praying his words are only vain boasting because of our rivalry, but he’ll be even bolder after last night. Do be careful of him.”

If Alton got any bolder, she’d slap him, regardless of what Papa thought of the man “I don’t know what to say.”

“You’re not angry with me?” Luke looked into her eyes.

She shook her head. “Only with Mr. Parker. I’ll not voice what I’d like to see happen to him at this moment.”

They resumed their walk in silence while Eugenia tried to sort through what she’d heard. No matter how jealous Luke was of Alton, she knew every word he’d spoken against his rival had to be true. She’d never known him to lie, regardless of the consequences.

He stopped next to a large leafless oak tree. “I assume you’d like some time to think and pray, so I’ll be going.”

“Thank you for being a true friend.”

His too-tender smile returned. “You’re welcome. I hope my next call will be more pleasant.” He tipped his hat before walking away.

Eugenia could only stare as Luke marched toward the

stable to get his horse. She walked around the house to the flower garden in back to keep Papa from realizing how short Luke's visit had been. She stared at the bleak beds of leafless rose bushes. The brown plants shivering in the winter breeze mirrored her desolation.

Luke's revelation could be the excuse she needed to turn Mr. Parker away. But if she managed such a feat, Luke would be emboldened to seek her hand. She'd already given her old friend too much false hope.

But fending off Luke would be better than dealing with Mr. Parker, once she found a way to rid herself of the scoundrel. Except she couldn't imagine Papa listening to anyone who said a single word against Mr. Parker, especially a rival like Luke. If Alton were so confident about winning her hand, had Papa already made his choice for her husband?

Chapter Twenty-Five

As usual, Eugenia's conversation with Belle reached his ears before Paul saw her. He didn't have the strength to keep the promise he'd made to himself to stay away from her this Sunday or any other. He'd prayed over and over for God to help him not to love Eugenia, but for some reason God was in no hurry to answer his plea. At least he'd have the money to leave soon.

He took a deep breath before he guided his horse alongside hers. "Good afternoon." It was good, simply because he could look at her face for a while.

"Hello."

She didn't smile the way she usually did. Eugenia always smiled at him.

She reined in her horse. "Help me down, please. I'd rather walk than ride today."

The desperate tone of her voice twisted his stomach into knots. He dismounted and walked over to help her. He relished holding her for even a moment. It took all his strength to release her so he could tie both horses to a fallen log.

Eugenia fell into step with him. He shoved his fisted hands

into his coat pockets to keep from reaching for her hand. Too often lately he'd caught himself imagining how her soft hand would feel in his. "What happened?"

"I must find a way to stop Mr. Parker from calling on me."

Paul sucked in the brisk air while listening to her tale of Parker's gambling debts. How he wanted to protect Eugenia from such a man. He clamped his mouth shut to keep from telling her what he was really thinking. His jaw hurt from holding back the words he could never say. "I'm sure your pa won't waste any time running that scoundrel off when you tell him."

"Except Papa wouldn't believe me since Luke is the one who informed me."

"Right."

"I fear Papa favors Alton over Luke."

Her words made it hard for him to breathe. She went on to tell him how the rascal had kissed her hand right in front of her father a few days ago. He kicked at a rock, sending it thudding hard against a tree trunk. Too bad he couldn't do the same or worse to Alton Parker. He sent up a desperate prayer for Eugenia's safety. He'd pray later about his angry thoughts toward the rogue intending to wed the woman he loved.

A gust of wind caught Eugenia's cloak. She pulled it tighter around her. How he wished he could put his arms around her to block the wind.

"I have to make Mr. Parker decide he doesn't want to be in the same room with me, much less anything else. I'd appreciate any advice you can offer."

A woman so experienced in dealing with men had no need to ask him for ideas for getting rid of a caller she didn't like. Which might mean she was more desperate than she sounded. Whatever her reasons, he'd be happy as a hound let inside on a cold night if he could help her get rid of Parker. "Do you know anything that he can't stand?"

She shrugged. "I haven't tried to get to know such a despicable man that well."

"Has he said why he's so interested in you?"

"Of course not. He'd never be honest enough to say he wants me for my money. I can't begin to remember all his insincere compliments. Why?" She stopped and gazed up at him.

He stared off at a clump of bare bushes. If he kept watching her full lips, he'd be in deeper trouble. "Try to remember what he don't like. Maybe he'll decide your money ain't worth the bother of putting up with you."

"He doesn't understand my love for riding. He'd prefer me to be more genteel."

Thoughts of the day he'd first seen Eugenia popped into his mind. He grinned at her despite the serious situation. "Tell him how you like to gallop that horse through the woods. Be as unladylike around him as you can."

"I've been as rude as possible and that didn't work, but I could try your suggestions. Perhaps if I could embarrass him in front of other people."

"Maybe. I wouldn't court a woman like that no matter how much money she might have." He started walking again. Standing still looking at her was too dangerous when all he could think about was taking her in his arms.

She quickened her steps to keep up with him. "What kind of woman do you like? You can't mind someone talkative, or you wouldn't continue visiting with me so often."

I like—no, I love you. He swallowed the words he wanted to shout but dared not whisper and concentrated on swatting away a spider web dangling in front of him. "It's what a lady says that matters. You used to not say much of anything important before you found the Lord."

"Thank you."

Her face lit up at his compliment. The way her long lashes fluttered, he had no doubt she was flirting with him. He had to put a stop to that for her sake as well as his. "What're you gonna do one day when I ain't around to talk to?"

She shrugged. "I don't know. Why?"

"I plan to leave by the end of next month, or the first of March for sure."

She stopped dead still as she gasped and covered her mouth with her gloved hands. The hurt look in her eyes made him wish he could crawl under a rock where a snake like him belonged for making her feel so bad.

"The end of next month? But that's only a few weeks." She ducked her head but not before he saw tears in her eyes.

"I have to go someplace where people accept me. You know that." He had to go away from her before he hurt them both even more.

"That doesn't mean I want you to leave. I'll miss you dreadfully—" Her voice cracked.

"You got more friends than just me. You and Clarisse talk a lot."

"But Clare is not you. What will I do without you?" Her anguished remarks stabbed his heart.

"Fall in love with some decent planter's son one day and marry him after you get rid of that rascal Parker." He couldn't stand to look at her. Such words hurt too much for both of them.

"I love *you*, Paul. I want to marry *you*."

She might as well have punched him in his gut. He stumbled backward and would have lost his balance if not for smacking into a huge tree. "You have no idea what you're saying."

"Yes, I do." She stepped toward him, staring up into his eyes.

The tree trunk pressing against his shoulder blades trapped him, keeping him from backing away from her.

"Please marry me and take me with you when you leave. We'd have to run away, but I'd go anywhere with you. Please." Her voice quivered.

He groaned and squeezed his eyes shut, unable to keep looking into her pleading eyes. "Jeanie, no ... Why'd you have to ask me that?"

"Because I—what did you call me?"

Another groan escaped. He forced himself to open his eyes. "I've just thought of you as Jeanie whenever I think about you lately."

A huge grin spread over her face as she sniffed away tears. "You have a special name for me, and you think about me when we're apart? You *do* love me. Don't you?"

He stiffened. The tree at his back was like the world's biggest mountain, cutting off his escape. "I didn't say that. I can't take you with me. You ain't got the faintest idea what you're asking."

She squared her shoulders. "I'm asking to become your wife. I love you, and you love me, even if you won't admit it."

He should tell her he didn't love her. End all this foolishness now. But he didn't have the strength to say what he should. He took in a shaky breath as he studied her. "It ain't that simple. How can you leave your pa, your home, and everything else? Illinois is a long ways from Tennessee."

"Yes, but I've come to the point of obeying my Heavenly Father instead of my ungodly earthly father."

He lifted his hands in exasperation. No matter how much

sense her words made about God's will, the two of them could never make a marriage work. "How can you be a dirt poor farmer's wife? You can't cook, clean a house, or wash clothes. You can't even put up your own hair."

She stared straight into his eyes the way she always did when he challenged her. "I can cook a little, and I can sew. If you wait until early March to leave, I have about six weeks to learn the other things."

He had to figure out how to talk sense into this woman before he wrapped his arms around her and never let her go no matter how crazy she sounded. Praying for the right words, he clenched and unclenched his hands. He folded his arms across his chest, hoping to look as stern as possible. The hard tree trunk poked him in the back. He was trapped in more ways than one.

"We're too different. I'll never buy one slave, and you see nothing wrong with owning a passel of them."

She stood as straight and tall as her small frame would allow. "Mama and Papa didn't agree on some very important things, and they were quite happy together."

He fought the urge to give in to her. He had to be sensible for her sake. For his sake. She took another step closer to him. He bumped his head against the tree trunk and almost knocked his hat off. He was going nowhere fast.

"Listen to me, Jeanie." He shouldn't call her that again. He had to dig himself out of this hole instead of making it deeper. "If I could buy a farm with a cabin already built, all I'd have is a place that's not much bigger than what your pa's slaves live in and maybe only a dirt floor at first. How would you live like that?"

She placed her hands on her hips. "Isn't being with the one you love more important than a lavish house or money?"

He sighed. She was getting the best of him again. "I can't let you throw everything away like that."

"Why not?"

"It ain't fair to you." He studied the fallen leaves carpeting the ground.

"Not fair?" She grabbed his arm. "Look at me, Paul."

Instead of gazing into her beautiful eyes, he wished for the strength to look over her head at the stand of trees behind her. He ached to pull her close. But he couldn't. No matter how much he wanted her. It wouldn't work.

"I won't take you with me no matter how much you fuss." He might as well have slapped her the way she looked at him, but he had to get her to see she couldn't go with him.

She released his arm and bit her quivering lip. "Alton Parker would marry me only for my inheritance. Would that be fair to me?"

He flinched at her words and hoped she didn't notice. He couldn't let her see how much it tore up his insides to think about her with any other man, much less with a rogue like Parker.

"Why are you forcing me to be with a man I don't love?"

"I ain't forcing you to do nothing like that."

She stomped her foot like a child. "Yes, you are. I'm afraid Papa will force me to marry—and soon."

The desperate look on her face made his heart stop. If only he could take her with him—but he couldn't. "What am I gonna do with you, Jeanie?"

"Take me with you. Please ..." Her voice broke. She clasped her hands behind her back and stared up at him.

No. He couldn't force the right words from his mouth while looking into her pleading eyes. "What if I pray about it and give you an answer next week if I can?" *Coward.* He wanted to take his ridiculous words back as soon they left his mouth. He was being unfair giving her false hope. The tree trunk at his back kept him from moving away from her.

She sniffed away tears. "I truly believe God wants us together."

He shook his head. "I can't say that."

"I know." She took a couple of deep breaths. "Since you have such serious things to pray about, I'll let you be on your way now. I want you to arrive home rested enough to start praying before you go to sleep."

Sleep? Sleeping five minutes tonight would be impossible. He wouldn't need coffee to help him stay awake. Especially since she was grinning at him like he'd already promised he'd take her to Illinois. "You don't seem the least bit worried about what God might say."

Her shining smile almost melted away his resolve. "Walk me back to the horses and help me to mount Belle, please. When you ride off, remember I love you."

He bit his lip to keep from telling her he loved her. Instead he followed her back to the horses and helped her into her saddle. "I promise to pray. Nothing else."

"I promise I'll love you for the rest of my life, Paul Stuart." She waved before she rode out of sight.

He clenched his jaw as tightly as he could to keep from yelling after her that he loved her. Instead of riding straight to Murfreesboro, Paul galloped his horse toward Hopeton. He needed Titus's advice and prayers as he never had before.

"What happened now that you need to talk to me alone?" Titus slid his office door shut then turned toward Paul.

"I got big problems." Paul perched on the edge of Titus's huge desk, not sure he could sit no matter how comfortable the leather chairs looked. He told his friend about his conversation with Eugenia.

"She proposed to you?" Titus chuckled as he slouched into a chair. His silly smile and twinkling eyes were ridiculous.

"Yeah. That's pretty much what happened." His friend had no business being so amused about something so serious.

"As quiet as you are it might be the only way you'll ever be married to anyone." Titus's expression reminded Paul of a happy boy with ten new tops.

Paul slammed his open palm on the desk. Titus jumped. "I should have been man enough to tell her no instead of saying I'd pray first. Now I'm going to have to hurt her worse next week."

"Aren't you going to ask God about it before you tell her no?" Titus leaned toward him.

Paul clamped his open mouth shut as he stared at Titus. He slumped into the chair next to his friend. If only he hadn't heard the man right. But he had. "Why should I pray about marrying her?"

Titus leaned back and steepled his fingers together. "You have to know how unhappy she is."

"What makes you think she'd be happy with me?" Paul gripped the chair arm.

"Because she loves you."

"But love won't put food on our table." *Our* table? Now he was talking more nonsense than Titus.

"There are worse things than poverty." Titus's expression finally sobered. "Her father prefers Alton Parker for a future son-in-law. I've seen it with my own eyes."

If Titus had dumped him in the nearest icy stream, he wouldn't have felt any colder. He'd had a bad enough time listening to Eugenia worry about a forced marriage. Hearing his trusted friend say the same thing terrified him.

"I'll pray about it then. God will have to work a lot of miracles if He wants me and Eugenia together."

"Miracles have never been a problem for the Lord." Titus's outrageous grin returned.

Paul let out a shaky breath. "We'll need bushels of miracles if God wants us to marry. What do we do about her pa? He'd kill me if he catches us."

"Just be sure you know what God wants, and then do it. I'll back you no matter what."

Paul swallowed hard. "Thank you." He needed to get to his cabin and try to sleep some tonight. Only God knew how he'd rest one moment. "I'd better go. I got a lot to pray about."

Titus rose and laid his hand on Paul's shoulder. "I hope God says yes to your marriage. Eugenia won't be the only one hurt if He says no."

"Yeah." His friend's words made it hard for him to breathe. He didn't want to think what he'd do if God said no now that he had his hopes up for a yes. "You can tell Clarisse and Jenette and ask them to pray."

"I'll tell my wife and allow Eugenia the pleasure of telling Clarisse when she comes calling. I'm sure Eugenia will be here tomorrow."

"Thanks for everything." He shook Titus's hand and strode toward the door.

Paul started praying before he mounted Rusty to head back to Murfreesboro. God was the only one Jeanie hadn't surprised this afternoon. He shook his head. Quit calling her that. But he loved her too much to let her pa force her to spend her life with Alton Parker. He'd gone plumb crazy.

The wind picked up. He pulled his coat tighter around him, hoping a storm wasn't coming. The storm in his heart was more than enough, and all he knew to do was keep praying. The last time he'd been so desperate, he'd been running from his problems with Noah.

He shivered as his thoughts took another direction. Jeanie might not love or want him if she knew the real reason he'd had to leave Nashville.

255

Chapter Twenty-Six

Eugenia spent much of the night praying and thinking. She read through most of the book of Acts before snuffing out her candle. The disciples had chosen to obey God no matter the cost. She'd lose more than worldly treasure by disobeying her father. She'd lose her papa too. Yet the longer she prayed, the more convinced she became God wanted Paul to be her husband. Now all she had to do was wait for Paul to listen to God instead of worrying over the differences between the two of them.

By the time the Hampton household stirred Monday morning, she'd thought of a way to obtain the skills she needed to be a good wife for Paul. If she could learn French well enough to almost speak it fluently, then she should be able to master housekeeping chores. After Papa left the house to discuss some things with his overseer, Eugenia walked out to the backyard to watch Polly wash clothes.

Polly jerked up straight from the washtub she'd bent over and stared at Eugenia. "Missy, what you doin' out here in dis weather?"

"Trying to learn how to run the household as well as Mama did. I'll watch and learn this way since I didn't listen to her as I should. Don't tell Papa what I'm doing. I'd like to surprise him after I've learned more."

Polly shook her head as she bent over the washboard.

"Why are you doing that with Papa's shirt?"

"You has to scrub a shirt to get it clean. That's what a washboard be for."

Just before lunchtime, Polly finished hanging the last of the laundry to dry. Eugenia hurried into the house to freshen up before Papa came in. She made notes on everything she'd observed. She must remember each detail correctly. Paul probably didn't have extra clothes if she ruined something.

After lunch, she went in search of her maid. "Lily, I need you to help me get ready to make a call."

While Lily did her hair, Eugenia sat perfectly still in front of her mirror and studied the maid's every move. She intended to start practicing at night how to put her hair up for herself. No matter that she couldn't manage the elaborate curls Lily could do for a party. She doubted she'd need such a style on the frontier.

"Am I doin' somethin' wrong, miss? You make me jumpy watchin' everything I do."

"I'm curious about how you can do my hair so well every time. I didn't intend to make you nervous." She couldn't recall apologizing to her maid before.

Paul's influence on her couldn't be denied. Something else Papa wouldn't be pleased about. Yet if he knew Eugenia had taught Lily to read all those years ago, his displeasure would know no bounds. But, Lord willing, she'd be gone soon. What if Papa found out about Lily after Eugenia was no longer here to protect Lily from him? He'd occasionally chided Eugenia for treating her maid too well before Paul had challenged her thinking about servants.

Would Papa suspect Lily had to have known about Eugenia's plans to leave? She'd pray about how to protect her loyal maid if God allowed Eugenia to leave with Paul.

The moment Lily finished her hair, Eugenia wanted to run down the stairs and out the door to go to Hopeton and tell Clare her news. Instead, she kept to her usual routine and walked into Papa's office before leaving. "I'm going to call on Clare."

"Enjoy your visit." He looked up from his ledgers to smile at her.

"I will." She bent to kiss his cheek. Her heart ached to think about how soon she'd be gone and unable to do this. Yet Papa's decisions were leaving her no other choice.

When she arrived at Hopeton, the Matthews' butler ushered her inside as usual. So many things could change soon. Eugenia began telling Clare how she'd asked Paul to take her with him the moment her friend took the usual spot on the couch beside her.

Clarisse covered her gaping mouth with both hands as she stared at Eugenia. "You proposed to him?"

"He'd never ask me to marry *him*." She couldn't suppress the laugh that welled up inside when she looked at her friend's wide-eyed expression.

"I could never be so bold." Clarisse shook her head.

"I did what I had to do."

"Are you absolutely sure about going with him?"

Such sobering words squelched Eugenia's mirth. "Yes." She told Clare about the hours she'd spent praying and reading scripture. "I'd much rather give up a plantation and my family than go against God's will for a husband."

* * *

Eugenia stayed busy for the remainder of the week. She watched the servants as much as she could to learn how to do everything she had assumed someone would always do for her. Luke interrupted her on Wednesday afternoon. Alton called on Thursday. How she wished she could refuse each man. She prayed she could end her life of charades soon.

"Missy, I still don' see why you is set on learnin' cookin' now when you never cared before." Nancy clucked her tongue while Eugenia watched her prepare supper on Friday.

"It's time I learned to see to things for Papa. He's always taken such good care of me."

"You is finally growing up." Nancy swiped the perspiration from her forehead with her sleeve.

"I should be at nineteen, shouldn't I?"

"You been surprising me for years. At least this idea is a good one. Your pappy will be real surprised one of these days." The cook smiled as she rolled out the biscuit dough.

"Yes, he will." Eugenia hoped she didn't look too smug. Nancy had no idea how shocked Papa might be someday —soon.

* * *

On Sunday morning Eugenia wrapped herself in an extra quilt before tiptoeing to the window to watch the sunrise. She prayed the remainder of the day would be as glorious and wonderful as the pink, yellow, and lavender hues decorating the sky. Thankful yesterday's clouds hadn't brought snow or ice. Enduring another week not knowing Paul's decision would have been impossible.

By the time Lily came to help Eugenia dress for church,

every nerve was on edge. God surely had revealed His will to Paul as clearly as He had to her. Which meant Paul couldn't and wouldn't refuse to take her with him. She shuddered at the niggling doubts she couldn't completely banish.

"Is you cold, Miss Eugenia?"

"No. I was just thinking." She didn't have to explain herself to her maid, but she must be more careful to hide her thoughts once she was downstairs with Papa, lest he worry something was wrong with her.

Getting through the church service proved more difficult than holding her emotions in check at home. She lost track of how many times she clasped and unclasped her hands while trying to sit still and not disturb the other worshipers. She forced herself to listen to the pastor while her thoughts centered on the red-haired man sitting in a pew toward the back.

After church, she chatted outside with Clarisse and tried to covertly observe Paul while he talked with Titus only a few feet away. "Don't you think Paul or your brother could at least nod our direction and give us some clue?" She covered her mouth with her hand.

Clarisse shook her head. "Not without creating suspicions."

"I know." Eugenia sighed. "I can't wait much longer."

Finally, Titus sauntered over to them. "Hello, Eugenia. I see you didn't get your father to come with you this week, either."

"No, but I'll keep trying."

Titus ducked his head. "He says to meet him on the trail this afternoon about the regular time."

Eugenia nodded. Dare she hope for a positive answer from Paul? She couldn't tell from his or Titus's expressions. "I should go home now."

Somehow, she pretended to be calm while eating lunch.

She barely tasted her food. Sitting in the parlor afterward for a few minutes was harder than listening to a boring lesson with a tutor. She found it impossible not to rise to glance out the window.

"I see the sunshine is calling you outdoors as usual." Papa chuckled.

"Yes, it is." Eugenia hoped he didn't see her hands tremble when she let go of the edge of the lace curtain.

"Dress warmly and don't be gone too long. It's too cool for a long ride."

"I'll keep my outing short." She rose and kissed Papa's cheek. Once out of her father's sight, she trotted up the last few stairs toward her room.

Eugenia gripped the reins when she neared the beginning of the trail. Belle tossed her head as if she sensed her mistress's anxiety. "I feel as if I've waited years instead of days, but I dare not let you gallop this afternoon." If she were going to persuade Paul to take her with him, she had to prove she could be sensible and prudent—not ride up to him at full speed.

PAUL PACED IN A CLEARING, watching for any sign of Eugenia, straining to hear the slightest sound of her horse approaching. Unable to sit still and wait, he'd dismounted and tied his horse to a bush. Before he could share the answer God had given him, he had to tell Jeanie the real reason he'd left Nashville. He hoped she didn't turn and run after he told her the truth about Noah.

A startled sparrow flew over his head. Paul spied Eugenia coming toward him on the trail and waved. The closer she got, the faster his heart beat. Sweat trickled down his back in spite of the cool weather.

"Let me help you down."

He spanned her narrow waist through the folds of her cape and set her on the ground, enjoying every moment he could touch her. Eugenia looked up at him in silence, her solemn eyes full of questions.

"You're awful quiet." He watched her as he tied Belle next to his horse. She shifted her weight from one foot to the other clasping and unclasping her gloved hands "You're usually chattering away by now."

"Don't tease me. Not today."

"I'm sorry." He walked over and gazed down at the woman he could observe all day. "You've cost me more sleep this week than anyone or anything in my life."

"Paul, please."

He stuffed his hands in his coat pockets to keep from caressing her cheek. No use living with the memory of touching her when she might run the other way after she knew what he'd done.

"I have to tell you something, but you've got to promise you won't ever say a word about it to anyone else. No one—not even Titus knows about this."

"I would never betray any secret of yours."

He took a deep breath, then another. He looked into her eyes as he took one last gulp of air. "I did more than make friends with a Negro in Nashville. My preacher friend pretended to own Noah so he could stay after he was freed. The man worked like an animal to get enough money to buy his wife. Then, her master went back on his word and refused to sell her." He sucked in more air as she continued to study him. "Me and that circuit-riding preacher helped them get away. A bounty hunter found out me and Noah were friends and got suspicious. I left after he started asking too many questions."

Eugenia stared up at him wide-eyed and silent for a few

agonizing moments. A smile slowly spread across her face and into her shining eyes. He let out the breath he'd been holding.

"If your revelation was intended to change my mind about marrying you, it didn't work. I taught my maid to read several years ago, so I have secrets too. I still love you."

He wanted to whoop for joy, but settled for a grin as he placed his hands on her narrow shoulders and looked into her eyes. "So you're still serious about coming with me in spite of what I've done and how hard it will be?"

"Yes."

"Then I'll take you with me, Jeanie."

She squealed, threw her arms around his waist and hugged him with a strength he'd never dreamed she had. Then stepped back and grinned up at him. "I surprised you again, didn't I? I love you so much."

"I love you too." He wrapped his arms around her and kissed her until he had to back away to catch his breath. "I was almost afraid I might go crazy, but God finally gave me His answer last night." He again placed his hands on her shoulders.

"Tell me about it." Her face glowed as she gazed up at him.

"I stayed up late praying and reading my Bible every night last week. I was almost too tired to work yesterday. Last night I found a couple of verses in the fifteenth chapter of Proverbs."

"I'd like to hear them." She leaned her head against his arm.

"I'd have to get my Bible out of my saddle bag."

"I'll wait."

He got his Bible then opened it to the verses he'd found. "'Better is a little with the fear of the Lord than great treasure and trouble therewith. Better is a dinner of herbs where love is, than a stalled ox and hatred therewith.'" He closed the Bible and set it on a nearby log. "Those verses jumped out at me."

"They say exactly what I told you last week. My treasure is proving quite troublesome to me." She placed her hand on his arm.

"Running away with you won't be easy, but it's right." He pushed a loose strand of her hair back. He'd soon know how soft her hair was. How and when was up to God now.

Eugenia took his gloved hand and pressed it to her cheek. He tried to imagine how touching her skin would feel. If only he could enjoy this moment without wondering how he'd ever make her his. "Herbs ain't much of a meal. And I still don't know how God will work the other things out." He placed his hands on her shoulders again.

"God has already helped me work on some things." She beamed as she told him how she'd followed their slaves around all week trying to learn how to be a good wife.

Her words filled him with awe. This wonderful woman was willing to leave everyone and everything she knew for him. "I still ain't sure what you want with the likes of me."

"You are one of the finest gentlemen I have ever met."

"Living with me will prove I ain't a gentleman."

She shook her head. "You never touched me or kissed me until you declared your love. You know I can't say the same thing about Mr. Parker."

Hot rage rushed through him as he recalled her telling how Parker had kissed her ungloved hand on her birthday. "If he tries anything again, you tell me."

"What could you do about it without giving away our secret?"

He groaned. "Not a thing." Thinking about how powerless he was made his gut ache. "You'll have to let at least one man call on you the next few weeks so your pa won't suspect anything."

"I thought six weeks would go by so quickly since I have so

much to learn, but this past week has felt like years." She sighed as she slipped her arms around his waist and laid her head against his chest.

He wrapped his arms around her, soaking in the thrilling warmth of holding her close. She's mine. A chilling gust of wind reminded him of reality. She wasn't his—yet. "We have more to pray about now than we did last week."

She raised her head. "What do you mean?"

"Only God knows how we're going to get away from here."

"Yes, but if He can help so many Israelites escape from Egypt, He can take care of just the two of us."

He grinned in spite of their serious conversation. "You're good for me."

"We'll be good for each other." She glanced at the sun filtering through the bare trees. "I should go. I promised Papa my ride would be short because of the cool weather."

"I'll help you up on your horse. We don't want your pa suspecting anything at all now."

"Kiss me goodbye first." She lifted her face, closed her eyes and waited for his kiss.

First, she'd proposed to him, now she was telling him when to kiss her. The feel of her soft lips kissing him back made him want her more. If only he didn't have to let her go, but he did. He had to save up enough money for two people now.

"I'll see you next Sunday as long as the weather's good." He walked her over to her horse and helped her up in the saddle.

She took the reins in her hand. "I love you, Paul."

"I love you. Now head that horse toward home."

"My home is with you."

"Not yet. Head Belle toward your pa's house."

She took one last look at him before urging her horse out of the clearing. He swung up in his saddle then stared at the spot where he'd just kissed Jeanie. If only they could run away today.

But they had to have a plan and more money. Otherwise, her pa and his hounds would track them down within an hour or two. His father might even help.

Chapter Twenty-Seven

While watching Nancy cook lunch Monday morning, Eugenia couldn't stop her mind from drifting to thoughts of Paul and his wondrously glorious kisses. He loved her. She forced herself to focus on Nancy as the cook tended to the pot over the fire. She must be on guard not to let anyone suspect she had other motives. So far, the servants were so thrilled she was finally behaving as a plantation mistress should. They were happy to go along with her plans not to tell Papa until she'd mastered what she should have learned from her mother.

In spite of all she needed to know, she called on Clare in the afternoon. Not keeping to her usual habits might make Papa suspicious. Clare flung open the front door as soon as Eugenia stepped down from the carriage.

"I've been watching for you." Clarisse hugged Eugenia before ushering her into the house. "Mama is off making a call, so you can tell me all about yesterday."

Eugenia followed her friend into the parlor before sitting next to her on the couch. "I assume Paul came by here."

Clarisse's sparkling eyes answered for her. "Of course, but I want to hear everything from you."

Eugenia gave Clare another hug before divulging the details her friend craved.

"I'm so happy for you, but I'll miss you terribly." Clarisse's expression sobered.

"I'll miss you too." Eugenia's voice cracked.

"We can write to each other once you're safely away from here." Clarisse squeezed Eugenia's hand.

Titus and Jenette walked into the parlor before Eugenia could reply. "Congratulations on your engagement." Titus smiled at Eugenia.

"We're both so happy for you and Paul." Jenette's eyes shone.

Eugenia laughed. "Not as happy as I am."

"We'll do whatever we can to help you and Paul elope." Titus reached for Jenette's hand. "If you need to tell Paul something during the week, get word to me. I'll ride to Murfreesboro and tell him."

"Thank you. I don't know what I'd do without all of you."

"You're welcome. If I needed to ride to Paul, how would I get a reply to you if Clare couldn't call on you?"

"I'll have to think about that. I should be able to tell you something by Sunday."

"Then we'll leave you to visit with Clare a while longer." He took Jenette's elbow and escorted her from the room.

Eugenia talked with Clare until almost time for Nancy to finish supper preparations. "I must be going. I forgot to watch the time, and I still have so much to learn about cooking if Papa isn't home yet."

After four days of shadowing the servants whenever possible, Eugenia had to have a diversion. The unusually mild weather was almost perfect for the end of January. An afternoon ride would be a delight. She strolled to her father's office to tell him of her plans. "Papa, I'm going for a ride. I might stop by to say hello to Clare. Would you like to accompany me?"

"Not today. My papers demand my attention."

While she guided her horse down the long drive, Eugenia drank in the beauty of the cloudless blue sky that contrasted with the brown front yard and barren trees. The sun shining on her face bathed her with contentment. A quick glance at the stone pillars marking the end of the driveway interrupted her reverie. A stone near the top looked loose.

"I think I've found a place to leave messages, Belle. That loose rock near the top of the left pillar might be easy to remove and set back in." She leaned over to test the stone. With a slight tug, it slid into her gloved hand. She couldn't suppress a laugh after she replaced the rock. "It's perfect. I'll have to tell Titus about this Sunday."

To celebrate, she urged Belle into a gallop. Paul wouldn't see such reckless behavior today, and she had to do something. She slowed her horse after almost losing her hat and dislodging several hairpins. Returning with her hair completely down would aggravate Papa. She must stay on his good side as much as possible.

She soaked in the beauty around her until she spied a rider coming toward her. The man closely resembled Alton Parker. How she wanted to gallop her horse in the opposite direction.

"Good afternoon, Miss Hampton." Alton tipped his hat as he rode up to her.

Eugenia nodded. His smug smile made her skin crawl as if a beetle had landed on her and worked its way under her sleeve. Since Papa wasn't around to see her, she didn't bother to greet the man. She tucked a loose strand of hair behind her ear. His smile reversed to a frown as his eyes followed her fingers. Her disheveled appearance must upset him. Wonderful.

"Your father said the trail to Hopeton is your favorite, and I should find you here."

"Papa knows my habits well."

"I finished talking business with your father, and hoped for the pleasure of seeing you also."

How she wanted to tell this hypocrite exactly what she thought of him. Soon she'd have the pleasure of never seeing him again. "I assume you and your father had a productive visit with Papa, then?"

"Uh … Father isn't feeling well today, so I came alone."

Whatever he'd discussed with Papa, she didn't want to know. "I hope your father is better soon. I hate seeing my papa ill."

"His ailment is minor. As I was saying, it's good to see you."

Eugenia busied herself with straightening her hat instead of acknowledging his remark.

"Could I ask you a question?" He looked straight into her eyes.

Her hand froze. Since he'd admitted talking to Papa alone, she prayed he wasn't about to ask the horrid question she never wanted to hear.

"Would you think me improper if I called you by your first name?"

She let out the breath she'd been holding. If only he knew all the ways she considered him improper. "I hadn't given it any thought."

"Then if you have no objections, Eugenia, I'd like us to be on a first name basis with each other."

"I suppose."

"Then shall we enjoy the remainder of our ride?"

She shook her head. "We have no chaperone."

As usual, his gaze traveled well below her face while he grinned at her. "I have your father's permission."

Her heart raced. What would Papa consent to next? Her fears of a forced marriage didn't seem the least bit unfounded now. "I'm on my way home to have my maid repair my hair."

"I'll savor spending even a short time with you. Though, you should chide your maid for not doing your hair well."

His barely disguised frown gave her immeasurable pleasure. Perhaps she could yet succeed in making him leave her alone as Paul had suggested. She might not be wasting her time after all. "I have yet to discover any style that remains intact after galloping my horse through the woods."

"I don't suppose so." The lines on his forehead deepened.

They rounded the last bend in the trail. Her driveway was almost in sight. "I don't intend to ever curtail my riding. I thoroughly enjoy a good gallop."

His eyes narrowed. "That's much too risky for a lady riding sidesaddle."

"Taking an occasional risk makes life more interesting, don't you agree?" She couldn't resist the allusion to risks, wishing she could tell him she knew the kind of chances he took with his card games.

"Well, yes, but I'm not accustomed to hearing a lady say such things."

"Always being a lady is stifling. I detest being stifled."

"Oh?" His eyebrows rose in surprise, or perhaps shock. She hoped the latter.

"Yes. My driveway is just ahead, so I'll bid you goodbye, sir." How she wished she could tell him good riddance instead.

"Good day to you, too, Eugenia. I'll call on you again soon. Your company is quite intoxicating."

"I must see to my hair."

She turned Belle up the drive and left him gawking after

her. By now any other man would have ceased bothering a woman as rude as she'd been. He must need her money sooner than Luke thought. How much sooner, she didn't want to find out.

* * *

Eugenia spent much of her time the next two weeks trying to discourage Alton. No matter how discourteous her behavior, he returned like a bad case of indigestion. His debts must be mounting, or someone was exerting more pressure on him to pay them. Nothing else explained the way the man kept coming back no matter how she mistreated him. If not for her calls to Clarisse, she wondered how often the rogue would pester her.

Since she'd gone to see Clarisse last Monday, Eugenia sat in the parlor with her needlework hoping her friend would be here soon. Clare now knew to come early enough in the afternoon to arrive before Alton might come.

Joseph stepped into the room. "Miss Matthews be here to see you."

"Thank you." Eugenia rushed past the butler to open the door for Clare and ushered her inside. "I'm so happy to see you."

"And I you." Clarisse smiled. "My family sends their regards to your father too. Mama says to greet him personally if he's in the house."

"I think he's in his office. He usually writes the family in Nashville on Monday afternoons." Eugenia guided her friend into the parlor, glad Clare had found a way to see if it was safe to mention Paul.

"Then I'll not disturb him." Clarisse settled onto the couch and waited for Eugenia to join her.

"I sent for refreshments when I saw your carriage coming up the drive. Papa might join us for that."

Even though they could only discuss mundane things with Papa across the hall, Eugenia enjoyed her visit with Clare. "I'll walk you out to your carriage. I need a little fresh air even if it is cold today. I left a heavy shawl draped on the coat rack."

"I'm sure we can talk a little longer." Clarisse grinned as she followed Eugenia from the room.

Eugenia closed the front door behind her as they stepped onto the porch. "You are such a dear. I'm glad I didn't have to worry about Alton coming by for one afternoon."

"I thought you'd like an excuse to turn him away if he came or force him to suffer visiting with both of us."

"Thank you." Eugenia pulled her shawl tight around her shoulders, wishing she'd grabbed her cape instead. But she'd endure a chill for the opportunity to enjoy an honest conversation. "I'd send Alton away, but then Luke would be encouraged. I hate to deceive such a good man more than I have already. I've so misused our friendship even though I've never made any promises to him."

"You could write him a note of explanation. I could deliver your apologies to Luke after you're safely away from here."

"What a wonderful idea." She hugged Clare. If only her friend were ready to think about accepting male callers again. She couldn't shake thoughts of how well-suited Clarisse and Luke could be for each other.

"You're shivering, and I should go home. I'll see you in church Sunday unless you need to come by before that."

Eugenia released her friend. "Thank you."

Clarisse walked toward her awaiting carriage.

* * *

Saturday afternoon, Eugenia sat on her favorite bench in the garden gazebo with her needlework. She thanked God for such a pleasant day. She needed to get out of the house and away from her father for a while.

A shadow fell over her as she stitched. She started and looked up to see Mr. Parker. He seated himself close enough to her that his trousers brushed her skirt. Shivers radiated through her body in spite of her wool dress and the warm shawl around her shoulders.

"I'm sorry to frighten you, Eugenia. Your father said he saw you walking this direction. Again, I'm glad he knows you so well."

She stabbed her needle through the fabric and resumed her stitching. "Any good father knows his child. Papa is an excellent father."

"I agree. I'm surprised to find you outdoors today."

"It had been pleasant here in the sunshine with no wind."

He smiled, completely ignoring her veiled hint. "I would much rather gaze into your beautiful eyes than enjoy the nice weather today."

What gall this man had. Her round eyes probably reminded him of Papa's coins he coveted. She clutched her shawl. "I'm feeling quite chilled now. I need to go inside."

When she started to stand, he grabbed her arm and held her on the bench.

"Release me now, sir." She spoke through gritted teeth..

He caressed her hand before letting go. "You act as if you're afraid of me. Is something wrong?"

"Very wrong. No true gentleman would ever sit so near a lady." She scooted to the edge of the bench, hoping for a chance to escape.

"I see nothing wrong with a man sitting next to the lady he's been calling on for so long." He slid over next to her.

She stiffened and sat as straight as she could manage before looking him in the eyes. "I am still in mourning." She gripped her embroidery hoop when he acted as if he'd reach for her hand again.

"Life is for the living, my dear Eugenia. It's past time for you to live again."

The cad pulled her into his arms. She shoved him away and jumped to her feet. Her embroidery hoop thudded onto the wood floor.

"Go and do not return, sir." She darted from the gazebo, grateful he didn't follow her. She ran the remainder of the distance to the house, not slowing her pace until she stopped to open the back door. Papa stepped out of his office while she was trying to catch her breath at the bottom of the stairs.

"Didn't Alton find you?" His ecstatic broad smile showed no care for her obvious distress.

She took a shaky breath. "I sent him away."

"What?" His smile morphed to an angry frown.

"He's worse about listening to me than Luke has ever been." She told him of Alton's improper behavior, down to the last detail. "He tried to kiss me. If he calls again, send him away."

Papa folded his arms in front of him. "I'll do no such thing."

Icy shivers of dread radiated up and down her spine. "Why not? You offered to speak to Luke before he listened to me."

"I didn't feel such urgency for you to find a suitable husband at that time."

Urgency? "I am still in mourning and not ready for marriage to anyone."

He fixed her with the kind of stern no-nonsense look he'd given her as a girl when she'd done something terribly wrong. "You should be ready at nineteen. I understand young Alton's behavior better than yours."

She gasped. "How can you say that?"

"He behaved in a normal fashion for a man in love with a beautiful woman."

"He loves me? How do you know?" She gripped the stair railing post to keep from collapsing.

"He told me last week what I had already suspected."

"Last week?" She was glad her full skirt hid her trembling legs.

Papa nodded. "He asked my permission to court you before he went riding with you."

"But why didn't you ask me first? You know how I feel about such things at this time."

His eyes narrowed. "Precisely the reason I suggested he not tell you of his intentions for now. I shouldn't have to remind you that your six months of mourning is almost at an end."

She shuddered as she stared into her father's cold eyes. She took a deep breath before asking the question she had to have him answer. "Would you force me to marry?"

His frown disappeared but his serious expression remained. "I shall."

Her pounding heart roared in her ears. Hearing him speak aloud the words she'd dreaded took her breath away.

"Since you won't choose between two excellent suitors, I've chosen for you. Alton is an astute businessman. He doesn't share your religious beliefs, which is refreshing to me. The two of you can work out what to do about your obsession with church later. We'll announce your engagement by the end of March with a wedding to follow soon thereafter."

Tears stung her eyes. She bit her trembling lip, lest Papa see her cry.

"I'm doing this for your good." He reached over to pat her arm.

She whirled then ran up the stairs. Slamming her bedroom

door behind her, she slumped against the wall, shaking and gasping for breath. She and Paul must leave as soon as possible. Waiting the three to four weeks Paul said he needed to finish gathering supplies might not be safe. Alton's debts must be due much too soon.

* * *

ON SUNDAY AFTERNOON she rode through the woods. Her heart was as dreary as the barren trees bending in the brisk wind. She urged Belle into a trot the instant she spied Paul standing in a clearing waiting for her. She didn't care how much he might scold her for riding so recklessly. She reined in her horse only a few feet away from him.

"You look as if you've been chased by a pack of hounds. What happened?" He helped her to dismount.

"Thank God you're here." She hugged him with all her might as soon as her feet touched the ground.

He pulled her close. "What's wrong?"

She soaked in the soothing feel of his strong arms as she pressed her cheek against his wool coat. Still sheltered in his embrace, she told him of Papa's dire plans for her. "I'm afraid if Alton pressures him, Papa will allow a marriage at any time." She raised her head enough to look into his pain-filled eyes. "We should leave tonight if possible."

He shook his head. "I've got a wagon coming soon, but I have to save up more money to take care of both of us."

She stepped away enough to pull a velvet pouch from beneath her cape. "I have emeralds and pearls I can sell, and—"

"No. I'll take care of you with no help from your pa's money." His large hands covered hers and the pouch. "If I didn't think I could, I wouldn't take you with me."

"But we could leave so much sooner. Please."

"No. A man should take care of his wife. Even though you ain't my wife yet I intend to provide for you the way a man should."

He caressed her cheek as he looked into her eyes. She tried to imagine how his fingers would feel on her face without his gloves.

"Your pa wouldn't want you marrying so soon that people would wonder if you and Alton had done something improper and had to wed quick. When that wagon comes, we'll find a way to leave. All right?"

She slipped the pouch beneath her cape before pressing against his chest. "I'm so afraid."

He cupped her chin in his hand and lifted her face. "Me too. Even more scared than when I helped Noah head for Canada."

Chapter Twenty-Eight

A loud knock on the front door interrupted Eugenia and her father during breakfast on Monday morning. The butler sprang from the dining room to answer the insistent banging. Eugenia prayed this interruption wouldn't bring another dreaded surprise. Papa set his fork on his plate and cocked his head to better hear the conversation between the butler and the unexpected visitor.

"Mistah Stuart, you know the masta don' want to be bothered at breakfast." Joseph's tone was stern in spite of the fact he spoke to the overseer.

"I have to see Mr. Hampton. Now." John Stuart's loud gruff voice carried into the dining room.

Papa laid his napkin on the table and pushed his chair back. The overseer marched into the room before Papa could rise.

"I'm sorry to bother you, Mr. Hampton, but I need to talk to you real quick. Please, sir."

"What could possibly be so urgent, John?"

Hat in hand, he glanced toward Eugenia. "Could we talk in your office, sir?"

Papa followed his overseer out of the room, leaving Eugenia to wonder what pressing problem could cause John Stuart to interrupt Papa's breakfast. One thing she did know, Papa would never welcome John's son here unless God worked a spectacular miracle someday.

Before Eugenia finished eating, Papa returned to the dining room. "One of the field hands ran away last night. I'll be gone most of the day unless we find him, dear girl."

He gulped down the remainder of his cold food. "Don't wait for me for lunch. I'll try to be here for supper." He kissed her cheek before hurrying from the room.

What sweet relief to have almost the entire day to herself. And how awful to have such thoughts concerning her own father. She longed for the days when they'd been close. But she'd lived with a dictator since the day Papa had told her of her impending marriage. She could follow the servants around without worrying about being caught since Clare had told her yesterday that she couldn't receive a call today. If Alton dared come again, she'd send him away.

Papa didn't return home until just before supper.

"I was beginning to wonder when you'd be back." Eugenia met her father at the front door. "Did you find the runaway?'

"Not yet. The dogs lost his scent a few miles from here. Stuart will try a while longer to find it again."

How nice Paul didn't live close enough to have assisted the runaway with his departure. "You look tired, Papa."

"Riding through the countryside all day does not agree with my old bones. I intend to retire early tonight."

Wonderful. Her heart almost shouted the words. Another excuse to turn Alton away if he came calling tonight. "I'm sure that would be wise."

* * *

THE NEXT DAY, Eugenia stepped from the carriage after calling on Clarisse to see Alton and Papa waiting for her on the front porch. No. Putting one foot in front of the other was like walking in leaden shoes as she forced herself to step toward the men.

"I told you she'd be home not long after four o'clock." Papa grinned at Alton.

"Yes, sir. You did." Alton turned and bowed to Eugenia. "Good afternoon, my dear."

Prickly shivers ran down her spine and lodged in her heart. "Hello, sir."

She ignored Papa's frown and kept her hands concealed in the folds of her cape. She had no intention of feeling this horrid man's lips even through a glove.

"I need to go upstairs and check my hair. Please excuse me. Papa, would you send Lily to help me?"

Eugenia dawdled in her room as long as she dared. She hoped and prayed Papa hadn't set a wedding date for her while she was at Hopeton. Half an hour later, she heard Papa and Alton's voices in the parlor before reaching the last stair.

She paused to listen to their discussion. They were talking about cotton instead of her. She might as well be a prisoner walking to her execution instead of into the parlor. Both men stood. Their beaming smiles chilled her worse than a howling north wind. The crackling fire offered no warmth.

"I invited Alton to supper." Papa's eyes sparkled.

"Then I should tell Pansy to set another place at the table." She turned to leave.

"No need for that. I've already informed her. We can visit until supper is ready." Papa took her arm and guided her toward the couch.

Eugenia sidestepped her father and chose the nearby chair to prevent Alton from seating himself next to her on the couch.

Papa would have to pick her up and set her on the sofa to force her to sit beside that horrid man. Since her father's age prevented such an action, she was safe for now.

She endured the dreadfully long meal by pushing the tasteless food around on her plate and forcing Papa and Alton to supply the conversation. Neither man mentioned a specific wedding date.

After supper Alton walked beside her to the parlor, his hand brushing her elbow. She wanted to scream at him to leave and never return, but Papa trailed behind them. Again, she took the chair next to the couch.

Alton pulled a chair up next to hers instead of settling for the couch. He smiled into her eyes as he laid his hand on her arm. "What a wonderful way to spend an evening."

Eugenia would have jerked away from Alton's grasp if Papa hadn't walked straight over to her. Instead of finding a comfortable place to sit, her father leaned over and kissed her cheek.

"I'll retire early. I'm still not rested from yesterday."

"I could have Nancy make you some tea to help you rest better." She started to rise. Papa laid his hand on her shoulder.

"That's not necessary. Good night. I'll leave you to entertain your fiancé and see him to the door later." He beamed at Alton before exiting the room. "Come again any time, son."

"Good night, sir. Rest well."

Papa smiled then left the room.

Eugenia stared after her father as she tried to ignore the man sitting too near her. If only she could send this vile creature out the door. Fiancé, indeed. Papa had called him son. She fumed to herself, but dared not voice her fear and anger. She couldn't risk either man suspecting the identity of her true fiancé.

"I hope Papa didn't overtax himself yesterday."

"He looks and acts quite well to me."

"And I want him to stay well." Alton caressed her fingers before lifting them to his lips. "I would so like to be the one to allay your anxieties over your father's health."

She yanked her hand away and glared at him. "If you would truly like to ease my anxiety, then respect my wishes as I expressed them to you only a few days ago."

"That is difficult to do when all I can think about is you." His thin smile never reached his cool brown eyes as he placed his hand over hers again.

"All I can think about is how disrespectful you are to my mother's memory." She pulled her hand from his. "My father has my best interests in mind. Whose interests are you most concerned about when you so stubbornly refuse to consider my feelings?" How she wanted to slap this impudent cad

He jerked back as if she'd hit him. She hoped he disliked her candor as much as he detested her reckless riding habits. She prayed for a way to get this rake out of the house.

"Perhaps we should continue our discussion another time. Would you be so kind as to see me to the door?"

Eugenia jumped to her feet. If Alton and Papa had settled on a wedding date, he didn't look to be in the mood to tell her tonight. She'd let him see himself out if she didn't want to lock the door behind him. She kept her hands clasped tightly in front of her as he walked with her down the hall. She wasn't sure why he'd agreed to leave. Perhaps he hoped to placate her or win her over. Either that or questioning his motives upset him. Whatever the reason, she'd one day be rid of this rogue.

Alton halted and pinned her against the wall by the front door. She gasped. Too startled to think, she could only stare up at him as he bent down much too close. His hands on her shoulders burned like hot coals as he looked into her eyes. His warm breath scalded her cheek.

"I'll continue to try to win your affection, dear lady. And I will win. I plan to announce our engagement as soon as your father allows and wed you the first day he deems it proper."

Prickly chills raced up and down her spine like marching ants. She shook her head, unable to force any words of protest from her constricted throat. She doubted she could scream if necessary.

"I'm looking forward to the time you no longer shrink from me." He twirled a loose strand of her hair with his fingers. "The day cannot come too soon when you long for me and welcome my kiss and my touch."

She darted from him when he tried to kiss her. "You said you were leaving. Please keep your word."

Her voice hadn't trembled, but she was shaking so badly inside, she wondered that she could still stand. If Papa overheard her words, she'd deal with him later.

"I shall return, my dear lady." He jerked his jacket from the hall tree and strode out the door.

Eugenia locked the door then ran toward the stairs and the sanctuary of her room, glad to see Papa's door was shut. She gulped in air as she collapsed onto her bed. Alton's wish to marry as soon as Papa allowed meant she and Paul had less time than he thought to make their escape. Especially since March was only days away.

Chapter Twenty-Nine

ugenia returned from calling on Clarisse and took her time walking inside the house. How wonderful not to hear Alton conversing with her father in the parlor this particular Monday. She hated that Mrs. Matthews was battling a terrible fever, but the need to comfort Clare had allowed Eugenia to stay at Hopeton later than she usually did. Perhaps tonight she'd eat supper in peace. Alton had yet to return after their confrontation last Tuesday night.

"How is Cassandra?" Papa met her in the entryway with a letter in his hand. He must have been watching for her return.

As Joseph helped her remove her cape, she braced herself for whatever dreaded news this unexpected epistle might bring. "Mrs. Matthews is a little better. I'm glad I went over there. It comforts Clare and Titus to know we're thinking of them."

"That's good. I've been waiting for you, dear girl."

Eugenia shuddered. She didn't want to guess what shocking announcement he might have today.

"Nathan sent a letter saying my runaway servant is in jail for theft in Nashville. I must leave tomorrow to tend to the criminal charges before I can bring the man back. Tell Lily to pack a small trunk for you so we can depart early in the morning."

She couldn't imagine riding alone that long with Papa. Spending even a short time in Nashville listening to her siblings congratulate her on her upcoming marriage would be much worse. "Can't Mr. Stuart go for you? What if we get another cold spell, and you catch a bad chill?"

Her words tumbled out before she thought better of them. She needed Papa to leave not stay. If he would travel without her ... Such a wonderful idea quickened her pulse.

Papa shook his head. "Nathan insists I come for the man due to the legal troubles."

Eugenia fought to control her soaring emotions. If she could think of a plausible excuse, she could stay here and elope with Paul. She sent up a quick desperate prayer for guidance. "I understand you must go, but my best friend needs me here now."

"No one in the Matthews family would expect you to stay home alone." Papa gripped the page in his hand.

"True, but I wouldn't think of not being here to comfort Clare if her mother took a turn for the worse. One of us should be here after all her family has done for us."

Papa's eyes widened. "Do you think Cassandra could get worse?"

"Mama never took any fever lightly." She wouldn't lie about Mrs. Matthews, but allowing Papa to come to his own conclusions might not hurt her cause.

"Perhaps under the circumstances, you should stay. But you've never been by yourself like that."

"I could never be alone with such loyal servants and reliable friends." She struggled to keep from sounding or looking too eager. "Grace stays home when David travels for business."

He took a deep breath. "I'll go without you. If the Matthews weren't such good friends I'd insist you come."

On the inside, Eugenia jumped up and down, shouting for joy as she worked to maintain a serious expression. "This will mean so much to Clare. And you shouldn't be gone too long."

"I'm planning on three days, possibly a day or two more. I can't imagine Grace allowing me to leave too quickly. You will be my concern here all alone." He placed his hand on her arm.

"I'll be fine. Give my love to everyone in Nashville."

Papa retired early to rest for his trip. Eugenia dismissed Lily as soon as she was ready for bed. She hugged herself and fought not to laugh out loud as soon as the door closed behind her maid. Perhaps the miracle she and Paul had prayed for would happen soon.

She sobered as her thoughts returned to Lily the way they'd done several times the last few weeks. Her loyal maid had helped her for almost eight years. Would Papa believe Lily when she said she'd had no idea Eugenia would run away? Papa's fury would probably know no bounds when he learned what his daughter had done.

The only way Eugenia could think of for Lily to escape Papa's wrath would be for her to run away too. If she and her husband were willing to take such a risk. Eugenia spent much of the night praying for a way to help Lily and Sampson obtain their freedom just as she would soon have hers.

By the time Lily came in to waken her, Eugenia had thought of a possible plan for Lily and Sampson to leave tomorrow night.

Holding in her wonderful idea took every ounce of willpower she possessed as Lily helped her dress.

Papa was already waiting for her in the dining room when she went downstairs. "I've told Sampson to ready the carriage and Elijah to be ready to drive. I'll leave as soon as we finish eating."

"I thought you might." Eugenia hoped her forced smile looked natural as Joseph seated her. Papa wasn't the only one concentrating on leaving. She had much to do today.

After breakfast, Papa waved goodbye to her from the carriage. This could be her last look at her father unless God worked a miracle in his heart someday, and he accepted Paul. She squared her shoulders then walked into the house. Leaving her father in God's capable hands was the best she could do for her stubborn parent.

Papa had been gone less than an hour when Eugenia walked to the stable and ordered Samson to saddle her horse.

The groom didn't move. "Is you sure you should be out as chilly as it is, miss? If you catches a cold, the masta gonna be terrible mad at me."

"I'll dress warmly. I need to check on Mrs. Matthews."

She battled the urge to gallop Belle all the way to Hopeton. She couldn't arrive there in any sort of disarray and have Titus tell Paul about it. Still, she couldn't resist running up the porch steps to knock on the door.

"I need to see Mr. Matthews." Eugenia blurted out her request as soon as the butler answered her insistent knock.

The butler ushered her inside and helped her remove her cape. "Mr. Matthews, not Miss Clarisse?"

"Yes." The puzzled servant showed her to the parlor then went to find Titus. She had a hard time not pacing while she waited. She couldn't sit unless someone tied her to a chair.

"Is something wrong?" Titus trotted into the parlor, a worried frown on his face.

"Everything might be perfect." Eugenia couldn't squelch a laugh. "How is your mother? I do hope you can ride to Murfreesboro today."

"Mother is better, but still in bed. Why do I need to go to Murfreesboro?"

She told him of her father's absence. "I know the wagon hasn't come yet, but please tell Paul we must leave tomorrow night. We'll have only a few hours before the servants discover I'm missing and notify Paul's father and who knows who else." She handed the sealed note to Titus. "He should burn this after he reads it."

Especially since the short letter told him of her ideas on how to help Lily and Sampson escape, but she'd keep those plans between the two of them. Hence the sealed page even though she had given it to such a trusted friend.

Titus nodded. "I'll leave as soon as I can think of a proper excuse to tell Mother."

"Thank you so much." Eugenia resisted the urge to hug him.

"Shall I leave you a message under the loose stone at the pillar as we planned?"

"Yes. Paul mustn't come before ten tomorrow night. I can't predict when Alton might pester me. My father insisted on sending the Parkers a message telling them to check on me. Paul should come to the front door so none of the servants will see him. I can hear the brass knocker from my room when the house is quiet."

"Clare is upstairs with Mother. I'll send her down and be on my way soon."

Eugenia placed her hand on his sleeve. "Thank you for being a true friend."

He grinned. "My pleasure. Don't worry about the wagon. The Lord will provide." He marched away before Eugenia could question the meaning of his words.

Happy shivers radiated through her body as she watched Titus leave. She'd tell Clarisse her good news and be on her way.

Her excitement waned when she walked through the front door of her house. She stared at the familiar surroundings as Joseph helped her slip off her cape. She might never see any of these things again after tomorrow night.

Yet this place had gone from her childhood home to a prison the day Papa had announced her impending marriage to Alton. She and her father were strangers now. She prayed he would someday understand what she was about to do. Perhaps losing her would finally convince him how much he needed God.

"Is you all right, miss? It ain't like you to stand, starin' at the walls." Joseph interrupted her thoughts.

She jumped. "Uh ... I'm fine. But I do need one thing. Send someone to get a trunk out of the attic. This should be a good time to sort through Mama's things since Papa hasn't been able to do it yet. Put it in my room. I wouldn't want to upset Papa if he gets home before I finish."

"Yes, miss." The butler left to do her bidding.

When Eugenia went upstairs, Lily was straightening her room. "You've already made the bed. Don't worry about anything else. My room will soon be in a mess." She told Lily of her plans to go through her mother's things. "You'll have more than enough to straighten after I'm finished."

"Whatever you say."

A servant soon brought in the trunk.

Lily wrinkled her nose as she eyed the grimy chest. "Whew. This thing got more dust than wood almost." She took her apron and started cleaning off the top. "Do you want me to help you?"

Eugenia sneezed as Lily finished with the dust. "Help me? Uh ... no."

She placed her hand on Lily's arm as she looked into her maid's wide eyes. "I might be able to help you instead." Eugenia's whispered words were barely loud enough for Lily to hear.

"Help *me*? Wif what?"

"*Shh.*" Eugenia placed her fingers on Lily's lips. "Have you ever wished you could be free?"

Lily shook her head. "Missy, you shouldn't be askin' that, and I cain't answer."

"Yes, you can. You know if I can keep our secret about your reading, I'd keep your secret about this too."

"Why you askin' such a thing?"

"Because I can't do anything for you if you don't want me to. We both know how dangerous trying would be."

Her maid chewed her lip as she clasped and unclasped her hands. "Sampson talk about it once. But I told him hush 'cause it be so terrible dangerous ..." She ducked her head as if unable to finish her sentence.

"Yes. It is and would be."

Lily's head jerked up. "You ain't makin' sense, miss."

Eugenia took more than one deep breath. "I know someone who can help you and Sampson get away tomorrow night if God works the miracles I'm praying for."

She wasn't sure how long Lily stared at her.

"You really mean that?"

"Yes." She'd been thinking and praying how to help them for a while now. The note Titus carried to Paul should have all the information needed for Paul to tell the proper person how to help Lily and Sampson.

"A man in a wagon will be here sometime after ten tomorrow night. He won't stay long. The two of you could hide by the huge oak at the first bend on the trail past our house. He'd pick you up there."

"How you know such things?" Lily cocked her head.

"I know the man."

"Enough me and Sampson should trust him wif our lives?"

"Yes."

Lily shook her head. "How you be so sure of him?"

No matter how quickly things were unfolding, she'd been certain Lily would immediately agree to such a wonderful plan instead of being skeptical and full of questions. The less Lily knew the better off they all might be, but offering her only general details didn't appear to be enough to convince her to take such a risk.

One shuddering breath, then another as Lily stared her down. "Because I love that man, and I'll be leaving with him."

Lily covered her open mouth with both hands, stifling her gasp. Eugenia doubted her maid's eyes could get any wider. And if her pounding heart got any louder, Lily would be able to hear it.

She grasped Lily's wrists with her hands. "I'm trusting you to keep my secret. You must trust me to get you and Sampson away from here."

"Oh, Miss Eugenia. You knows I trust you. But why is you doin' this?"

"Papa intends to force me to marry Mr. Parker soon. I can't and won't. My father's unexpected trip is the miracle this man and I've been praying for."

Lily nodded. "I'll talk to my man tonight. If he say we go, I tell you tomorrow. But if we stays, I won't say nothin' about what you gwine to do."

"Thank you so much." She hugged Lily before thinking about it.

Her maid stepped back. "We bof got lots to do today. We'd best get started."

"Yes, we should. I've a trunk to fill before I leave." Eugenia glanced around her room, not sure where she should begin. "Tell everyone not to disturb me the next two days. Leave Papa's room alone so I can get things from there without anyone knowing. I don't want any callers unless Clarisse or Titus Matthews needs me."

"Yes, miss." Lily nodded as she usually did, then left to deliver Eugenia's message to the rest of the household.

Packing the trunk was a step of faith, since Paul still wasn't sure how soon his—their—wagon would arrive. But with Titus so certain of God's provision, Eugenia felt compelled to fill the chest. God knew how much they needed a wagon to carry Paul's precious plow and their supplies.

Eugenia opened the doors to her wardrobe, shoving aside her ball gowns. She'd have no need for such finery. Her sturdy riding clothes should work well on the frontier, as would some of her simpler day dresses. A year ago, she couldn't have left all these things behind. Paul was right. God had changed her. But she'd bring her favorite blue muslin. Frontier people must do something special once in a while.

She spent the day prowling the upstairs for things she could pack ahead that no one would miss. In her parents' room, she laid some of Mama's dresses across the bed in case one of the servants came in against her wishes. She walked to her mother's nightstand and ran her hand over Mama's Bible. Papa had no use for it. She carried the precious book as well as one of Mama's brooches to her room and placed them in the trunk with her other treasures.

The day crawled by while she made notes of everything she

should finish packing after the servants went to their cabins. Alton and Marissa came by, but the servants turned them away as Eugenia had ordered. She dismissed Lily then paced and waited. The parlor clock struck eleven before she ventured outside to check for a message from Titus.

Twinkling stars guided her steps down the driveway to the stone pillars. Her hand shook as she stretched up on tiptoe to tug on the loose stone. She pulled a folded piece of paper from its hiding place and clutched it close to her heart. As quickly as possible, she made her way inside. She threw open her bedroom door then ran toward her dressing table where a candle still burned.

Be ready at the time you suggested with your goods. Will meet you where you said to be.

Eugenia watched the sun rise from her window the next morning. She should take a nap sometime during the day, if she could manage to sleep. She climbed back in bed before Lily came in to stir the embers in her fireplace and help her dress. Only God knew where she'd be tomorrow.

As soon as Lily entered Eugenia's room, she shut the door behind her then pushed on it as if to be sure it was closed tightly. Eugenia tossed her covers back and sat on the side of the bed. "Have you decided what you'll do?" She kept her voice low.

Lily walked over to her. "We'll go wif you."

"Wonderful." Since she'd shocked Lily by hugging her yesterday, she refrained from doing it again.

Eugenia spent the morning trying to think of anything else she should bring with her. She and Paul could use so many things her father would never miss. But she dared not pack more than the one trunk Paul could handle alone. Her Bible went in after she finished her daily reading.

After lunch, she went to her room to rest. The servants

didn't question her when she said she was exhausted from going through Mama's things. She and Paul needed to get as far away from here as possible before sunrise tomorrow, so she'd better sleep while she could.

A knock on her door interrupted her nap. She blinked as she rolled onto her elbow. "Yes?"

"You has callers, miss. We couldn't get them to leave." Lily's agitated voice drifted through the door. "Miss Parker and her brothah be here."

Eugenia sprang from her bed, ready to march downstairs and insist the intruders go home. She flung open her door to find Lily still in the hall. "Joseph told them you still don't want no callers, but that man was comin' up the stairs to see about you till Joseph blocked him." Lily wrung her hands as she whispered her comments.

"I see." Perhaps she'd better humor Alton this afternoon. She didn't want him coming back tonight. "Have Nancy prepare refreshments. I'll tend to these people myself."

"Yes, miss."

Alton rose as Eugenia walked into the parlor. "Good afternoon, my dear."

She fixed him with a glare she hoped looked as cold as his soulless eyes while tucking her hands behind her. Never again would she have to endure the awful feel of his lips.

"We came by yesterday, and your butler insisted we couldn't disturb you while you sorted your mother's things. When he wouldn't allow us to see you again today, I felt compelled to ascertain you're all right." Alton stepped closer to her.

Eugenia backed away. "As you can see, I'm quite well, but very busy. I want to finish my tasks before Papa comes home." She patted her hair. She hadn't thought to have Lily check it, but this way she looked like she'd been working.

Marissa occupied the chair farthest from the sofa. Eugenia forced a smile at the woman as she took the chair closest to the couch. Alton seated himself on the couch and leaned close. She clasped her hands in her lap and hoped he wouldn't touch her.

"You're so courageous to undertake such a chore to spare your father." Alton laid his hand on the arm of the sofa. "Another thing to admire about you, my lady."

I'm not your lady. She wanted to scream the words loudly enough to be heard all the way to the carriage house. She'd settle for counting the hours until she'd be rid of him forever.

"We came to ask you to supper tonight." Marissa's glib smile looked as if their visit were perfectly normal.

Eugenia wished she could throw the silver serving tray at the woman instead of pretending to be happy to see her. "I have much to do and only a short time to finish. Tomorrow would be much better." They had no idea how much better tomorrow would be for her.

"But I've been looking forward to spending the evening with you." Alton reached over and covered her hands with one of his.

She jerked away. "Not tonight. Papa won't be gone much longer, and I must use what time I have."

Her unwanted callers droned on for another hour. Eugenia emptied her tea cup for the second time and checked the clock for what must have been the tenth time. She had to rid herself of these pests. "I can't believe the time. I must end our visit and return to my work if I'm to finish before Papa returns." Eugenia set her cup down.

Alton's brow furrowed into deep creases. Marissa snapped her open mouth shut as she almost dropped her teacup before returning it to her saucer.

Eugenia rose without offering another pretend smile. She'd be the talk of the county after tomorrow, anyway. No use wasting more of her precious time being polite to these boorish people. She couldn't believe she'd ever thought of Marissa as a friend. The woman had to see that Eugenia wanted nothing to do with her brother. One of them angered her as much as the other now.

"I'll see you both to the door before I resume my efforts." Eugenia walked out of the room, leaving them no choice but to follow her.

"Until tomorrow, my lady." Alton reached for Eugenia's hand as soon as he caught up to her in the entry hall.

She slid her hand behind her back. "Goodbye, sir."

He ran his finger tip along her chin. "I'll never say goodbye to you, my dear, no matter what."

Chapter Thirty

Eugenia went up to her room after supper, glad for the excuse of going through more of Mama's things. Alton's last words had unnerved her to the point she'd had a hard time eating. God had orchestrated a way for her and Paul to leave. She'd trust Him to take care of everything else.

She squared her shoulders as she sat at her small writing desk. Her beloved father deserved some sort of explanation. Mere words would never be adequate to tell him goodbye for the last time, but words would have to do.

A half dozen or so crumpled pages littered the floor before she settled on what to write. She tossed the discarded papers into the fireplace. Lily would soon be up to go through the ruse of helping her prepare for bed. Keeping to normal routines would prevent anyone from suspecting what they planned for tonight. She'd reread the letter after Lily left.

Lily knocked on Eugenia's door a few minutes later. "Ise here to help you get ready for bed, miss."

"Come in."

"What you want me to do?" Lily whispered her question after closing the door behind her.

Eugenia pointed to her favorite green wool day dress lying on the bed. "I won't elope wearing black." She kept her voice low as a precaution. With Papa gone, Joseph should already be in his quarters. But neither of them wanted to risk being overheard in case someone still lingered in the house.

Lily nodded. She helped Eugenia change. "Now what, Miss?"

"Now? We pray and wait."

"And pray a heap more." Lily ran her fingers up and down her apron.

She placed her hand on Lily's arm. "Godspeed to you."

"To you too." The maid left the room as quietly as she'd entered.

Eugenia's hands shook as she took the letter for Papa from the nightstand drawer. Tears stung her eyes as she went over the note one last time.

Dearest Papa,

I'm sorry to cause you such heartache, but I will not marry Alton Parker. He is not the man you think he is. I wish you would accept the godly man I love, but I realize my hope is futile. That man is Paul Stuart. We will be gone by the time you read this letter.

I hope and pray someday you understand and can forgive me for the distress I've caused you.

Always your loving daughter,
Eugenia

P.S. Don't be angry with Paul's family. They know nothing of our plans to elope. They will be just as shocked as you are when they discover what we've done.

She sighed. She'd given serious thought to mentioning Alton's gambling and his debts instead of hinting about them, but Papa wouldn't believe a word she said against the man. Her father would have to discover the harsh truth from someone else. She placed the letter on her pillow.

"Goodbye, Papa." She'd never stop praying for his salvation or that he'd change his mind about Paul.

Tears spilled down her cheeks as she sank onto her bed. In spite of her pain, peace engulfed her. She hated hurting Papa, but he'd left her no other choice. She'd disobey her earthly father instead of her Heavenly Father.

The wind rustled through the tree near her window. She jumped and peered into the darkness outside. Any shadow could be hiding Paul while he made his way up the driveway.

Papa's hounds barked from somewhere close to the house. The dogs should have been in the barn for the night. Eugenia raced from her room and bounded down the stairs. She threw open the front door. The dogs had cornered Paul near the porch.

"Hush, Brown," Eugenia whispered to the oldest hound as she grabbed Paul's hand. "Run inside before one of the servants comes to see what the dogs are barking about."

They dashed hand in hand into the house. She shut the front door and gulped in air. "I'm sorry." She took another breath. "I don't know why the servants forgot to put the dogs up tonight."

Paul reached for her arm to steady her. "Let's get out of here."

The back door banged open.

Paul took the stairs two at a time—half pulling, half carrying her up with him.

"Miss Eugenia, is you all right? We heared the dogs." Joseph's voice bellowed up the stairs.

"I'm fine." Eugenia sucked in air. "Since the dogs quit barking so soon, everything must be all right." She paused to take another breath. "Put them in the barn where they should have already been."

"Yes, miss."

Eugenia slumped against Paul and listened for the back door to close. He gave her a quick kiss before releasing her.

"Let's go, Jeanie."

"I have a trunk in my bedroom in case you found a wagon."

"We have a wagon. How big is the trunk?"

"It's average size I suppose." She took his hand and guided him to her room. "Getting it downstairs will be difficult, but there are things in there we can use."

"How much did you pack?"

"My clothes, some linens, candles, soap, candlesticks, and other things we can use. My jewelry is still in the drawer in my dresser. I'd take it if you'd change your mind."

He shook his head. "The wagon is at the end of the driveway. I was afraid to drive up to the house. Get your cape on, and we'll go."

"My cape is on the hall tree by the front door."

Eugenia followed as Paul scooted the trunk down the stairs. When they reached the bottom, she paused in front of the shadowy paintings of her grandparents hanging in the hall. Her hand trembled as she reached out to touch a gold frame.

"Please don't change your mind." Paul's voice cracked. He kissed her hair as he gently touched her shoulder.

She turned to look at him and clasped his hand in hers. "I can't stay here without you."

He kissed her forehead. "Titus has a preacher waiting for us at his house."

"He does? Who would risk marrying us?"

"The circuit rider who helped me get Noah and his wife on their way to Canada. Thank God, he was in the area."

"What a perfect answer to prayer." Her words rushed out as she told Paul where Lily and Sampson were hiding. "God *has* worked everything out. Hasn't He? I can't wait to become your wife." She pressed his hand to her cheek.

Paul helped her with her cape. "I wouldn't think of traveling alone with a woman who ain't my wife. Walk in the shadows of the trees and not on the driveway. Don't say a word until we're at the wagon."

Eugenia shut the door behind them. This house would never be home again unless Papa someday accepted Paul. Her true home was with the godly man she loved. Together they pushed and slid the trunk on the ground until they reached the end of the drive. Paul loaded it into the bed of the wagon then gave her a quick, tender kiss before helping her up onto the seat.

"How did you find this?" She whispered as she looked over at him after he scrambled up beside her.

He snapped the reigns and started the horses on the way. "Titus. He said this and the other horse are our wedding presents from him and his family." He kept his voice low.

"We'll have to thank them somehow."

"You can do that tonight. Titus, Jenette, and Clarisse will be waiting for us at their barn."

"They will?"

He nodded. "None of them want to miss our wedding."

Our wedding. Eugenia clasped her hands in her lap. Such

joyous yet sad words. Neither of their families would be present for the momentous occasion. She'd never thought God would answer her prayers to marry Paul in this fashion. Only God knew why He hadn't answered her countless pleas and worked a miracle in Papa's heart so he would accept the man she loved.

Paul laid one hand on her arm. "You're awful quiet. This is hard for you, ain't it?"

"I'm following my heart and God's will at the same time, so leaving is easier than I thought."

"I hadn't looked at it like that." The moon shone through the trees just enough to reveal his wide grin.

"My only regret is Papa, but I must leave him in God's hands. I pray he'll accept God, and you, one day." The moon went behind a cloud, obscuring the trail. How she prayed Papa wouldn't always travel in similar darkness.

"I don't expect my pa to understand what we're doing any better than your pa. Both our families will turn against us."

"Then we'll have each other. You are more than enough." The wagon lurched. She grabbed the seat to keep from falling.

"Are you all right?"

She nodded but didn't loosen her grip.

"Sorry this ain't the carriage you're used to. There must have been a hole or rut back there."

"The wagon is ours. I'll manage." With God's help, she'd deal with ruts or anything else in order to be with the man she loved. The heartache of leaving everything she knew behind was worth the love she'd gain with Paul.

A few minutes later, Paul halted the wagon near the big oak tree. Wordlessly, Sampson and Lily scrambled into the wagon bed. Paul hid them under the canvas covering his plow. He jumped up next to Eugenia and snapped the reins.

"We'll drop them off a little ways before we get to Hopeton.

The preacher told me where to hide them by the stream until he can come get them." Paul's soft voice barely carried to her ears.

She nodded. As dry as her throat was, she doubted she could speak, even if it was safe. She'd never done anything so dangerous in her life. Nor something so right.

They talked only when necessary as they drove toward the place to leave Lily and Sampson. Paul halted the wagon near a clump of brush and bushes by the stream. Their passengers slipped off into the shadows, but not before Lily turned to give Eugenia a quick wave. Eugenia waved back as she sent up a prayer for their safety.

They talked in hushed tones until they neared Hopeton. Paul drove toward the barn. Titus appeared from the shadows. He closed the barn doors behind them as soon as they were inside.

Clarisse hugged Eugenia when Paul set her on the ground. "I'm so glad I can see you once more."

"I wanted to see you too."

"We don't have time for the two of you to visit." Titus gently tugged on his sister's arm. "Eugenia, you and Paul need to be on your way as soon as possible."

The ceremony was brief but meaningful. Paul gripped her hands in his as they repeated their vows. The hay and horse smells disappeared as she looked up at the man she loved.

In spite of the shadows cast from the lanterns, his eyes shone as she'd never seen before while he repeated the preacher's words to her. "To have and to hold from this day forward until death do us part."

The preacher grinned. "I now pronounce you man and wife."

Paul took her into his arms and kissed her soundly despite

their audience. He kept her hand in his after releasing her and turning toward their friends.

"I'm so happy for both of you." Clarisse dabbed at her moist eyes with her handkerchief.

After hasty hugs and goodbyes, Paul helped Eugenia up onto the wagon seat. Titus opened the barn doors, and they were on their way.

Paul stared straight ahead as he guided the horses down the dark road. "I'm thankful to God for stars and moonlight with hardly any clouds and such nice weather for early March."

She placed a gloved hand on his coat sleeve. "I'm thankful to God that we're married."

"So am I. But as much as I don't want to, I have to pay real close attention to keeping this wagon on a narrow road instead of thinking about you."

"Are you asking me nicely not to talk too much?"

"Sorry, but yeah. I don't mind if you sit close and lay your head against me."

"That would be wonderful." She complied with Paul's suggestion. How nice to be near her husband.

A strange peace flowed through her entire being as she looked out on the moonlit road. She'd turned from the only life she'd known to step into the unknown. This new adventure was a true walk of faith. Neither she nor Paul knew what lay ahead. But God knew and cared. If only Paul hadn't asked her to be quiet so she could share her thoughts with him.

They traveled for what Eugenia guessed to be three or four hours.

"We'd better rest for a little while." Paul took his eyes off the road long enough to glance at her. "I figure the way your head's been drooping the last few minutes you're ready to stop."

Eugenia covered a yawn with her hand. "I've been too excited to sleep well the last two nights."

"Me too."

A few minutes later, Paul found a thick stand of trees to hide the wagon from view. He jumped to the ground and walked over to help Eugenia down.

He enfolded her in his arms and kissed her with an intensity she had not dared dream about. "When we're far enough away to be safe, I'm going to hold you and kiss you all night and all day long."

"I'd like that very much." She couldn't think of the words to describe the deliciously warm feelings coursing through her.

Paul kissed her again before releasing her. He climbed up into the wagon and pulled out rolled-up blankets and quilts. "It ain't much, and it sure ain't fancy."

"I don't mind." Eugenia watched as he made an inviting-looking pallet beneath the wagon. Tonight, sleeping on the ground would be better than the nice bed she was used to.

He halted next to her. "I wish we didn't have to spend our wedding night in the woods like this, but—"

She placed her fingers on his lips. "We have God's moon and stars for our canopy. What more could we ask for?"

Chapter Thirty-One

The night shadows were creeping from the forest when Paul rolled over onto one elbow and looked down at his sleeping wife. She was his in every sense of the word now. *Thank you, Lord.*

A breeze stirred the bare tree limbs over their heads reminding him of reality. They needed to put more miles between them and whoever might come after them. He brushed Eugenia's soft cheek with his fingers and let them travel down to her neck. She didn't budge. He'd never have guessed a lady like her would sleep so soundly on a pallet spread on the ground. He gently nudged her shoulder.

"Jeanie, it'll be light soon."

"*Mmm* ...what?" She jolted awake.

He pushed her loose hair from her face. "I wish I could let you sleep longer, but somebody will soon notice you're gone."

She shuddered. "Papa's hounds will be after us in no time." She scrambled from under the wagon then snatched up a quilt and folded it. "The sooner we leave, the better."

"Don't worry about dogs. Our scent trail ends where I helped you up into the wagon, so anyone trying to find us will have to guess which way we went." He tossed the quilt she'd folded under the wagon tarp. Then he took her in his arms and kissed her soundly.

She grinned up at him. "We must not have too much to worry about if you have time for a kiss like that."

Her words forced his thoughts back where they needed to be. "We should probably worry about my pa maybe catching up to us on horseback. He'll be the first person coming around for the slaves to talk to."

Eugenia shivered and pulled her cloak more tightly around her. "You really think your father will come after us?"

"Not after me. It'll probably be a while before he knows I left. But he might try to find you if he thinks he could talk you into coming back. He'd probably like to stay in good with your pa and keep his job." He jerked a knapsack from the back of the wagon. They *did* need to hurry.

Eugenia laid her hand on his arm. "I wrote Papa a note to tell him I'd left with you and no more, so only the Matthews family knows where we're going."

He wished she hadn't done that, but no need to scold or worry her now. "Pa knows about my dreams for a farm in Illinois."

"Oh." Her grip on his arm tightened "I'm sorry about the note. I only wanted to tell Papa goodbye. I didn't think about your father coming after us on his own. How easy will it be for your father to find us?"

"Pa's a terrible tracker. Just the same we'll eat a cold breakfast instead of risking a fire someone might see. Jenette sent us biscuits and ham."

Paul handed her the food. He said a quick prayer of thanks for their breakfast before adding a longer plea for their safety. He grinned at his wife as he leaned against a tree. "There's one good thing about a wagon even if it's slow."

"What?"

He swallowed a bite of bread before he could answer. "It's pretty hard to tell one bunch of wheel ruts from the other. We shouldn't be too easy to track." If only a wagon didn't travel so much slower than a good horse ridden by a man who knew which direction his son would head, but he wouldn't worry Eugenia more by saying such a thing.

They finished their simple meal in a few minutes. Paul helped his wife onto the seat and jumped up beside her. He snapped the reins and guided the wagon toward the road then took his eyes off the trail long enough to kiss her. "I have enough supplies so we don't have to go into any towns for a while, and I ain't taking the main roads."

"How long do you think it will be before we're safe?"

He shrugged. "That depends on how determined your pa is."

"Or how badly Alton still wants my money." She turned to him with a look of pure terror in her eyes.

He clenched his jaw. That scoundrel better know what was good for him and stay home. He'd do whatever was needed to keep his wife safe. "A man like him won't want you after he finds out you ran off with someone like me."

She leaned against him and squeezed his arm. "I pray you're right."

So did he. Neither of them talked much as the wagon bounced along the rutted road. Better to be quiet than chance another traveler going by them and hearing information to help his pa.

The drive through the barren winter countryside would have been monotonous if both of them weren't listening so carefully for anything that sounded like an approaching rider. Paul kept his hat pulled low, and Eugenia made sure the hood of her cape hid her face. The few times they came across other travelers all but took Paul's breath away.

He looked up at the sky. The last of the sun's gold and pink rays were barely visible above the treetops. "It'll be dark soon. No matter how tired we are, we'd better use this clear weather to travel a while longer."

Eugenia shifted. "You're still worried someone will find us, aren't you?"

"My faith ain't as strong as you always think it is." He glanced over at her.

"God will protect us, but being sensible and careful isn't a lack of faith, dearest." She laid her hand on his arm.

He wondered if she could feel his tense muscles clear through his coat sleeve, but she could call him dearest any time she wanted. "Pa knows me well enough to know I won't be on the main road. He could crisscross and cover a lot of territory since he has such a good horse."

"Alton's father also has excellent horses." She shivered.

Paul shifted the reins to one hand then reached over to pull her to his side. "We better not risk a fire once we stop to eat. Hope you don't get tired of cold food."

"Eating a few cold meals is better than looking into Alton Parker's cold eyes the rest of my life."

"Yeah." Paul kissed her cheek before forcing himself to return his full attention to the horses and the darkening trail. He prayed for God's help to keep Jeanie safe.

* * *

THE NEXT MORNING, they resumed their journey at first light. Paul continued to listen and watch for fast approaching riders. "If we don't have any trouble today, I'll think about a fire and a hot supper tonight." He was so tired of cold food, he could almost smell beans cooking.

"I'd like a hot meal, but only if it's safe." Eugenia leaned her head against him as she clutched his arm.

The thin smile she'd given him didn't light up her serious eyes. He could feel the tension in her body. Her expression signaled she was as afraid as he was. They both knew they weren't far enough away to keep a man on a good horse from finding them.

About the time the sun was straight over their heads, Paul heard horse's hooves galloping up from behind. He hoped someone was in a powerful hurry and that the rider wasn't his pa. Or worse, Alton Parker. The rider caught up to them before he could stoop to get the loaded rifle at his feet.

Alton yanked the reins from Paul's hands. The horses halted. Eugenia screamed and pressed against him.

"I'll not waste time on conversation. Eugenia, come with me. Now." With his free hand, Alton whipped a pistol from under his coat then aimed it at Paul's chest. The pure evil in the man's eyes chilled Paul to his soul.

Alton tossed the reins in Paul's face, his gun never moving from its target. He extended his free hand toward Eugenia. "Choose now whether you return with me in peace or not, my dear."

"Don't move, Jeanie." Paul locked eyes with the fiend in front of him and prayed. He had to find a way to reach his flintlock.

"Paul and I have been lawfully wed since Wednesday night." Eugenia's voice sounded calm and strong even though he could feel her fingers trembling while she held tightly to his arm.

Alton's lip curled. "Your father will be happy to see to an

annulment, or I'll see you come back to him as a widow. I'd prefer the latter."

Eugenia released her grip on Paul's arm. From the corner of his eye, he watched his wife as she sat up straight and inched away from him. He fought the urge to grab her and shove her down by his feet. Taking his eyes off the brute with the gun could get either of them killed.

"Forcing me to go with you will solve only part of your problems."

The serene look on her face didn't make any more sense than what she'd just said. Surely she wasn't trying to draw Parker's cocked weapon away from him. He prayed for the Lord's help. If only he could move and get his flintlock.

"*Au contraire,* my lady. You *are* the solution." Alton's jaunty grin never reached the hardened eyes he kept trained on Paul.

"Only if I haven't already told others about your gambling and the debts you can't pay."

Rage burned in Alton's cold eyes as he glared down at them. Paul thought he saw the man's hand tremble for a moment as he kept the gun aimed at Paul's chest. "I'll have you or—"

Horse's hooves thundering up from behind them cut off Alton's reply.

"It takes more than you spooking my horse to get rid of me." Pa aimed his cocked pistol at Parker's head as he reigned in his horse. "Throw that gun on the ground if you want to live. I'll be hanged before I let you make my new daughter-in-law a widow."

Alton's face went whiter than untrampled snow. He turned his head to stare straight at Pa and the weapon pointed at him. Paul took advantage of the distraction his father created and grabbed the rifle at his feet. He aimed the loaded flintlock at Parker's heart.

"You can't shoot me and Pa both. Throw your gun down now or decide which one of us lives to kill you."

Alton looked from one Stuart to the other before tossing his weapon on the ground. He glared at Pa. "I'll see you never work anywhere in the county again."

"I already figured that. Throw down the other gun I saw under your coat. Then git." Pa didn't lower his pistol until after Alton galloped off.

Paul laid his gun at his feet.

Eugenia let out a shaky breath. "Thank you, Mr. Stuart."

"I couldn't call myself a man if I didn't watch out for my own."

"Thanks, Pa."

His father nodded then looked from Eugenia back to Paul. "I hope I didn't lie to that scoundrel calling this lady my new daughter-in-law. You did make an honest woman out of her, didn't you?"

"Yes, sir." Paul reached for Eugenia's hand.

"You've made a terrible mistake, son." Pa's eyes were tender in spite of the hard set of his jaw.

"No, sir. We're doing what's right in the eyes of God."

"And helping Negroes run away is fine in God's eyes, too, as far as you're concerned?"

Paul stared unblinking at his father. He'd wondered when Pa would accuse him of such a thing. "What do you mean?"

"I mean your wife's maid and Mr. Hampton's groom were as gone as you two when I got to the Hampton's place yesterday."

"They were?" How Eugenia managed to sound so surprised was more than he could do. "Are you sure they weren't already looking for me?"

Pa shook his head. "I'm sure."

"Check our wagon. We ain't got any idea where those people are." Paul motioned to the bed.

"I'm sure you don't." The sarcastic tone of Pa's voice said more than he did "I ain't got any more to say to either one of you if you both want to be such fools." Pa's shoulders slumped. "Grab the pistols that young coward left behind before you start off again. I'll see he goes home where he belongs."

"Thanks. We didn't plan on costing you your job." What could be his last words to his father were hard to force from his tight throat.

Pa shrugged. "I'll find another one. Titus Matthews has the hounds out after the runaways. He offered to watch over the Hampton place for me so I could ride with that fool Parker and keep him from hurting anyone. I'll tell Mr. Matthews you're safe when I get back." He headed his horse south without another glance their way.

The moisture in Paul's eyes made it hard for him to watch his father ride away.

Eugenia reached up and caressed his face, wiping away a tear with her glove. "I'm sorry, dearest."

He pulled her close and pressed her head to his chest. "I'll never be sorry I married you." He slipped her hood back and kissed her hair. He held the one who mattered most in his arms. "I figured Pa would be mad. Now I don't have to wonder."

Eugenia pulled away enough to look at him. "At least he said he'd see that Alton doesn't bother us again."

"Yeah. That's good."

She snuggled against him. "I'm so grateful to God to finally rid of that horrid man."

* * *

As they resumed their journey, Eugenia strained to hear every sound. Paul took a less direct trail just in case Alton somehow eluded Mr. Stuart. Watching him look over his shoulder or twist to see behind them became routine.

As the sun dipped closer to the tree tops, Eugenia shifted and rubbed her stiff neck. She'd sleep well whenever Paul decided to stop.

"You have to be as tired as I am." He slipped the reins into one hand and reached over to pat her shoulder.

"I'm all right. We'll travel as late as you think necessary."

"We should be safe now. I'm sure Pa hasn't let Parker out of his sight after he caught up to him. That coward is probably more worried now about protecting himself since he ain't sure who else knows about the money he can't pay back."

"I'm glad to hear you say such things." She relaxed for the first time in days.

"I'll stop soon and get a fire started. I'd like to find a rabbit or something so we can have fresh meat and a hot meal."

Eugenia's stomach growled. "Hot food sounds wonderful."

By the time the moon rose above the trees, Eugenia breathed in the wonderful aromas of supper cooking as she set their tin plates and cups on a log next to Paul. She could do something useful while he finished preparing their meal.

"Everything smells wonderful."

He rose from tending the rabbit roasting on a stick over the fire. "Coffee, beans, and wild game ain't what you're used to, but I promise we'll have better later."

"There is nothing better. Nothing I left behind can compare to what we have, dearest."

"Is that so?" He caressed her cheek.

She reveled in the feeling of his work-hardened hand on her face as she leaned into his arms and laid her head against his chest. "You are the only treasure I'll ever need."

About the Author

Betty Woods has been a storyteller since childhood. She still has the notebooks of her handwritten tales, plus the first "book" she wrote in fourth grade. An incurable history buff, she was mistaken for the tour guide at an historical site while answering her grandchildren's questions. Touring museums or old houses to research for her books is fun instead of work. She can tell you more interesting tidbits about our past than you might want to know.

She and her husband enjoy their grown children and spoiling grandchildren and great grands. They share their Texas home with a spoiled Chihuahua. Spending time with family, especially going on multi-generational vacations is one of her favorite things to do.

When life hands you lemons, don't just settle for lemonade. Taste and see that the Lord is good! Psalm 34:8

Love's Twisting Trail

Trails of the Heart—Book One

Stampedes, wild animals, and renegade Comanches make a cattle drive dangerous for any man. The risks multiply when Charlotte Grimes goes up the trail disguised as Charlie, a fourteen-year-old boy. She promised her dying father she'd save their ranch after her brother, Tobias, mismanages their money. To keep her vow, she rides the trail with the brother she can't trust.

David Shepherd needs one more successful drive to finish buying the ranch he's prayed for. He partners with Tobias to travel safely through Indian Territory. David detests the hateful way Tobias treats his younger brother, Charlie. He could easily love the boy like the brother he's always wanted. But what does he do when he discovers Charlie's secret? What kind of woman would do what she's done?

The trail takes an unexpected twist when Charlotte falls in love with

David. She's afraid to tell him of her deception. Such a God-fearing, honest gentleman is bound to despise the kind of woman who dares to wear a man's trousers and venture on a cattle drive. Since her father left her half the ranch, she intends to continue working the land like any other man after she returns to Texas. David would never accept her as she is.

Choosing between keeping her promise to her father or being with the man she loves may put Charlotte's heart in more danger than any of the hazards on the trail can.

Get your copy here:

https://scrivenings.link/lovestwistingtrail

* * *

Redemption's Trail

Trails of the Heart—Book Two

Newly widowed with her second child due in a few months, Lily Johnson has nowhere to go until Toby Grimes, her late husband's boss, asks her to stay on as housekeeper at his ranch. Remaining in the house Mr. Grimes built for her and her husband is an answered prayer. But malicious gossips see her godsend job as a ruse for a sinful dalliance since her employer is a nice-looking, single man.

God and a lot of others turned their backs on Toby during the war, so he returns the favor by keeping to himself. Yet the need to care for and protect Lily overwhelms him. The way she tugs at his heart scares him more than going into a losing battle.

Unwilling to allow anyone to destroy a fine woman's reputation, he proposes a marriage of convenience. After much prayer, Lily accepts. Her first marriage was a love match made in heaven. The second leads down a trail only God knows. The peace she has concerning a marriage to a troubled man she doesn't love begins a walk of faith to a destination neither she, nor Toby, can guess.

Get your copy here:

https://scrivenings.link/redemptionstrail

* * *

Independence Trail

Trails of the Heart—Book Three

To escape an arranged marriage to benefit her father's business, Heidi Schultz runs to the ranch owned by her sister, Lily, and brother-in-law, Toby. No one will ever run or ruin her life again. She'll find a job in nearby San Antonio and fulfill her dream of living on her own. She'll never surrender her independence to anyone, especially not to a man. But when her father finds her, Heidi agrees to Toby's idea to postpone her plans for a new life and stay at the ranch a while longer just to be safe.

Jethro Bannister likes his life as foreman for Toby Grimes. Memories of the way his Georgia family turned on him don't plague him while living on a secluded Texas ranch. With God's help, he's made peace with his painful past. Until Heidi interrupts his carefully arranged, placid world of quiet. The too talkative woman could worry the horns off an entire herd of longhorns. Plus her family problems remind him too much of what he left behind.

Watching Lily and Toby love and depend on each other chisels away at the wall of independence Heidi has built to protect herself from being betrayed again. Despite their misgivings, Heidi and Jethro form a tenuous friendship based on their common wish to be left alone. They understand each other better than anyone else around them does. Confiding in one another deepens their friendship more than either intends. Will Heidi and Jethro's past wounds bond them together in an unexpected love or push them apart?

Get your copy here:

https://scrivenings.link/independencetrail

Stay up-to-date on your favorite books and authors with our free e-newsletters.

ScriveningsPress.com